THE LOVERS

Alice Ferney is a writer living in Paris. This is her fourth novel.

THE LOVERS

Alice Ferney

Translated by Helen Stevenson

ATLANTIC BOOKS
LONDON

First published in France in 2000 by Actes Sud as *La conversation amoureuse*
This translation first published in Great Britain in 2001 by Atlantic Books, an imprint of Grove Atlantic Ltd

This paperback edition published in Great Britain in 2003 by Atlantic Books, an imprint of Grove Atlantic Ltd

Liberté • Égalité • Fraternité
RÉPUBLIQUE FRANÇAISE

This book is supported by the French Ministry for Foreign Affairs, as part of the Burgess programme headed for the French Embassy in London by the Institut Français du Royaume-Uni.

1 3 5 7 9 8 6 4 2

A CIP catalogue record for this book is available from the British Library.

1 84354 027 4

Typeset by Patty Rennie Production, Portsoy.
Printed in Great Britain by Mackays of Chatham Ltd, Chatham, Kent.

Atlantic Books
An imprint of Grove Atlantic Ltd
Ormond House
26–27 Boswell Street
London WC1N 3JZ

CONTENTS

I	*Early Evening*	1
II	*The Meeting*	79
III	*Time to Eat*	105
IV	*At the Height of the Party*	165
V	*Full-Blown Lies*	197
VI	*On the Phone*	219
VII	*In Bed*	241
VIII	*Years Later*	271
EPILOGUE	*It Never Ends*	289

I

Early Evening

I

A pair of future lovers were walking down the middle of a pedestrian street in the hour before dinner. The town was ablaze with the colours of evening. As the sun sank low, the stones of the grand old apartment buildings glowed orange like heated metal. Young people clustered like grapes, chattering as they strolled along, laughing, flirting a little. The old university quarter still had a festive, carefree feel. June had been a fine month, and the warmth of the day hung heavy in the air. The woman wore a light summer dress, its modest neckline concealed by a yellow chiffon scarf. Without even looking at her face you could tell from her figure and from the way she moved that she was young; at the same time, something else about her – her grace, her sense of ease – suggested she was more than a girl. She had lost that awkward look, that inward fearfulness which, like a seal, both signals a girl's virginity and protects it. In its place was her obvious pleasure in being flirtatious, which marked her out as a woman who prefers the company of men. The man at her side had outgrown the age of passion. He had reached the time in life at which a man, in the presence of younger people, is most conscious – and admiring – of their youth. He was forty-nine. His hair was still blond and thick but his features were starting to sag a little. He was not handsome, and was not trying to be. This was not a small point: it was proof of his considerable self-confidence. He was casually dressed in a light-coloured suit and a white shirt with one button undone at the collar beneath a rather dull tie. His suit was crumpled. Though a breeze lifted now and then, it only briefly disturbed the warm air hovering over the asphalt. He must have been sweating and you could see that he had not gone home to change for their rendezvous, unlike his companion, who had prepared herself at some length. It was also clear that their meeting was not professional, nor that of a married couple coming together to round off the day, but was more in the nature of a date. All this was obvious at first glance.

They seemed to be performing the steps of some lively dance, as though they were in a hurry, but in fact there was no rush at all. What looked like haste was simply a wish to escape the throng. They came close together, parted, moved closer again, then split again, coming and going as they moved on through the surging crowd. Whenever they found themselves on opposite sides of the street, he would increase his pace to catch up with her, his eyes always on her, as though he himself were invisible while she walked on happily alone, skipping up onto the pavement edge, darting through the crowd of strangers like a mountain goat, dangling a minuscule handbag from her fingers. No one would have guessed that her relaxed and easy air was in fact a disguise for anxiety, the graceful mask of an inner fear. She desperately wanted to please, and, as is often the case with women, this desire quite cancelled out her self-assurance.

And there, right at the very start, she lost her spontaneity. Whenever her companion looked at her, she tried to look composed. And he looked at her all the time. At first she wondered if there was something wrong with her appearance. Was she perhaps too this, or too that? She wanted so badly to strike the right note. Now she even began to question the way she moved. Why am I skipping? she wondered. It's childish. So she stopped. He looked at her, smiling. It was not a flirtatious smile, just a smile of simple pleasure. She was pretty, he thought, no wonder he'd picked her out at school, and she looked lovely in that little yellow dress. It was made of fine poplin, simple and fresh. He knew the names of fabrics because he was a man who loved women: whatever interested a woman interested him.

There's a young woman with real style, he'd said to himself, when he'd first noticed Pauline Arnoult. Even though she was blonde, the yellow gold of her dress looked wonderful on her and the skirt hung just perfectly, short of the knee. She could afford to show her legs. He felt proud to be in such good-looking company. He would be very attentive to her. He admired her face, as smooth as a polished stone, and her fair, close-grained skin. It was one of those faces that seems to yield where in fact it asserts itself. Not because it was more secretive than the average face – a face does not hide easily – but because you had the sense of stealing a look at it. He forgot he would probably tire of it. He had been swept over the boundaries of common sense, transfixed by the image of a woman. She was statuesque, not so much in the perfection of her features, but in their perfect continuity of line: a face cut from a single block. This was the privilege of youth, an uninterrupted brow, smooth down to the eyelashes, a regular nose, carved in one stroke stopping just short of the mouth, full cheeks, not a line to be seen – just like stone. Naturally, she was blissfully unaware of her firm white loveliness. Does anyone ever fully appreciate their own face? The harmony of beauty is so fragile, so intangible and inexplicable, that she probably didn't know she was so privileged. All she saw were the effects, which made her smile. When she smiled you could see her teeth, with a gap between the two front ones, lucky teeth, she was often told, which was really a way of talking about her, of telling her, without being too obvious, that she was much admired. When it became too much for her she would blush, and continue to mesmerise those around her, even if her big blue eyes sometimes made her look rather thoughtless.

They emerged from the crowded pedestrianised streets and at last could walk close together. The space between them lessened until eventually their upper arms occasionally brushed. He could smell the summer perfume on her skin, a hint of vanilla. He had deliberately moved up close. A force was pushing him towards her. How would she react? He couldn't say. He didn't know her well enough. But she had turned up. . . . She couldn't be as timid as all that. He kept up the pressure. She did not move away. What was going through her mind? He was watchful, but mostly plain admiring. His eyes were constantly upon her. Although she had not turned once to look at him, she could feel the weight of them upon her. Aware that he was observing her, she went on walking as though she hadn't noticed. A natural gambler, he decided to stay in close, and still she did not flinch. It was as though he simply wasn't there. She was bluffing, but nervously, he could tell. She was bothered by the closeness of his gaze, but was feigning indifference. In the end you could always turn a blind eye to things. We are playing games, he thought. He must know every one of these games inside out by now. But this time was different. He felt romantic. The slightest contact of his arm against hers gave him an intense pleasure, a childlike pride, just to be walking along beside a gorgeous woman, a woman all other men looked at. He noticed this the moment he took his eyes off her and became aware of the motley swarm of people around him, all taking their evening walk, no more to him, just at this moment, than energy swirling around his desire, an anonymous herd on the move, at the heart of which he pursued his vision.

They were exactly the same height (she was tall, while he was short for a man) and the rise and fall of their shoulders as they walked fell into a common rhythm. The delicate figure in yellow and his darker form, the one always inclined towards the other, seemed somehow to belong together, to make a pair, a harmonious couple of sorts. As they walked along, they considered one another in silence, and their pleasure in this made them both smile. And yet the secrets each appeared to harbour were in fact no more than the natural reticence of new acquaintances. Gilles André and Pauline Arnoult had spoken on only two or three occasions: they were new to each other. And their bearing towards one another, its undue eagerness, their sense of joy, unmistakable but contained, the extravagance of some of their gestures, the way one would quickly glance at the other then look away, the fullness of their movements, the air of intoxication which shrouded them, weighed them down, all this indicated as much. They stood together on the brink of pleasure. There was no mistaking them for man and wife. And the thing that immediately declared them lovers, though they were not lovers yet, was as difficult to define as it was plain to see.

They were becoming lovers. An inescapable future lay ahead. Whether they resisted or accepted, it would enfold them just the same. They stood trembling on the threshold of intimacy. Trembling, because they both knew that love had told them their destiny. Perhaps the strangest thing was not their destiny but their awareness of it and the fact that with such a destiny, foresight was no protection. They were trapped, as though by a spell, in the secrecy of their meeting, in this unavoidable encounter, in their freedom. A storm of feeling had thrown them together. What kind of life had they made for themselves before this fatal meeting? They did not ask this at the time, but their impulse towards one another was already stirring up a force which might be either their joy or their destruction. The secret impulse was visible to others. It spread all around them in beaming smiles and peals of laughter. They might have sensed danger if all sense of caution had not already been lost. How did others see them? They looked like lovers; if they weren't lovers yet it must be imminent.

They'd been watching each other a great deal, and for some time now. They retained that furtive awareness of the other, the mute but lustful searching, the million urgent glances. They exuded the fervour of people struck by passion. They were at their most conspicuous just when they would have preferred to go unseen. Desire always advertises. Whatever lies in the hearts of lovers, their palpitations, their surges of emotion and sudden changes, says it all. Only four walls can conceal an irresistible attraction. The two of them were simply walking, but their enchantment was clear for all to see. He was lost in contemplation of her, a contemplation which held her utterly enthralled. There was a blissful sense of newness about them which drew the eye. The rhythm of their movements, attuned, conspiratorial, poised and graceful – she was like some winged creature – would soon break up in laughter and nonsense, because anyone could see they had nothing in particular to do and no place in particular to go. Their encounter this evening, their miraculous affinity, their joy, their silence and their smiles, were out in the light. Their desire was expressed in a kind of courtship dance, which was also a show, as perhaps it always is: for the steps are always the same, and anyone who has traced them, even if only once, will instantly recognise the characteristic motion of two people flying towards love.

They had been walking along in silence. While they were parted by the crowd, there was no need to speak. But now they were alone and unhindered, someone had to break their first silence. Neither of the two lovers knew what to say. Did they really need words? Their silence spoke for them. She, for one, was a little embarrassed by what it said. When a man and a woman who have no business with each other are alone together in the street, in the early evening, isn't it obvious what they are about? So obvious perhaps that he took a disarming short cut, saying, 'I wondered if you'd come. I wasn't sure you would' and because their shoulders were just touching the young woman's face was suddenly caught close up, soft and full of sun, so close he could make out the tiny hairs on her cheekbones and the point below the eyes where the skin thins out. Why? she asked. We'd made an arrangement. She pulled in her lips, as though to even out her lipstick. He looked at her mouth. She felt uncomfortable, so close to him. Why was he staring at her mouth like that? She gave a little smile in an attempt to disguise her embarrassment. You might have changed your mind, he said. If I make an arrangement I stick to it, said Pauline Arnoult. And as she said this her voice was controlled, clear and strong, even though her thoughts were all caught up in a tangle of motives and dreams. I believe you, he said, but since I was the one who asked you to come . . . She had moved away from him when he started speaking. And since he had moved towards her again to murmur this, she moved away again. And you know nothing about me, he said, amused by this silent to and fro. It's quite forward of you. You think I'm forward? she asked, suddenly concerned. Should she feel insulted or flattered? No, I don't think that, he answered smoothly, slightly mockingly. Even so, you could have sent me packing, and you didn't, he said, laughing outright. She turned quite pink and said, almost like a little girl who's been found out: It didn't occur to me! Deep inside this woman pursued, voices made themselves heard, secret little admissions and whispers of surprise. Even if I'd wanted to I couldn't have escaped. It's strange, the way I was captivated from the very first time he looked at me. The way I immediately began to imagine things. She translated all this for him, coyly, in a voice which pretended to reproach him, but was still conspiratorial and relaxed: I hoped you wouldn't dare come up and talk to me like that. It was a back to front admission as well as a lie she wanted to believe, and was uttered so quietly he didn't hear. She kept her head lowered and watched her own feet walking. And once again, mumbling, as though her lips were stuck together, she tried to amend what she wanted to say: that the sensible, conscious part of her had hoped he wouldn't speak, while every other part of her, which was neither sensible nor conscious, hoped he would. I thought . . . Her words were lost in the laughter of a group of girls in their path, obliging them to part again (this time there was no skipping). He didn't answer, and she didn't know whether he had heard her or not, and so herself fell silent. They were still walking, as though they were on their way somewhere, but they had arranged nothing. (She had arrived slightly late. He'd seen her coming from afar, they'd shaken hands, embarrassed, pleased, and he had gone on walking in the same direction, with her following.) I have no idea where I'm going! he said. I'm following you blindly! she said. For the first time, they laughed together, simply. They felt as if their laughter summed up and somehow resolved everything.

Pauline Arnoult pondered the romantic memories of the past few weeks: to think that she had once dreamed about this man. At that point he had still been the stranger who caught her eye at school when she dropped off her son. She had ended up thinking about him at night, just as she was going to sleep, because he kept on and on staring at her with an admiration which was blatantly sexual. How could she not notice? Lying in silence next to her husband, she would summon up the memory of his face, the way he looked at her (even if this meant she had to invent bits here and there). She was thrilled at the idea that she inspired this look of loving reverence. Surely it was both shameful and absurd, the way she was suddenly, unjustly giving precedence in her mind to some absent man over the one whose presence confirmed her very existence? He'd turned his eyes upon her and she'd lost her head. Some spell had been cast, and suddenly his look was her command. Who could have resisted such enchantment? She knew perfectly well what was happening to her: all flirty, all of a dither, suddenly besotted with some man, simply because he happened to be besotted with her, that's what it was, she was drawn to him by way of imitation and incapable of refusing to meet him, even though she knew there was no future in it. She hadn't heeded the voice of common sense and run away.

What had happened, exactly? He'd made the first move. That was the trickiest bit, and she'd been completely stupefied. Admiring, even. She would never have done it herself. She was impressed, having forgotten how commanding a man who is no longer young can appear to a woman he finds attractive. He had made the first move because he knew she never would and she had followed him without a second thought. She had not proved incorruptible. Her words, her gestures, her smiles, had all been signs of welcome, there was no mistaking it. Struck by this thought, she raised her head and began to walk taller. There was something shameful about the whole business which was making her act more furtively than she actually felt. She would have much preferred not to have lied to herself, to avoid cheating, whatever else she then went on to do. But maybe that wasn't actually possible. We can't always be what we'd like to be: she had no intention, either, of simpering, and yet she caught herself doing it every now and then. She was tangled up in a whole web of sensations. I'm walking along with a man I don't even know! she said to herself. There was no other way of putting it. This sensual feeling was pulling her in irresistibly. As she walked along beside him, matching her steps to his (at the same time as he was trying to fall in with hers, which was what created the impression that they were somehow in harmony) she studied him for the first time, and registered with astonishment: he was not a handsome man, he was not elegant, the minute he stopped talking his charm vanished too. Was he not a very ordinary sort of man? He certainly wasn't very refined. And yet his presence provoked a response, an attraction in her, the feeling that things were awakening, things were stirring, long buried, secret things, taking over from all the usual things that made up one's life, those sensible, useful other things. Most magical of all, however, was not the emotion itself but the fact that it was clearly shared. Not for a moment, even while she was dismissing all these so-called questions, did she doubt the attraction she held for him. In short, it was a very common sort of enchantment. And we all know where that can lead.

Right now Gilles André was opting more or less for silence. He had no problem with the absence of conversation. His ability to remain silent in the company of someone he scarcely knew, to rely simply on gestures and looks, discomfited his companion. Not that it was deliberate. He simply created his own inner calm. He needed to soothe something inside, a secret part of himself. If it had been up to him he would have dragged this young woman off to a hotel room without further ado, any old place would do as long as he could overstep the bounds of convention. He wanted to run his hands all over her, impose silence with kisses. And the truth was, she wanted it too. He was quite sure of that. Yes, that's what was in her mind. She was preoccupied by this inexplicable desire for intimacy and he knew it without her saying a single word. He was one of those men who is a stranger to conformity and to vulgarity, who acknowledge the reality of their emotions, and don't go in for pretence. If a man felt the impulse and the tenderness which leads to intimacy, why should he have to wait? All he need do was lie down beside her. That was how he looked at it. He had a libertine amorality and the determined clearsightedness that goes with it. And yet he was a true lover: he was delicate. And he could sense that she was not yet ready. She was waiting. That was what she wanted, just now: to defer the inevitable for a while. With his long experience of seduction he recognised it intuitively. That was how it was. And why not? he said to himself. He was capable both of adjusting happily to her feminine rhythm and at the same time wishing it was otherwise. He was aware he was making a conscious effort. Forcing himself to see it her way. She knows nothing about me, he said to himself. So he simply said, Would you like a drink? Yes please, she replied. And they sat down at a pavement café full of people. All of which, he thought, looking at her sitting there, all the lovelier for the desire within her, was just a detour, a way of wasting time, sheer cowardice. While she, on the other hand, was simply excited, suddenly convinced of her beauty in the golden evening light, drugged with delight, unhurriedly savouring the sense that this was a holiday, a special occasion, spiced up by secrecy and novelty. She had all the time in the world to dazzle him. The hands on love's clock move more slowly for women than for men.

And so, since he had to, he began to talk. He used his best cajoling voice, velvety smooth, cushioned with a sigh, as though murmuring in a hidden alcove. His intimate voice, as she would come to think of it. Whispered words, like those of a man on the brink of exhaustion. Pauline Arnoult had been instantly hooked. Did he do it deliberately? When he spoke she almost had the feeling he was tired of loving her. And when he laughed – as he did sometimes, suddenly breaking into laughter – she felt it was all around her, provoked by sheer delight in her. She thought she could detect in his voice exactly what it was she wanted to achieve: to be unique and to make this man subject to her charm. She believed she had already achieved it. She was wrong, but the illusion was as persistent as his voice was smooth. And he excelled in the casting of spells. You listened, you looked, you admired, you laughed, you murmured the familiar clichés, and the flower obediently opened – it never failed. He could not have said quite how it worked (though he knew it did, having observed its effects). He played around with the sensual, even suggestive, power of a phrase: when it came to sweet nothings and winning ways, he was master. His voice, hushed and almost prayer-like in its dedication, kindled the vanity of women.

He was a narrow beam of bewitching light, and this beam spoke her name. I know your name, he had whispered, laughing, in her ear. Ah yes, he used that part of the language which is not quite language, is less binding than words, but just as explicit. Pauline, he murmured, that's it, isn't it? And he said again: Pauline. All the while looking into her eyes, with a tiny, subtle smile. She felt the look was rather overdoing it, but he did it deliberately, as though he knew that women, for all their intuition, fell for it every time. It's a beautiful name, he said. She replied: I've always been very fond of it. She paused, then added, until those films came out, with that tall girl on a beach in a swimming costume. Mmm. She looks a bit like you, he murmured, as though speaking to himself. I hope not! She's not that bad, he said, laughing. He was still watching her with genuine pleasure, a pleasure which came simply from being with her and being able to look at her. She was flustered, so she didn't notice. She was too taken up with herself to be properly aware of her companion. He pursued the question of her name: she was the first young woman he'd known called that. What could she say? She said nothing. And so the voice asked: May I call you Pauline? The request, too, was excessive: outmoded, ridiculous, almost. Of course you can, replied the poor, lovely creature, aware he was play-acting, yet, to her annoyance, enjoying it.

How many women had he used this line on? The question stood between Pauline Arnoult and complete appreciation of the pleasure of being pursued in this way. How many women? And another thing: might he not be making fun of her? She was terrified of being made fun of. The greater the grip of love, the more one suspects the other of trying to trap one. Was she simply his prey? Was he sincere? She was happy to play along, but only on condition it really was just a game. A game of seduction: she didn't really like to think of herself caught up in that. And so, imperceptibly, she tried to behave in a way that was simple and straightforward. But the game pulled her in. Here she was, smiling, laughing, blushing . . . perhaps one could only be oneself when completely alone? She wished she could just be totally herself. You're so quiet! he exclaimed. Don't you want to answer my question? And he repeated: May I call you Pauline? Of course you can, she said. You can't exactly call me 'Madame'. Why not? he replied, laughing, relaxed, flirtatious. After all, you don't know me, he said. His face was set in a smile. I don't know, she said, with a directness which astonished her future lover, I feel as though I've known you for ages. And anyway, she said, seizing her courage with both hands, stop going on about how I don't know you. I'm here with you now, aren't I? Besides, if I'm a stranger, how come you know my name? He laughed, yet again. I heard a woman at the school one day call you Pauline, he said. And he added: It was my grandmother's name. Mine was called Marie-Pauline, she said. These things go through fashions, like everything else, she said, rather coldly, in a voice which lacked his singsong gentleness, was altogether lower and more masculine. She was making a real effort to dispel the mist of desire clouding their meeting. But there was no point trying, these things are either there or they're not. They don't suddenly disappear. Have I done something to annoy you? he asked. She shook her head. The message in his wordless murmur had made her miserable. He didn't like it when she pressed her lips together like that. He liked it when she smiled. He looked deeply, daringly into her eyes. She was just that moment blushing. Enough was said.

And so he took up the reins once more. Enough had been said, but it wasn't quite that simple. Nothing had been done! Some men never quite seem to get round to making the transition from silence to gestures, from words to actions, while certain women are satisfied with virtually nothing. The mistress of temptation who disdains to sin. He'd known a few of those, but had always made a point of sniffing them out right at the start. This one wasn't a flirt, he thought, far from it. You had to hand her that: she had an utterly seductive kind of charm, without ever attempting to seduce. He began to give this some thought. Surely that wasn't possible. She must be trying somehow to please. In any case, she wasn't being completely natural. You could tell she was holding herself back. He glanced up at her. She existed. She was a woman with presence. Why did some people have presence, others not? he wondered. She must have an inner life, a strong sense of inner self. He'd always believed in it. He looked at her with genuine interest. She was even more gorgeous in his dreams. She had attracted him and now he was completely hooked. He was ecstatic. And meanwhile she said nothing, sat there in silence! Surely she'd say something? He waited. Silence. She was watching people drinking and chatting in the warm evening air. Once again he noticed how busy the streets were. The two of them were not exactly alone together. And yet she was all he could see. She's fairly got me in her clutches, he thought. Had she still not spoken? No, she was looking elsewhere. What are your children called? he asked, just for the sake of saying something. Instantly he was horrified to hear himself. What was he saying? He must be feeling pretty intimidated, despite everything. Sometimes one was such a cheat, it was laughable. He wanted to say 'I want you' and here he was asking her about her children. And he knew perfectly well she only had one. That wasn't like him. Normally he couldn't even be bothered to talk. He smiled at her, feeling almost sorry for himself. Her cheeks were still flushed red. She was as bad as him. The silence was crackling. . . .

No, they hadn't yet found a way of talking to each other. They were bogged down in trivia, caught by the openness of their secret, caught in the exchange of feeling as their eyes met, looked down and looked away again. Whether open or furtive, no glance was innocent. But she entered into the fake conversation. She had just the one son. His name was Theodore. And your daughter? she asked him, politely. She was one of those women who have no fear of politeness, and who are capable of saying or doing the most spectacularly uninteresting things, out of sheer urbanity. My daughter's name is Sarah, he said. Then he added, as though in self-defence: But I didn't choose it. He explained: My wife felt that since she was the one who'd been through the pregnancy and labour, she had the right to name the child without consulting me. And you don't like the name? she asked, slightly embarrassed by the way these confidences brought his wife into it. Not much, he admitted. He thought for a moment and then added: For me Sarah's an old woman's name. He went on: My daughter took the place of the old woman. But the old woman took the place of my wife. It wasn't entirely clear what he meant, but he was funny and sad and this combination in a man was somehow touching. She decided to laugh, because that was obviously what he was trying to get her to do. He noticed she had nice teeth, pristine as a child's. He noticed that her eyes narrowed like those of a Chinese woman, and her lashes were very dark for a blonde. No man will ever dare admit the importance of a woman's body, how it either wins him over or leaves him cold, how it asserts itself before overcoming him, reveals its secrets and of itself attracts or repels him. That a body should be the thing that decides everything! A body. It seemed so un . . . and yet that's what was there before him, moving, breathing, giving off its subtle and overpowering scents: that was what had him hooked. He saw her laugh. Her nose creased just at the point where spectacles would rest. He wished he could stop staring at her in fascination like this, but he couldn't help himself. He was captivated by her face. And she kept it before him like a net, reading his unwavering expression, aware of what it meant. Here was a man falling in love with her. No doubt about it. She was part thrilled, part troubled. Torn between lucidity and shyness, one minute she was a goddess, the next a lumpen schoolgirl. Her confusion blinded her to him. He wasn't handsome, but she'd stopped noticing. Her mind was frozen, like that of an animal attacked: she had no words left, only feelings. She felt stripped of her own self by a man's gaze. Women who are admired without seeking to be so will understand this better than those caught up by their own frantic efforts to please. She was aware that the confusion of the woman who is looked at blinds her to the feelings of the man who looks. The obvious questions arose. He was in love. But seriously in love? Could she be wrong, getting carried away when in fact he was only teasing? The dance of certainty and doubt was under way.

He was considering her in a state of rapt delight. He had a smiling air of mild amusement. That was it: he radiated a kind of uncomplicated and complete happiness in his contemplation of her. She was somewhat overwhelmed. (She was acutely conscious of the presence of his body.) She was smiling as much as he was, with the same sense of wickedness almost tipping over into laughter. But ridiculous though it seemed, she was also plagued with doubt. She could not tell what he was really looking at, what the object of his inner gaze was, the cause of his pleasure, the source of his desire. She would never be able to see the world through his eyes, those eyes which were not hers. There was simply no way of knowing what he thought when he looked at her, or even whether he thought anything at all or just remained blank. She was sucking away at the end of a straw in her confusion; she set the straw aside and drank from the glass, sitting there right beside him, aware of his silence. What was he thinking? Was he bored? What did he want? He was genuinely taken with her, caught by her charm and obliged to charm her back, not in any way playing or hunting surely, but how could she be sure? How many women . . . ? Intentionally or no, his face was closed off from her, a mask which could be doubted at any moment simply because he could perfectly well lie if he chose to, simply because others before him had lied. She would never be quite sure what he felt, she would never really know quite what he thought of her. The best thing would be to pretend to have stopped asking questions. Do you love me? The lifelong refrain. We just have to forget the opacity and everything else that stands between us and the other. We have plenty of words and gestures to communicate with. It's the thoughts we can't get at; we don't know how to say everything, or what we would want to say, even if we could. We can scarcely get round to thinking own our thoughts in the time we have. We can't even admit everything to ourselves. Was he just playing with her? It would always be like this – conjecture; feeling, sensing, guessing, but never knowing for sure, sowing doubt and fear on the site of all that remains unspoken. Were they doomed to keep everything between them secret? Yes, it was a bad joke, a twist of fate, the fact that all their thoughts, their feelings, their love must remain forever trapped inside their flesh, behind the iron bars of the face: inaccessible, improbable, never to be taken for granted. There they sat, facing each other, doomed indeed, awkward in the knowledge that they could never more than guess at, or take on trust, what was being said through this silence. It was terrible, this need to actually prove the one thing which more than any other might be pure and true. Even love required proof.

How many women? she wondered, as she listened to him. And how should she respond? How could she tell him what was happening, that this time it was different? There is no end to the misery of those who are sincere. Why couldn't they just be there, facing each other, like open books? he wondered, noticing her reticence. She was unsure of him. Of course she was. What did she know about him? He would have liked to say to her straight out: I'm not playing games. But he didn't dare. It wasn't the right moment to make this remark. She was lost in thought, watching a woman sitting alone at a table, a woman just at that crucial age for her sex, who had ordered a Kir Royale. Solitude. The Kir Royale woman must have been beautiful once, and she was very striking in her turban. Don't you think she's beautiful, that woman over there? asked Pauline Arnoult. Nodding slightly, he pulled a little face. The face meant that he couldn't see past her age to her beauty. And indeed, he was thinking: she looks a bit past it. She was disappointed. He was like all the rest, in thrall to the freshness of youth. Which was why this woman was alone and why she herself, young and so pretty, had a husband. The companionship of marriage . . . You had enough and to spare precisely when you actually needed it least. Life was all back to front: the happiness of great love is given to those who already have youth. This led Pauline Arnoult to think of her husband. She recalled the way he had paused for a moment, then replied, the first time she had allowed herself to mention Gilles André, since the thought of him, the silent determination in his eyes, occupied more and more of her waking moments. Her husband had said: Yes, I know who you mean. He's going through a divorce, I think. She'd casually talked about the man she'd met at the school, who looked nice enough. Nice! Yes, that was the word she'd used! She blushed to think of it. She plunged back into the conversation without thinking what she said. Didn't you get divorced recently? she asked. He was surprised. How did she know that? Someone must have mentioned it at the club, people talk. So it would seem, he answered. Even so, she must be feeling uncomfortable to ask such a question. Ever supple, he switched his voice back into a sweeter mode: How do you know about that? he asked gently, with a sad smile. I just know, she said. Oh well, if you want to get all secretive, he murmured. Maybe I do, she said. There was no way she could have told him about her conversation with her husband. She kept her silence. He, meanwhile, had recovered from his surprise. Yes, he said, I am getting divorced, apparently it's coming along very nicely! His dark eyes sparkled – it was a painful subject. Why do you pretend you don't care? she asked him. I don't know, he said. Because I didn't want it to happen in the first place. It's my wife's idea. I just let her get on with it. I'm not dealing with any of it, he said, as though that was all he really cared about. Her lawyer's doing it. He suddenly looked determined as he said: I don't want my daughter to go short. Or my wife either. I'm not going to start counting pennies. I can understand that, she said. But she didn't quite know what to say. Women can be so hard when they think they've fallen out of love, he said, speaking almost to himself. Then he turned to her, smiled and added: I say 'when they think' because they're often wrong. It was not the moment to contradict him. So she agreed, and he laughed at the sight of her lovely face, with its slightly crestfallen look. You're adorable, he said. And this time she countered: Don't say that. It sounds absurd. I don't like it when you speak to me like that. Nonsense, he said. You love it. He drew his face close to hers: You just don't want to admit it. . . .

He turned serious again, to wind up the subject of his divorce. Do you mind if we don't discuss it any more? It's not my favourite topic of conversation. To reassure her (for, of course, he was not trying to keep anything from her, no, he was as honest as the day is long) he added: I've told you everything there is to know. I'm getting divorced, he said, just like everyone else. His mouth drooped wearily. Not like you, though, he said, after a short silence. She liked that thought. And yet – how did she manage it? – she seemed to hear a note of regret in his voice. She almost believed he was asking her to get a divorce. He warmed to his theme: I don't know why they all start wanting divorces. Sheer stupidity. God only knows, women just aren't meant to live alone. You're made for company. Above all, he loved the idea of a woman who loved and it was in an attempt to draw close to her purity that he said again: You're not going to get divorced. And very wise too. He said he was glad to see she'd got more sense than the rest of them. Again she thought she detected a note of regret, and wondered if she was imagining it. She was indeed imagining it. It was a projection of her own desire, a flirtation with the absurd but somehow comforting thought that a man wanted her free so he could love her completely. But then he said: You won't ever divorce, I'm sure of it. Still she thought he must be asking her in a roundabout way. But she was simply wrong. He wanted in fact to be reassured that she would never do anything so silly. Again she was faced with the irreducible opacity of the other, the great danger of believing or not believing that such and such is the case, and then getting everything wrong – depth, width, colour, everything. And finally of shedding tears over it. Surely tears are the last words of every love?

How subtle, how numerous they are, our misdemeanours: our secret thoughts, our concealed hopes, the moves we expect of others and those we fail to make ourselves, the words we long to hear, and those we do hear but which were never said. And yet in the turmoil they foment within us, we find some kind of answer. There was one thing which at this point she had not openly admitted to herself – why, that is, she was sitting there without her husband's knowledge, or anyone else's either – and the fact that her being there was a secret conditioned everything she heard or said. The secrecy unsettled her. Better to be open, she thought. It was impossible, or at best idiotic. But she attempted the impossible anyway. She said the stupidest thing she could think of to say. She said: Why did I come with you? What am I doing here with you?

Now she'd put the cat among the pigeons. She'd reached a point where she was so irritated by their flirtatious banter, she had just blurted out the words without thinking. What really irritated her was the sight of herself from the outside, playing the game, enjoying it. So she had asked him this stupid question. Now look at her, simpering away! All in an effort to disguise her instinct, the inner tremor which was itself a kind of warning. Wasn't that what was really going on? The truth of it was, she was already in love with him, and wouldn't admit it. She both knew it and didn't know it. Deferment and seduction gave her the same pleasure as the outcome itself. She was playful, captive, guilty, all in one, as it is entirely possible to be. Why did I come here? she had asked. She had asked him the very question she could not ask herself. She felt stupid and fake, and then, since she didn't really think she was either, aggrieved. First that crackling silence, now this stupid question! She felt so lost that she said it again: Why did I come with you? He smiled at her like an elderly man smiling at a young girl. She was charming; he loved it when she blushed. He would give the little darling her answer. The intimate voice murmured: Because there is no reason you shouldn't. It was almost as though he was putting this to her as a question, a question that she didn't really hear, she was so completely thrown by this remark. No doubt she came across as stupid or naïve right now, a pretty silly young thing, determined to blurt out things you're not supposed to say, things better left unsaid, which, being unsaid, remain half known and half dreamed of. Her reluctance to be honest with herself had made her brutal. She had simply succumbed to the need to speak. But would he be able to answer her straight out, to admit his desire, his rapture, the vast eternal plan? To say right out: We are here because I want to sleep with you and because you are going to say yes. Or would he beat around the bush a bit and say, murmuring low: We are here to seduce one another, because I like you, because I can't stop thinking of you, because I suppose I must have fallen in love with you, and I know you like me too, even if you cheat and pretend not to realise. No, these were not words he could possibly say. There were certain things that shouldn't be said at this stage. She wouldn't like it. But if he did choose to speak, everything would suddenly be out in the open. He felt a huge sense of regret. The words were there, and he didn't say them. He knew the answer, but all he did was repeat her question. A parrot, and a liar too.

Yes, he said, rocking back on his chair, why are we here? Why are we here together? His eyes were laughing. He was an echo, ironically giving her back her words. And all they could do was laugh at these questions, to which they held the key in their bodies (out of sight), in their eyes (magnetically drawn to each other), and which they both knew they could unlock. No doubt this knowledge, hidden away like a foolish secret, is what sets off the fever. And so of course they lapsed into laughter yet again. Laughter lay at the heart of their flirtatious manoeuvres. It was the sign of their awkwardness, the sound of their disloyalty, because however obvious the meaning of their words, their gestures, they liked to pretend, in the midst of the courtship ritual, not to hear the thud of their racing pulses. I've got a present for you, she said, opening her bag. . . . Why had she wanted to give him a present? It was one more question she refused to answer. And so she blushed as she handed over what looked like a book. Where's this all leading? he said. They laughed again, because it was all they could do. The way was opening up – they could lie a little, for elegance, laugh a little, for cleverness, admit everything, and then let themselves go completely. He tried to imagine her body. He found he couldn't. Her face was too much present. Its magic exerted a taboo. But that wouldn't last for ever. As soon as he got close to her he felt sure of that, because he liked her smell. It wouldn't last for ever. The sun had disappeared behind the rooftops.

They sat side by side in their respective postures, and continued to chat for a while. She sat with her legs crossed under the flimsy fabric of her dress, hunched over towards her glass and the tabletop, while he leaned against the back of his chair, his legs spread, more relaxed than she was, for now – she was inhibited by their physical proximity. On the pavement, people came and went, some leaving, others taking their seats. He began to ask her a series of very straightforward questions, to get an idea of the kind of life she led. There are many things which preoccupy a young adult which he had now forgotten about, and on top of that, he was a man, but he tried his best to find a way in. Who's looking after your son tonight? he asked. He's with my mother, she replied. Do you work? What do you do? A designer – you make a living from design? Designing wallpaper? I'd never have thought of that, he said. People need it, though. And always there was the threat of silence breaking in. He was really making conversation. What's your favourite colour? he asked. The question struck her as original. No one's ever asked me that, she said. I count myself a happy man, he said, looking deep into her eyes. You're exaggerating again, she objected. Okay I'll stop. Promise, he said. But you know you like it really. He was so brusquely perceptive, she had to blush. A silence fell. Then he began again. What about your husband? he asked. What does he do? Where were you born? And then: Do you like living here? How long have you been married? Are you going to have lots more children? When he asked this she blushed. Are your parents still alive? he asked. Then, remembering: Of course, stupid of me, I'd forgotten your son was with his grandmother. And your father? Is he retired yet? Seeing her surprise at the question, he realised that it was something an old person would ask. At her age, of course her parents weren't retired. He smiled as he said rather boringly: And how do they feel about having such a pretty daughter? They must be very proud of you. My parents are wonderful, said Pauline Arnoult. When I was little we lived in a big house near L'Isle-Adam. . . . She told her story simply, smiling happily. Then she said: And you? It was his turn to tell his story. He was far more discreet. She sensed he was omitting the most important fact, which was that he adored women, but she didn't press him, since in any case she preferred not to be told. Each acquired a version of the other's life made up of details. It didn't change anything. He even felt a slight surge in his desire when she talked about her husband. One might say it gave him a secret pleasure. She turned a little red with the effort of speaking. He found her prettier than ever, her face flushed with a pink glow, the glow of desire. She leaned back in her chair. For the first time they sat in identical poses. And she found she was able to sit there in silence without feeling awkward, just smiling, watching him. It was almost as if talking loosened the knot that bound them, as though words somehow brought calm, replacing her initial resistance with ease and the ordinariness of what had become apparent.

2

It was the end of that same sun-soaked summer day. They were in the bathroom, getting ready, discussing who would be at the club that evening. The husband was very much looking forward to it. (The men would watch a boxing match and it promised to be a good fight.) His wife was not so keen. She didn't like this way of splitting up the men and women. It's never a good idea, she said, as she'd said before. The mothers always got to talking about their children (but she had none herself) while the fathers went all silly, laughing first at nothing, and later at obscenities. These evenings were pointless. And you didn't have to be psychic to know what the men talked about. We talk about you, Guillaume Perdereau said to his wife. He was laughing, but not at her. So he said: It's not true. You know perfectly well we talk about work. It was a time when professionals were working very hard. The men devoted their lives to their jobs. It was no exaggeration to say they hardly ever saw their families. As Louise said: You get home late every night of the week and then on Friday evenings you all get together to talk rubbish. She thought back to a few recent dinner parties. How terribly ordinary we all are on these occasions, she thought. She was sick of wasting her time like this. She needed to achieve something. Or else she preferred some real human warmth, not these superficial shindigs, full of silly gossip. These days she preferred intimate occasions, where you could talk properly, really get to know someone. I've gone off this sort of thing, she said. To which her husband replied: You say that every time, and then you enjoy yourself. He was right. She shook her head and said: It's true. I do enjoy myself because there is always something touching about other people. It makes me realise how much we all help each other, just by being close together. And that's what bothers me about tonight – we won't be together. But you don't want to watch the fight with us, do you? She shook her head.

He couldn't see past the end of his own nose: he had no idea what women talked about when they got together, he didn't even notice that he and his old pals always talked about the same things, in the same way. Basically he was a man of action: he was far less interested in what was said or done than he was in the saying or the doing. And as for the personal or psychological problems (since that was what it was really about) of his partner, he believed he did his bit, acted – tried genuinely to be – concerned, and no doubt the very effort he had to make convinced him that he succeeded. But it was an illusion. He was incapable of understanding the unhappiness caused by not being like other people: of not being a mother. Of having a flat stomach when others are complaining about putting on too much weight, of being free to do what you like while they pick up their children from school, of knowing that once the holidays are over you'll still be there just growing older, alone. Because, let's face it, husbands die before their wives, and widows grow old alone, sometimes with no one even to discover their corpse in some little bolt hole that's never been quite clean since their eyesight failed. She sighed. You can come with us if you want, he said, again. He insisted: No one's forcing you to stay with the women. I know, she said, but I don't want to be on my own surrounded by men either. He raised his hands and let them drop. At that very same moment, Pauline Arnoult was considering her own gestures, and resolving not to skip and jump. Well then, my love, what do you want me to say? said Guillaume Perdereau.

He had sticking-out ears, which wouldn't have mattered if the rest of his face had any kind of harmony or cohesion, but he was pretty much cobbled together, with coarse features and a large head. In fact, the way he'd been assembled, each imperfection seemed only to accentuate the others. A great big head and a bull neck: Louise thought this almost every time she looked at him. But she loved him. He was intelligent and romantic: astonishing but true. When he clenched his teeth and puffed out his neck, with its prominent veins and tendons, she would laugh, and kiss him. In public she might make a single gesture to indicate how much she loved him. And he was happy to have such a pretty young wife at his side. He was happy to be with her. Come and watch the match with us, he said again. Oh no, she said. I don't fancy watching you all shouting at the television. He had begun to shave, and the only answer she got was the sound of the electric shaver. She was barefoot, dressed in a faded kimono, her hair was loose and brushed and a little static around the collar. She had finished putting on her makeup and went into another room to fetch a dress. Louise! he called. What? she replied. Her voice was muffled – she was speaking into her wardrobe. Should I put a tie on? he said. Not to go and watch a fight, said Louise. You're right, he said, I'd forgotten. I hadn't, she said drily. Is it really such a bore? he said. He was genuinely surprised, since he himself could never have got upset over something so trivial. He would never get used to the way certain women have of wanting to control everything, of wanting every second of every day to run according to their plan. His first wife had been a despot and he had imagined Louise would be easier to live with. But he would end up believing that actually no one is easy to live with – instead of realising (as he might have done) that he always went for the same type of woman. He broke off getting ready and went and stood in front of his wife. What would you rather have done tonight? he asked, simply, looking at her, weary of these endless discussions, but obliged somehow to have them, because he didn't want to leave her in the lurch. Would you rather we just stayed home together? he asked. She seemed to be saying yes, but in fact she didn't know what to say, she didn't know what she would have preferred. She often found that she knew what she didn't want, but not what she did. He was irritated by her point-blank rejection. If you don't want anything in particular, he would say, you should let other people choose what they want. He allowed his displeasure to show. Louise immediately went into a sulk. She ignored him completely and pushed the hangers along the rail to get at a dress. She was angry, since for once she could see he was right. She thought – without saying it – that she was not a very nice person. She could picture her own face, set hard and obstinate, and she started to laugh. I'm sorry, she wailed, turning towards him like a cat, I'm such a pain.

He was fifteen years older than her, which is to say he was past the halfway mark, while she was in the full bloom of her thirties (though she was not in fact blooming at all). Here, side by side, as he bent to pick up the hanger and she puzzled over what to wear, the age difference was very apparent. His body had begun to spill over, he was a bit paunchy, it was clear that in old age he would swell up rather than wither away. He wasn't the kind of man who kept a close eye on himself, he used his time to go out and live: a happy man. She, on the other hand, was a woman of passion. She was eaten up with anxiety. Anxiety over what? he would ask. She bit her nails. Stop it! he'd say. She would place her hands on her slender thighs. Her pale wrists were so delicate! I could break you in two, just like that, he would say, clasping them. She was thin, but not bony, and not just slim either, she was a truly thin woman, burning herself up – that was her temperament, a hungry fire, unhappiness beneath it all. Perhaps that was why she liked him: for his life force. She was fascinated, she wanted to get in the boat with him. Time was, she had known how to enjoy herself, to have a laugh. Before she had shrivelled up with this unrequited desire for a child she had looked the part of his young mistress – which was what she had been. In choosing to pursue her, his choice had been purely sexual. At the time neither one of them had imagined he would leave his wife. Louise was just a bit of escapism. And the experience had taught him what escapism meant for a family man: it meant an adventure from which you safely return. She expected nothing. But when he discovered, or believed he had, that she was not a tyrannical woman, he had married her. He'd left everything, the children, the mother, everything. Louise had not really appreciated the cost, she wasn't a mother, and had even despised the abandoned wife a little, who threatened suicide, and actually went beyond threats. . . . She had gone out and bought her little white outfit, turned up at the Mairie with this man of action, who was deeply in love with her. He never took his eyes off her, as if she was his first. In fact she would be his third and last wife, and the idea that he couldn't afford to get it wrong again had crossed his mind. But it was an unworthy thought, since it had more to do with money than emotion: he had two families to look after, two wives, three children. With all that in your wake, all that love, all those words, those caresses both given and received, you are somehow fated to stray. You know in your heart that you have always broken all your promises and will leap at the chance of an adventure, at any price. Louise was quite conscious of the balance of power between them. She could leave him, start a new life with another man at any time, while for Guillaume, it was basically his last shot at married life.

She looked at herself in the mirror. The fertility treatment had made her stomach swell. I'm deformed, she thought. Guillaume couldn't bear her saying such stupid things. If you were lucky enough to be pretty you should have the decency not to complain. But she wasn't complaining, she was simply stating a fact, and admittedly once she had her clothes on she looked perfect. How awful those people who look ugly with their clothes on must look when they take them off, thought Louise. In the end she slipped on something brightly coloured. Is that a new dress? said Guillaume. It was simply a way of resuming conversation – in fact he'd seen the dress a dozen times. Don't you like it? she asked. Yes, yes, of course I do, he said, I just thought I hadn't seen it before. You don't look at me properly, then, she said crossly. Then, with an abrupt change of tone and manner: Do you? she asked playfully. Do you really look at me? I've worn it at least ten times! She was laughing. He breathed a sigh of relief. (Picture him as one of those men who are a little bit spineless about facing up to their wives, not because they're really frightened, but because they live with them and want to avoid conflict.) Arguments wore him out, he didn't want to have his life ruined by stupid rows, but Louise was an expert at them and he always ended up avoiding a scene just to keep her happy. Which is how it was that she, with her awkward personality, usually had the better of her conciliatory partner.

3

Where would you like to eat? he asked. Oh, I don't know, said Pauline Arnoult. I'll leave it up to you. I never dare choose for someone else. What do you feel like eating? he asked. I don't mind, I like everything, she said. She began to laugh: You lead and I'll follow. You can take me where you want, like a parcel! Her teasing made her provocative – perhaps it helped her to relax. She behaved towards him with an astonishing mixture of grace, forwardness and expectation: the fusion of a genuinely loyal disposition with profound femininity. Did she realise she was provocative? he wondered. He was beginning to get to know her better, and asked himself: Would she be a tease? He wouldn't be surprised. She'd turned up. She was beautiful: she must be used to being pursued. She had a husband. And she was shy, joyful and flirtatious all at once. Let's go and have dinner then, he said, pushing back his chair sharply and standing up. It's still early, but that way we'll have longer to get to know one another. She was embarrassed by the joint allusion to 'us' and appetite. Hence the little gesture with which she touched her hair a moment, before fiddling with her scarf. Might she be a tease? he asked himself again. He got up, still wondering, still preoccupied with the mystery of what makes others tick. His eyes glanced over her flat white shoes, the yellow stitching on her dress and then up to her face, which had lost its golden glow. It was then he realised that the sun had gone. Aren't you cold? he asked, at the same time thinking, Why am I asking that? He himself was boiling. Something about this woman made him act like a fool. No, not at all, she said. Are you? she asked, surprised. Absolutely not, he said. But you make me say stupid things, he said with calculated honesty, drawing a smile from her. She was beginning to overcome the shyness which had almost made her shameless and now looked him full in the face. She was quite obviously happy to be there with him. Ah! There was only one real reason why she would be here with him. She radiated desire, he thought, and now here they were, off to have dinner, instead of filling each other and their darkness with light, without need for food, drink or talk. He thought: We are unspontaneous, fearful. I certainly am. But why? I daren't take her arm, I'm too scared, too feeble, too complicated, perhaps, to simply lay my desire before her. How compliant we are.

The thought absorbed him: We are very compliant. Both of us. Oh yes, she was being very proper, and unfortunately, as a result, she was also dreadfully predictable. Like many women, she demanded little, when in fact what she really wanted was the whole man. It was really rather silly. Once again he wondered: why did women usually prefer endless foreplay to the immediacy of making love? Why did they refuse to simply open up? He'd never worked that one out to his satisfaction. Women are always said to 'give' themselves, he thought, but in what way do they 'give' themselves so much more than we do? They too feel desire. Surely they too are 'taking' us to some degree. Using us even, he reflected. Hadn't his own wife used him, like a stallion, simply to have a baby? Having a baby – that was one thing they couldn't do alone: they could only appropriate a baby. It made him shudder to think this. He could get quite angry thinking about women. They always came out on top. They were such flirts. A woman loved to arouse a man's desire, to get him to pursue her. This one was no different: she was thrilled that he was courting her like this. If he wasn't careful he might suddenly feel incredibly weary of it all. He turned to her, looked at her carefully. She was quite stiff, she walked like a doll which has been wound up tight with a key in her back. There was something slightly clumsy and shy about her, which was touching. He found it not so much naïve as moving, this fledgeling beauty in her, which troubled her with its new-found power. It lent a kind of purity to their encounter. That was the feeling he had. He also liked the fact that she wasn't divorced, as so many others were, that she seemed even to have woven a web of familial harmony about her, a kind of grace which could be seen in the face of her child. She was so young! That was what was so good, that was what turned him on, the feeling he got that she was just a beginner.

This girl's turning me into an old-fashioned suitor, thought Gilles André, laughing mildly at himself. And she's completely thrown by me. She's a bit lost. She doesn't quite know what to do. Whereas he knew perfectly well. So he said: We both know what's going on here. It was as though he was making an announcement. Regret, avowal, appeal, hope, delirium – they were all present in the words. What makes you say that? asked Pauline. He fell silent, and gave her an ironic look. What do you think? he said, looking her straight in the eye. I'm right, aren't I? She knew perfectly well what he meant, how they were both fobbing each other off with decent delaying tactics, and how disingenuous it was to pretend that they could end up anywhere but in each other's arms. She felt as if she were the guilty one. Guilty of feminine wiles. She was: she was pouting and acting coy, playing a part because she was afraid. I'm afraid because it isn't a game, she thought. Should one really make light of desire and its upheavals? She felt the thrill of sexual engagement with a man she didn't know. Maybe it was true she was feigning reluctance, but she could hardly fling herself at him. How could they find a short cut, without being crude? she thought, by way of an excuse. Don't say that, I don't like it, she said. Then convince me I'm wrong, he said. (Thereby finding a short cut.) So he said again: We both know what's going on here. She didn't contradict him (though what she was thinking was 'women don't like short cuts') and he laughed suddenly, as though he had her cornered, exposing her as a flirt, but was prepared to forgive her anyway. She hated this feeling of being caught out, got the better of. Her cheeks flushed abruptly red. She wished she could stop blushing, revealing that she was thrown.

She still didn't realise that being close to her moved him, or that her confusion actually made her even more appealing. He really did find her very attractive. She was very much his type. More than that, her smell, her skin, some indefinable quality, they were all exactly to his taste, so as to match the minutiae of his desire, though as yet he had not considered the minutiae. She, for her part, felt the same startled thrill at the affinity between them: an affinity between lovers, of the kind that wears out our attempts to understand it and overcomes our attempts to feel. There was no point trying to talk. Better not to speak of the languor they were both feeling. How quiet they were – stunned. She was thinking how the absence of any future, and the craziness of her being here at all cast a black pall over the playfulness of their meeting. They would have to part. At this prospect, her desire dwindled down within her to a tiny melancholic stream. Maybe the only way to avoid the anguish lovers feel when they are parted is to disappear altogether, to shut oneself off completely from the light, to break the spell? Nevertheless, they stayed where they were, already bound to each other, more lost even than they knew, slaves to an impulse, oblivious of their fate: their future deaths, the course their lives would take, their pasts so full of others they had loved, their separate, single bodies.

Perhaps there are people whose fates are sealed, the stories of whose loves are already, somewhere, written down. We often say as much but rarely believe it. But it's true there are so many men in the world and so many women and so many possible combinations of the two, that lovers are constantly getting together, as inevitably as if they were predestined. Here? asked Gilles. Are you happy to have dinner with me here? They were outside a pleasant-looking brasserie. He stopped to inspect the menu and take a look inside to see if the place was a decent size. It's fine, she replied. The outline of her form was like a flame. For the first time he allowed himself to imagine what her body might be like. All legs and arms, he decided. I love your dress, he said to her. Me too, she said, with the very simplicity she had risked losing in the urgency of her wish to please him. I told you, I like yellow. She smiled her wonderful smile, revealing her lucky teeth. Her face glowed with pleasure. Are we really so lonely, even when we have someone who loves us, that the slightest flirtatious compliment gratifies us and lights up our lives? She let him go in ahead of her and followed him, her hips swaying slightly. Her eyes sparkled as though brimming with tears. She ran her hand through her hair, embarrassed by the way people looked at them as they presented themselves as a couple. Or perhaps by the very fact that they presented themselves as a couple at all. The maitre d'hotel was saying sir, madam, as though they were man and wife. Pauline Arnoult watched Gilles André's purposeful stride. She yielded to the temptation to lay on the charm. For there is a moment of acquiescence in these things, and she had just made up her mind to fall in love with him. To be looked at, to listen, to laugh, to cajole, to be intoxicated, to go no further, and to wait. Infected with a fever which wouldn't break, Gilles André dwelt in the moment, a moment full of signals, stolen words and potential dangers. When it comes to happy events, no occasion requires so much finesse as the first meeting of lovers.

4

It was the moment when Gilles André was saying, with a weary set to the side of his mouth: Women are so hard when they think they've fallen out of love. And Guillaume Perdereau was trying to soften up Louise, asking: Is that a new dress? Just then, in another bathroom, another young woman was getting ready for the same evening. She too was looking for the right clothes to wear, making her face up, putting on perfume, getting dressed, alongside the man with whom she shared her life. Just now she was vigorously brushing her great mane of curly hair and asking her husband: Who'll be there tonight? Everyone, I think, said her husband (whose name was Jean). She went on tugging at her hair with the brush. 'Everyone' who? she said. The usual crowd, he said. He ran through the list for her. Guillaume and Louise, Eve and Max, Tom and Sara, Penelope maybe, Melusine and Henri, Gilles and Blanche, Pauline and Marc. Gilles and Blanche? asked Marie, in surprise. Do you think they'll turn up together? Why shouldn't they? he asked. Don't you know they're getting divorced? said Marie. No, said Jean, I didn't know that. Well I never, he thought, saying nothing.

He wondered what could have brought about the break-up. Has he met someone else? he asked his wife. No, she said, I don't think so. Why do you say that? she added, in a different voice. She turned towards him, saying: There are other reasons for splitting up. They just don't get on any more. She said this energetically, with some irritation. It was an important point for her. There were definitely other reasons for getting divorced. Of course, it was one possible reason for breaking up a relationship, that you'd found another one that was still in its heady early days. And it wasn't the fault of the person left behind. But she wanted to believe it wasn't the only possibility. Besides, she said, it's Blanche who wants the divorce. Anyway, Blanche is coming this evening, she phoned me this morning to tell me, he said. She phoned you this morning to tell you? said Marie. And to what do you owe the honour of a phone call at work? she said. I never disturb you at work even when I need to. She had taken on the righteous indignation of the angry and dissatisfied wife. He tried to calm her upset: It lasted all of two minutes, he said. She reminded me about the do this evening, said she was coming, that was it, nothing else. His tone was a mixture of pleading, apology and irritation in the face of stupidity, the tone you employ when you can sense a silly, pointless argument coming up. I knew we were going, said Marie. Just because she hasn't got a husband doesn't mean she has to suddenly start ringing *you* up. He sighed. Don't be ridiculous, he said, and please, don't be unkind. She doesn't deserve it. It infuriated his wife still further to hear him being compassionate to another woman. He realised this, but the harm was already done. The conversation had taken a wrong turning and he must find a way to head it off. Well I never, he said, you're jealous! Yes, she said, that's right, I'm jealous, I'm entitled to be, and it doesn't seem to bother you. What a crafty one she was, he thought, not to deny her jealousy, simply to admit it and inflict it upon him.

Don't get cross, he begged, trying not to laugh. Marie. He went over to her and placed his hands on her shoulders. Oh no you don't, she said, laughing with him. Don't you touch me. Stop it, he pleaded. She answered merely by pulling a little face. What are you thinking? You think Blanche is making a pass at me? That I want to have a fling with her? he asked, teasingly. The only person I want a fling with is you, he said. Huh! . . . she exclaimed. He shouted: I love Marie Def! She's the only one for me! Do you hear me? She burst out laughing. But did she really hear him? She was so jealous. With a problem like that a woman could become blind to your love for her. But I don't have a problem, Marie said. Oh yes you do, said Jean, you're feeling insecure, and you're taking it out on me. He added kindly: Why are you feeling insecure, my darling? It really annoyed her when he said my darling like that. He sounded like her father-in-law. And it wound her up when he treated her like a little child. I'm perfectly sure of myself thank you, she said. Everyone feels jealousy. If they don't they don't feel love either. There was no point even trying to convince her otherwise. So do you think I'm a jealous person? he asked her. Of course you are, she said. She added: It just doesn't show because I don't give you any reason to be. But you . . . she said. Marie's jealousy had first erupted the day her husband lied to her and by chance she happened to find out. Marie Def didn't really think her husband would leave her and their four sons. In actual fact she believed that a woman with children had her husband hooked. The thought almost made her laugh. It was a horrible thought, actually. Because the six of them were basically happy, she felt free to indulge in this kind of little game, which might not have been a game for everyone. With four boys all under eight, no one would consider walking out. Her Jean would never do anything stupid like that. But that didn't stop him adoring women, turning on his charm. Marie had seen him doing his stuff. He was irresistible.

As chance would have it, he had lots of female friends. They seemed to need to talk to him all the time. And he listened. The friends in question all absolutely swore by him. Other women had wept at the news of his marriage. And even then he had the nerve to claim they were only friends. At any rate, Marie was not prepared to accept that he might have intimate friendships with other women. She didn't want to have to deal with the thought of female friends who confided in him, friends whom he in turn admired and tried to help out. You're being very selfish, said Jean. It's not as though I'm depriving you of anything. You're not missing out. I know, Marie said, hanging her head. She wasn't proud of herself. Just because you loved a man, and lived with him, didn't mean you could detach him from the outside world. She had no rights over him, she knew that. But one thing was stronger than all her resolve: the images in her head. Jean sitting beside a woman at one of those little round restaurant tables, their smiles, the closeness between an available man and a woman who confides in him, the things they say, the things they leave unsaid, the kindness and compassion, the comfort offered, the mutual respect and the final embrace in which all this is expressed. The thought of this possibility drove her crazy. She couldn't stop herself having a go at him. It was a vicious circle, because it simply made him more inclined to stray. But she went for him anyway. And naturally he began to lie to her. Without the slightest scruple he would say: There's nothing you want to know that I haven't told you.

She wasn't dressed yet. He came and slipped his arm round her waist, showering her fragile shoulders with kisses. I love you, he said. And as though to reinforce the point, he ran his hands over his wife's belly and breasts. She had dark, smooth skin, with a soft coating of invisible hairs. Her softness was entrancing. He continued to get in her way as she tried to get ready. He gave himself up to the pleasure of touching her. His hands took the message to the rest of his body. His wife stirred him profoundly. He considered himself a lucky man. She was still slim and attractive, even after bearing four children. He held her and let his hands wander. His instinct got the better of him. Marie detached herself. It was hardly the moment to give in to that particular impulse. He caught hold of her again. She let him have his way, so as not to annoy him. He murmured extravagant compliments in his wife's ears – things he often said and still truly believed. He loved her body, and the slightest contact with it aroused him. Let me get ready now, she said. She knew he never stopped once he'd got this far, that the strength of his desire immediately swept him away. You don't love me, he sighed. He was laughing. It's common knowledge, she replied. She'd lived so long with him, she'd started to talk like him. She kissed him. He was reassured. They had narrowly avoided a scene.

5

A silence settled between them once they'd sat down at the table, face to face, and this brief moment of awkwardness led Gilles André to think of the evening which was going to unfold in their absence, bringing together their secret, their partners and their friends. He said: Thanks to you I'm missing a great boxing match. She didn't reply. She realised he was letting her know just how precious she was to him. Pauline Arnoult looked instead at the tablecloth, and fiddled with her knife. The fight was a special evening at the club, he said. Your husband didn't mind that you weren't going with him? No, she said. As though that was just the normal way of things in her marriage. He was amused by her reply, the way she gave no further explanation. A very slight smile began to form on his lips as he continued to ply her with questions. He wanted to get a sense of what her marriage was like. She didn't seem like a woman who was available to men, and yet here she was. He needed to get his head round this paradox. Did he have any chance of success with her? Success at what? he wondered. He really didn't know. He was attracted to her, but as to where it might lead, he had no idea at this point. He said: Didn't he ask you what you were doing this evening? No, she said, smiling this time. Or who you'd be with? No, she said, he didn't ask me anything like that. She understood perfectly what he wanted to know (what approach she'd taken with her husband), but she was more comfortable keeping him guessing than telling him direct. I didn't know such husbands existed, he said. What a treasure. They laughed, but she felt ashamed. She was laughing with a stranger, and over her husband at that. It was a form of betrayal. She tried to clarify things: He works very hard. I often go out for dinner without him, with friends. Girlfriends, she added, to be more precise. But he's not working this evening, said Gilles André. True, she admitted. He trusts you, said Gilles maliciously. His eyes were sparkling, and he turned them upon her as though, far from concealing his passion, they might display it to her. But she forgave him everything. She was mesmerised by him. She knew and yet did not know. . . . Let's say that she would not have been surprised to be told that she was experiencing a massive crush. I'm not doing anything to undermine his trust, she said, ceasing to worry about whether or not she was exposing herself to his warped sense of humour. He could go ahead and laugh if he wanted: she was in on the joke too. It was quite obvious to both of them, so he laughed and she laughed with him. Which explains his daring, his stupidity even, in then making his little joke: Not yet, he said. Insolent, provocative words to which the young woman offered no answer, underlining the stupidity of the remark, but simply went on laughing, showing no reaction, not even blushing. He marvelled at her teeth, those virgin white teeth, as though she had never come into contact with food, sweet little Pauline . . . he'd never seen an adult with such a perfect set of teeth. Suddenly he felt old. He looked across at her minute, sharp-edged incisors. There was a purity there which drew his eye, which explained why he stared insistently at the young woman's mouth. After a bit it began to embarrass her. Was that why she got up from the table? She stood up and said, 'I'm just going to wash my hands', leaving him sitting there with his napkin folded in front of him on his plate. His eyes followed her quite openly across the room. He had never been one to stop himself looking at women. Any woman sitting in the restaurant at that moment would have known who it was he had eyes for. As she turned her back on him and walked away, he watched her with something approaching indecency, not just her general gait and manner, but also in order to work out for himself what might lie underneath the dress – her legs, her hips, her waist, her bum. Some men are blind. The simplest camouflage completely floors them. Others, however, know exactly how to read a woman's body beneath her clothes. They can pick out a fine pair of legs, and won't mistake flat buttocks for a nice behind. And so Gilles André read, since he knew, by simple force of habit. Pauline Arnoult, twenty-something. Tall, very tall. Slim. Walking through a brasserie on a cloud of romance. He watched her. He couldn't make out much – a slim waist, long legs, nice arms. A streetwise sort of walk. No curves. She was a young woman with wings, one of those astonishing, weightless women. No breasts, of course: she was too thin for that. But she was perfect, she had a most unusual presence, true charm, something . . . These were his thoughts, once she had disappeared down the stairway, as he unfolded his napkin and began to read the menu. He was happy to have her there, under his spell, to have her for a whole evening, all to himself, happy that he'd had the nerve to ask, and to have got what he wanted. She could have no idea what a pleasure it was for him to capture a woman. The fact that she was keeping the evening secret was the icing on the cake.

It was impossible to say where Pauline Arnoult got her looks from. You wouldn't have expected it, looking at either her father or her mother, but her beauty was undeniable: the obscure pathways of inheritance had conspired to make a fine-looking woman. Although she was very tall (one metre seventy-four), she had true feminine grace: there was always a smile on her face and her long silhouette was willowy. At twenty-five, she was naturally slim, but with the peculiar luminosity which motherhood gives to young women. This combination of delicacy and fullness created the impression of natural sensuality heightened by desire; a sensuality expressed in all the usual ways but enhanced by her little games and inconsequential sparring. It should be understood by this that Pauline Arnoult was one of those women who owes what she is to men – self-confidence being largely sexual in its origins. She fed off the admiring looks of men. Pauline Arnoult had a face other people noticed. There was nothing perverse or manipulative about it, and even if it had something of that seductive power which some people can exercise over others, Pauline Arnoult herself remained above suspicion. Her pale beauty suggested she had not lost her innocence. Her dinner companion realised he was in the presence of something unsullied: one might almost say it amused him. He had fallen precisely for this simple happiness in one so uncrumpled, so smooth. As though ripping open this cold surface would be an ecstatic celebration, a sacrifice a man might wish to be made to him. Just for now – and it would not last indefinitely – he was in the phase of attraction and affinity, magnetised and dazzled by a face. A woman may not understand this – unless she is a mother who knows how the flesh can be suffused with the excess and greed of love, and unless she remembers her true nature in the throes of the act of love.

She had stopped at the top of the stairs and was watching. Gilles André was not what you would normally call handsome. Of only average height, and quite solidly built, he was not an elegant man. His movements and his appearance were awkward, but he didn't seem to care. He had been born short and broad and, having always been keen on sport, was well-muscled. *My mother always swore I'd shoot up late, like my father, but I waited and waited to grow tall*, he'd say to women. And his words would touch them, finding a way to their 'maternal' hearts. He smiled. One of his incisors was yellow with tobacco. The worst that could be said of him was that he was not a handsome man. No one had ever actually said this, just as no one would have thought to deny it. Given the choice, one would have remarked on quite different things. He was as witty as he was discreet. When he chose to, he could crackle with wit and fun. Women saw only him, because he in turn only had eyes for them. He was mad about them. Women all knew this instinctively. Men were equally charmed by him. Presumably they were not jealous of him, since he was not good-looking – luckily for him – nor ostentatiously wealthy. In short, people did not envy him. Such sparks of happiness as he had known he kept secret and most of these secrets were linked to women. His face sparkled vivaciously: he possessed that most attractive form of intelligence, which asks questions rather than provides answers. The constant invention of his wit depended on huge vitality, and the combination of this with a capacity for observation and accurate detective work rendered him a formidable presence in any company: a clairvoyant. It wasn't his floppy, dull blond hair that was so attractive, nor his face which was a little chubby for a man, nor his imperfect teeth; it was a different quality altogether, something non-physical, a wickedly humorous look, the exercise of his charm – for he exercised, rather than possessed charm. Passionate with women, intelligent with men, he managed to connect with other people without actually revealing anything of himself. He didn't set out to be enigmatic, but the combination of silence, words and gameplay created an impression of perspicacity which suggested he was a man of hidden depths. This was somewhat short of the truth, since in fact he was more a man who relished secrets. He never talked about himself, or his life, or his family. This policy of orchestrated silence might have led one to think him insincere, but his care to reveal nothing came across simply as attention to the words of others. And it was true, he did pay very close attention. He went out of his way to please.

No one was surprised he was so popular with women. First he made them laugh, then he made them cry. Oh, they gave him a hard time, his abandoned mistresses. . . . It is no easy thing to detach oneself from someone who seems to have eyes for you alone. Some men have a natural gift, or develop one, for making a woman feel intensely alive, at the heart of the world, eclipsing all others, able at last to see the reflection of their own bright light. He was one of those men who cast the everyday world into sleep and carry you off into the secret cave of their passion: skilful, obstinate, and full of love.

She came back and sat down opposite him at the table. What would you like to eat? he asked her. The menu is excellent. Here, take a look. He offered her the menu without looking at it, looking instead directly, impertinently, into her eyes, a look which stirred up that part of her which responded to the desire expressed in his telepathic smile. I'm not all that hungry, she said, beginning to look at the different menus. He said: Women don't eat these days. You're right, she said. She was trying to be gracious, and was not, just at this moment, being entirely herself. Such is the banality of language that, even as she was saying this, inside her she was struggling against her femininity, her attraction to him, this charm between them, her temptation, her pride in his scrutiny, his flattery, his desire. She murmured: I never eat much in the evening. That's the secret of good health, he said, without really believing what he said, simply mouthing a common belief. But she took up the idea: I think that's true. Do you know what Hippocrates said? she asked. (He shook his head.) Hippocrates said: everything I don't eat does me good. Are you sure about that? Who told you that? he asked, laughing. It's incredible, the number of facts or opinions we are prepared to believe without proof. Have you ever actually seen a baboon or a sperm or an atom of carbon? Or an electron? Isn't it strange, that many things we confidently believe in are actually invisible? She didn't answer. Her eyes narrowed as she smiled. And yet, he continued, other things, no more invisible, we question: God. Spirits.

Love. If you tell people that spirits are like radio waves, invisible and yet entirely real, at best they'll think you are eccentric, at worst they'll get angry with you. Many things are invisible and important, she said, with the sense that she was saying something idiotic or banal. In fact the most important things are the least visible, he said with a smile. She suddenly thought: like this child in my womb. In that respect he had no idea what was going on in her head. She was sure he hadn't noticed. And immediately the secret of the child felt like an intolerable burden. She ought to tell him: You can't try to seduce me, I'm carrying another man's child, I'm more mother than woman. She was about to say it, plainly and simply, but she wanted him to carry on seducing her, even after she had told him. And course she couldn't say that. Could one ask for such a thing? Or would he understand this anyway, without her needing to tell him?

Another silence intervened, and she took advantage of it. There's something I must tell you, she said firmly. He smiled at her worried expression. What's the matter? he asked, kindly, with concern, as he might have with a young child who was unhappy about something. But she didn't relax, so he sat up straight and said: I'm listening. I'm going to have a baby, she said. When? he replied, without hesitating, surprised, but still using the intimate voice, which was gradually turning into an instrument of torture for her, the very sound making her shudder. In five months, she said. You don't look very big, he said. I find it hard to believe I'm having dinner with a woman who's four months pregnant. Without knowing it, he was giving her pleasure. She said nothing. Well, he said, here you are, in the happiest of states – I'm very happy for you. And are you happy? he asked. She thought: it doesn't bother him at all, why not? Doesn't he understand – this child thwarts all his plans? She was astonished, almost disappointed. She answered lightly: Yes, I'm very happy, I really wanted this child. I didn't want Theodore to be an only child. It was an unfortunate remark (Sarah André would never have a brother or sister) but he didn't notice. Unhappy father or not, he said without flinching: You're right. Then he asked: How old is Theodore? Three and a half, she replied. She appeared to be relieved to talk about her son. Or was it relief at having told him she was pregnant, as a woman might confess to being married, or engaged, in short, unavailable for love? You like children, don't you? he said. I think that was what touched me when I saw you at school. She smiled. The memory of their meeting made her heart beat faster. Yes, children are very important to me, she said, and yet, it's funny, I keep thinking I could perfectly well have lived my life without having any. I often thought I would, before I got married. I wanted to design, to be an artist, I didn't *need* a child. I even thought a child would get in the way. He said again: I understand. He was still reeling from what she'd told him. She warmed to her theme. When I got married, everything turned out to be different, she said. He murmured: In what way? She considered. I don't think a relationship has much of a chance, long-term, if there aren't children at some point, said Pauline Arnoult. I suppose there's a lot of truth in that, he said, but no one likes to think it.

Then he murmured: You don't believe in a pure kind of love, detached from everything else? She shook her head, smiling. Well, actually, yes, she said, in very special cases. I really admire men who stay with women who are sterile. They must truly love them. She said: I think love usually needs good reason to exist. Our feelings have to have a practical purpose. If they don't lead anywhere we abandon them. He nodded, and she couldn't tell what he was thinking. She blushed. I don't know why I'm telling you all this, she said. Even as she'd been speaking she'd wondered if she wasn't sounding a bit young and stupid, so she broke off what she was saying. My husband wanted children, but I didn't feel the need, she said. I'd be equally happy without. Of course you would, he said, trying not to smile. You've got me. She laughed. They were both still playing the same flirtatious game to the tune of their shared laughter. You're right, he said, people shouldn't have children by default, just because there's nothing else going on in their lives – that way they've nothing to give them. Some mothers make that mistake, he said, they give up their own lives and want the child to have everything. It leads to terrible conflict, he said. He was serious again as he said this. She would often be thrown by the way he could see-saw between joking around and perceptive remarks about people or situations, a sudden solemnity in his words. He wanted to teach her things too; he believed she was worth the trouble, she could be improved upon, he might almost have gone as far as to feel a sense of responsibility towards her. But in fact she knew very well what it was he wanted to teach her. She didn't have that much to learn from him because she was like him (though several years younger). Indeed, she said to him: I think that too, that you should be able to give your children something of what you experience away from them, something of the world they aren't part of yet. He smiled. Why are you smiling? she said. Don't you agree? she asked, mischievously, sensing that his approbation came in the form of silence. Yes, of course, he said, I'm just smiling because you look so stern. I was trying to picture you with your son.

She sighed and sat back in her chair. Are you tired? he asked solicitously, which bothered her. She felt it was slightly indecent for him to worry about her condition. No, she said, I'm fine. In unguarded moments she recaptured the impetuosity of her youth and a certain brusqueness, which came from sudden waves of shyness. I'm very happy to be here, thank you, she said abruptly. It was quite true: she was basking in the feeling that she was the centre of a man's world. She was astonished to find she could actually say so. Just at this moment she was happy with herself, happy too to have mentioned the child without a shadow being cast over their meeting. Several times she lowered her eyes, then looked up again. Each time he tried to catch her eye: she felt as if she'd been hooked. Me too, he said. I'm very happy to be here having dinner with you. It's like a fairy story, he said. He meant it. I can't believe that, she said (truthfully). Believe me, he said, in a low whisper. And hearing the exaggeration in his tone, she wondered whether he was doing it deliberately, if it was all a calculated ploy, and was tempted to ask him to stop putting on such an act. All this pretence was increasing her discomfort. She wanted too much to believe it was sincere. His devotion seemed like the real thing. By making her so precious he was subjugating her.

A voice had begun to whisper inside her head: they could tell each other everything. She was brimming over with desire, the intimate voice set her blood racing, but the magic between them was surely a total disaster – secrets, lies, remorse, memories, pain, it would all be there, and she would be unhappy. She already was: tortured, split in two. All she wanted was to lie down next to him, and this she could not bring herself to do. Would anyone understand that – this mixture, so typically feminine, of desire and extreme modesty? She herself was wretched at the thought, incapable of speech. She could tell him everything, and still not actually touch the truth of this moment. That truth had to do with sex: I want to sleep with you but I don't think I dare just yet. How honest was she being with herself? She wondered this when he murmured: You and me, I don't know what we have here. Did he really say that? She scarcely dared believe it, and pretended she hadn't heard. There was always this doubt in her mind: was he lying so as to seduce her? The way men did with all the women for whom they felt desire, but very rarely love. That was what went through her mind. How many women had he put on this act for? She had gone quiet. He could see her thoughts flitting across her face. But he chose to hammer his point home. What's happening between us? he said. It's not sexual, he said, with an intonation which allowed for the possibility that he was asking a question. He supplied the answer himself. No, he said, that's not it. She had to smile. She was quite sure the key to their meeting was sexual; she could feel the sharp twinge which had awakened her body. She had never realised she was so fast asleep. What had he done, besides look at her? It was a mystery to her, but she felt present, in the moment, passionate and full of love. She thought he must surely be aware of this, and that his denial was just a game. But no, she was wrong, he was being sincere. She was mistaken because she was younger than him. He did desire her, but there was something more than desire, an affinity which he valued more, because it was far more rare. Wrapped in this sense of their closeness and of a sensual urge which their words, their smiles, and their sense of expectation had already satisfied to some degree, he sat there, simply contemplating her. And now there was suddenly nothing more to say. They sat there looking at each other, in total silence. Since the moment she had decided to let herself fall in love, he could feel a force propelling her towards him: she was attracted to him, she was offering herself, she wanted to get to know him, she was voracious, she was powerful. He smiled at the sight. The best thing about you, he said, isn't your beauty. It's your temperament. And, being of a truly feminine disposition, she failed to recognise the compliment.

It lasted a full minute. They looked at each other as though they each saw – and each knew the other saw – what they would become (inextricably bound together), what they would do (tell each other their life stories, then sleep together), what they believed they had always been (destined for each other, perhaps former lovers who had been driven apart and had found each other again). And they did not feel awkward as they looked at one another, although the exchange was passionate and insistent, because all this was utterly clear, in the way that things which have been said, repeated, promised and believed are clear, without brutality, since here there were no words, only that strange naked vision, something acknowledged in silence. The look which passed between them expressed something that speech cannot convey, and yet its message passed, as if through faith, by a miracle, giving strength and provoking doubt, as is the way with things invisible. And yet it is a fact that such a look, such a moment of perfection, can never last. As always happens, this moment ended, and with its end came the resumption of normality between them: talking, trying to work each other out, asking questions of themselves, wondering, doubting, hoping, holding back – and so the essential remains unsaid. The waiter arrived with their food. He guessed he must be disturbing them in an intimate moment, but he was carrying hot plates in both hands, and had other diners waiting. He apologised, and slipped the plates between the forearms resting on the table. Excuse me, madame, he said. Excuse me, sir. She glanced up at him, thanking him twice over, anxious to make the service run smoothly, embarrassed to have been caught out in a moment of intoxication. My God, she was so pretty!

Gilles André thought as he watched her. Even the waiter was blushing, poor boy, caught in her radiant glow. She was in a state which was not normal, exalted by the certainty that what they were experiencing was a true and mutual passion. We must be a sight to behold, she thought, my feelings must be apparent to the naked eye. She tried to get a grip of herself. I'm floating, she thought, my legs are cotton wool, I can hear the words I'm saying but as though someone else had said them, my whole being is angled towards him (she had suddenly become aware of the way she was sticking her chest out). She smiled. I am in love, enchanted by love, that was the message written in those eyes, with their narrowed gaze. Was she genuinely in love? She didn't care either way. Is it ever really possible to separate out desire and emotion? Her feelings were swift, torrential and sublime. She admitted the truth to herself: what I love is his desire to sleep with me. I love egging him on. I love his curiosity about me.

Because he was trying to discover the real, inner Pauline, he showed a greater interest than anyone ever had before. She was enchanted to be the object of such interest. He contemplated her, as she sat there daydreaming in her typically feminine way. This too thrilled her, since contemplation itself is perhaps the first expression of desire. What are you dreaming about? he said, placing a hand on her wrist. It was the first time he had touched her. Then, as though he held her at his mercy, he said with a smile: Tell me your dreams. The young woman was briefly aware there was something a bit ridiculous in this but she agreed to go along with the game of gallantry, as though accepting the truth, the future, a promise. It was all very typically female: to be caught by the interest in a man's eye, his inexplicable attention, to surrender with pleasure to seduction, to respond, to be found pleasing, and to imitate. She was trapped in her own femininity. Her face felt as though it was on fire. She had flushed a deep red, a mixture of excitement and shyness. She didn't dare remove her hand. She didn't want to. Her hand was in a place of sweetness, headiness and bliss. Her hand was held fast by the complicity, the warmth, of a man. Her hand took all the struggle out of life. Her wrist whispered secrets, secrets she heard and understood: everything connected with this man was erotic.

6

Meanwhile, elsewhere, the preparations continued. I knew you wouldn't be ready, Tom Laragole was saying, as he walked into Sara Petersen's apartment. She was just getting undressed to take a shower. Then you should have come later, she answered, disappearing into the bathroom. She had been his mistress for two years, was madly in love with him, while he was quite openly unfaithful. She was trying to leave him. He just didn't love her enough. But he could count on her, she always came running when he called, all dolled up and in love with him. What did 'enough' mean anyway? It doesn't start till eight, she called. You're early. He paced about the room, the panels in the back of his lightweight jacket flapping behind him. Don't wait for me, she said, I can go in my own car, I don't need you. I know you don't, he said, not believing a word of it. She quite clearly needed him at her side to get through life. What woman wouldn't be utterly content with the company of a man like him? He was sure he was everything the woman of his choice could wish for. He smiled a smile which seemed directed at himself. A man can be satisfied with a simple conquest, be sure of himself, of what he's doing, as long as the standards he sets himself and his life are not quite as high as he likes to believe. Tom Lagarole had made himself a huge amount of money, sacrificing his first wife, three children, all his early friendships and the level of his intellectual interests, to his career.

What did you do today? he asked, at the very moment when Gilles André was asking: May I call you Pauline? and when Louise, who was upset, shamefaced and trying not to show it, was flicking through her dresses and deciding what to wear. Sara Petersen was just doing her hair, having now showered, and dressed. Tom followed her everywhere: standing outside the glass shower door (she could make out the dark masculine outline), walking after her from cupboard to cupboard, and now, in the tiny bathroom, looking at his image in the mirror. Move over a bit, she said. And stop looking at yourself. But he didn't budge. So you like this shirt? he asked. You don't think it's a bit dowdy for me? No, it's very nice, she said. Such a vain man: there was something ridiculous about it. Come on, out you get, she said, pushing him out of the room. He went reluctantly. Can't you let me get ready in peace? she said, exasperated now. And since he seemed to be enjoying annoying her, she changed tactics. Please go and wait for me in the drawing room. I'll be ready in a couple of minutes, she said more gently. Go and pour yourself a drink. He went into the drawing room. And it struck Sara Petersen how easy it was to manipulate people. Did they stop to think what they really wanted? Or did they just bob around like corks on the waves of the sea? When a couple was unhappy it was always because of this uncertainty.

Shortly after, she came up behind him (he was sitting with a drink in his hand) and ran her hands through his hair. So, he said again, tell me what you did today. She didn't like telling him about her days: it merely revealed how empty they were. Nothing special, she said. What? he said, pretending to take offence. My woman did 'nothing special'? He could be very crude. Just now she found him so. I'm not your woman, she said. Very sorry, he said, laughing. She wasn't laughing. Men liked things to be kept comfortably vague. But she didn't like him calling her his woman when he didn't have the guts or the will to marry her or live with her. He flung back the last of the whisky he'd helped himself to, and stood up with his characteristic energy, bordering on restlessness, saying: Shall we get going? I'm ready, said Sara Petersen. She was wearing a sleeveless mauve dress, which showed off her well-covered upper arms and slender, square shoulders. It was not just that Sara was pretty, she knew how to achieve the effect of being so. Nothing in the overall picture of harmony was left to chance.

7

So, said Gilles André, you were pregnant all this time, and you didn't tell me. Pauline Arnoult smiled, blushing. She would never have dared admit what she had really thought: that he wanted to be her lover, but he couldn't, because she was expecting a baby. Did he know that that was what she'd thought? At any rate he said: You thought it would bother me? She nodded. Why? said the intimate voice. Of course it doesn't; I'm delighted for you. She smiled a wretched, regretful little smile. She would have loved to be free, and knew she wasn't. No doubt recognising her dilemma, he said: Surely you're not sad about it? Though she shook her head, she was. It was dreadful to feel both the warmth of desire and the flesh of a child in her belly. And she was disappointed by his lack of jealousy. But how could a man who had always been free and available, as is the way of men, possibly understand this feminine despair of hers? Crestfallen, she was silent: though she wouldn't admit it to herself, she was already waiting for him to make some grand declaration. She would have liked to hear him say what she herself was feeling. There were indeed things he could have said. For example: Don't worry, we've got all the time in the world, I'm in no hurry. Or something rather more expansive, such as: This thing – you and me – it's inescapable. She would have loved that. But he didn't say it, because for him it was perfectly obvious. Because he wanted to savour this first encounter, their hovering sense of expectation. And perhaps, though he didn't realise it, because he was already anxious to protect her against those impulses and agonies he seemed to provoke in women. It never occurred to him for a moment that she felt impatient and wretched, that the way to relax her would have been to speak openly.

Instead he said: Anyway, it certainly suits you, you look radiant. I love pregnant women. She smiled, but didn't answer, so he went on: Why does that make you smile? Don't you believe me? Men find it fascinating, you know, this whole thing of carrying an unseen child. Women are at their most distant, unfathomable and mysterious when they're pregnant. What a cliché, Pauline thought. The thought that it was also rather naïve gave her a bit more confidence. She shook herself and tilted her head towards him, still smiling. You say that because you see things in abstract terms, she said, but you don't really know what you're talking about. True, he said. And he asked her, with a careful edge to his voice, Don't you like being pregnant? I hate it, she said. I'm tired, I feel like sleeping the whole time, I feel really heavy, really ugly. . . . But you look divine, he exclaimed, trying to make her laugh. And laugh she did. I didn't even notice, he said. What further proof do you need? How young she was, he thought. He looked at her again, enchanted, unflinching, and astonished. She thought he was blasé, that he'd had mistresses up to his ears. The thing that drew them together (that he was a man and she was a woman) was the very thing that held them apart: he couldn't understand her thought processes, or what she expected of him. The gender difference spoiled the harmony between them: it was one thing to wish to love someone, quite another to be able to do so. She thought: he's playing with me. At that same moment he would have loved to hold her in his arms like a little girl. Everything between them was clandestine. Honesty, even sincerity, were trapped in flesh, and there was no way out. Their knowledge lay upon them like a curse.

For a moment she was thrown off course. She sat in silence. Sensing something was not quite right, he let the silence run on. He was so moved by the unspoilt, youthful beauty of her face, he just sat there, looking at her, saying nothing. She could almost have been his daughter. His desire for her was gradually mingling with a kind of paternal tenderness. Meanwhile she was trying to assess the damage caused by her revelation. No one was ever quite satisfied, she thought. Her silence was heavy with hope and feminine devotion. She was the victim of a love potion. A magic spell had cast her into a man's arms. The cause of the happy laughter she'd shared with him was the knowledge of their shared, intoxicating future. Her desire had swept the rest of the world away. She was in love. There was no denying it. What would happen? Was it possible to turn down the chance of such pleasure, simply on the pretext that one had already tasted it elsewhere? Again her right hand played around with the knife. It was one of those pieces of brasserie cutlery which has a number engraved on the metal handle.

Pauline Arnoult turned it in her hand. And Gilles André buttered himself some bread. A heavy silence. She was thinking again of her husband: was she already 'being unfaithful' to him? In her mind the words were laced with all the venom they carried when people uttered them. But that didn't mean she wasn't already doing wrong: there was something her husband didn't know, because she had hidden it from him. She didn't feel guilty about it. She couldn't bring herself to accept that one must, or might, let a grand passion pass one by. True passion was like a life: it had to be lived. They would all die and sooner than any of them thought. Who would thank them then for having neglected their impulses, their passion, their tenderness and desire? They were all dying and they would take their secrets with them to the grave. All torment gone. How pitiful their lives would seem then, their little cares. Of course the purity of married love was a good thing in itself. But you couldn't simply say no when a new love came along. Not if you were truly alive. The answer was to harness one love to the other, somewhere in the very depths of your soul. She was pretty sure of that. In the great catalogue of possible misdemeanours, under the subsection 'marital infidelity', a true love affair had the double beauty of being both unspoken and deeply felt. For that, however, it had to be the real thing. Not just a quick roll in the hay. The key to their innocence lay in this phrase: not just a quick roll in the hay. But how could you be sure of that, with a man? How can you know, at the outset, whether you are putting your initials to a joke or a solemn vow?

They resumed their chat. She grew languid, lulled by the tenderness of their words. As she listened, she relaxed back against the chair. When she spoke, she leaned forward, wallowing in the moment, riveted by his presence, bewitched by the pleasure of being looked at, far more deeply involved than him. The words issued from her pretty lips burnished by desire. The intimate voice had made her long legs weak, as though struck by lightning; a sweetness had found its way to the top of her thighs, where it lay tightly coiled and tingling, bringing a glowing smile to her face. She looked him straight in the eyes, waiting. How would he go about it? She wanted to be seduced, to be worshipped. She expected no less. I know the words you'll say. Say them to me now and I will be yours. I'm waiting, for a word, for a gesture from you. I am a woman, waiting, suppressing my fear, smothering it with a smile, and if I've judged it right, you will sense the storm in my troubled breast, but not be frightened off by it. Inside I'm burning, but outwardly I'm calm – so calm it almost makes me shudder. Don't be afraid. Here I am, smiling at you, I think you're wonderful, and if I wasn't quite sure that our love will burst spontaneously forth, I'd break down, howling and weeping. And when it is accomplished between us, that's no doubt what I'll do. That was how far gone she was: in a feverish condition of suspense, speechless, wrapped silky and warm in a coquette's dream. Of course she was – for her dream had already come at the price of a lie.

8

Because of his marriage, Max de Mortreux had chosen the wrong career. He didn't know this yet. The fact of it hadn't yet come knocking on the doors of his consciousness, but slowly, gradually, it was destroying him. He had his family, but he himself had become invisible: a sadness he would not acknowledge had wiped everything away. His wife, who had sized him up, chosen him, courted him, married him, set him to work, was the last person to want to acknowledge it.

It was that time of evening when the sun disappeared behind the building opposite. Max had just got back from the office and his wife, Eve, was in the bath. Can you put a pan on the stove with some water in? she called, when she heard the front door open. I'm in the bath. He put his large briefcase and summer jacket down on the sofa and went straight through into the kitchen. The children were playing in their rooms. The water's boiling, he came to tell his wife, a little while later. Eve de Mortreux was soaking in a bath full of foam. Throw the rice in then, she said. He could sense that he got on her nerves. Once again she was thinking how he could not do anything without being told. You could never get a moment to yourself in this house. They all constantly seemed to need something. She was their slave. Max knew she thought this. Poor Eve, he said to himself, wondering how other mothers managed to find fulfilment.

When she emerged from the bathroom, with her hair up, barefoot and in her dressing gown, she came through to check that the children were eating their tea properly. They were just about to sit down at the table. Well done, she said. Then she crossed the room and ostentatiously, with ill humour, put away his jacket and briefcase in the place assigned by her for them since the dawn of time. Max had become invisible.

He had given himself a side parting, after wetting his hair in order to comb it. He did this in the kitchen, so as not to disturb his wife in the bathroom. You look like a choirboy, said Eve. She had not a single kind word to say to him. He had often noticed this over the last few months: nothing she ever said expressed concern or tenderness for him. She had been odious throughout each of her pregnancies. And yet she was the one who'd wanted a third child. Now she was pregnant, she resented him for being the same as he ever was – intact. And he was every bit as tired as she was. Whatever state Max had been in, whatever colour the mask on his face might have been, whether his eyes had been sparkling or dead, Eve wouldn't have noticed either way. He thought: If I dropped dead tomorrow she wouldn't notice. I'm just a cheque book to her. He was bound to think this, but he didn't actually have to believe it. Can you organise their tea, yes or no? she asked, shoving past him to get out of the room. I'm sorry – am I annoying you? he asked. She didn't have the nerve to say yes. No, not in the slightest, she said, but I'm in a hurry. You're ready and I'm not even dressed yet. So I'm asking you to do something for me: supervise their tea. She was talking about their children, to her husband. She'd put that black mascara stuff on her eyelashes to make her eyes look more 'mysterious'. She had completely lost her looks, he thought. He stopped short of actually thinking: the warmth of a person on the inside creates the glow on the outside, which was precisely what Eve had begun to lack. He really did try to love her. He was determined to love her as she was, or even as she had become. That was what marriage was about. Accepting that people change. Max looked at his wife, but said nothing. He was too tired to fight this evening. He didn't even have the energy to ask her not to talk to him as if he was a dog. He looked at her dispassionately: her face had grown hard, her mouth had developed two curved lines leading outwards and downwards from the corners, she almost never smiled these days, nothing ever pleased her, she just ordered everyone about. Did it make her happy, at least? Possibly, incomprehensible though it might seem. (He thought this because he didn't actually understand the first thing about his wife or about what was going on in their lives.) Were they on a dangerous and slippery slope, or was this just one of those bad patches all marriages go through? It's always so difficult to know. You can't draw comparisons with other people's experience, because you don't know what their experience is. Max de Mortreux sighed. He laid the table, two bowls, two glasses, one with Lucky Luke and the other Snow White. He felt a mixture of sadness and tenderness. He was determined to love his wife. Why was he so intent on this? Because that was the way he'd been brought up. You can't change what you are. He let the question drop, and called the children for their tea.

He was now supervising them as they ate. The children were laughing. Thank goodness the children were laughing. What else was keeping him here in this house, except the children? It was a question to which there was no answer, because it *was* the children who were keeping him there. He never spoke to anyone of the things he did but didn't want to, the things he longed to do but never got round to, his daily life, everything he put up with. Silence was a perfectly possible option: bury your unhappiness in silence, and then stand up straight, next to the grave. Certain little phrases would have been enough to expose the extent of his error. But he had never uttered any of them. Even in the heat of an argument, he would never have said: I stay because of the children. You think I don't earn enough money. We hardly ever make love. His feet were planted firmly on the ground; he had no illusions. He would never leave Eve. But what were they going to put in the place of love? A smiling child, of course. Wouldn't it just be the same with another woman? There'd be no point going and falling in love with someone else. All he'd achieve would be to lose the children. Eve had come back into the kitchen. Eat up, she said to the children, who were being slow. Mummy and Daddy are going out this evening, she told her eldest. Max was washing the saucepan, thinking. Loving someone else . . . the possibility had never crossed his mind. Anyway, he did feel something like love for his wife. She was the one who had stopped loving him. Surely something must be left of the old magic, a genuine tenderness, the white light of a shared emotion? Give me a kiss, he said to her, with a weak little smile. Surely love between two people was bound to come and go? Give me a kiss, he said again. She came up behind him, and with a silent sigh, gave him a peck on the cheek. On the cheek, he thought. That was all she could manage.

Once she was in the car, in the passenger seat, she said: This do tonight really pisses me off. He was appalled by the sound of these words coming from the mouth of his wife. What sort of woman had he got himself involved with? He didn't reply, not because he wanted to annoy her, but because he just didn't know what to say, perhaps not even what he felt. You might at least answer when I speak to you, she said. He replied quickly: You didn't ask me a question. How was I meant to know you wanted an answer? I'm telling you this party bores me rigid, she repeated, and you just listen, you don't do anything. At last, something began to stir within him, an irrepressible surge of anger. What do you want me to say? he said. It was a rhetorical question. The sudden firmness in his voice petrified her. Yet again she had crossed a fateful line. How many times are you allowed to cross such a line? He continued: Everything pisses you off, you're never happy with anything, everyone gets on your nerves, you talk to them all like dogs. He corrected himself: No, that's not right, you wouldn't talk to a dog in the way you talk to me. You scorn my friends, you despise my parents, you criticise everyone, I daren't ask anyone to our house any more, I don't know how to please you these days, I just try not to get in the way. And he rounded off with the subject of money: The only thing you care about is that I bring home the money to pay for your smart apartment and your cleaner. There. He'd said it. For the first time ever. They were beginning to slide.

Eve was as still as a statue. He couldn't see her eyes, she wasn't looking his way and anyway he had to concentrate on the road. But he got the feeling, without quite knowing why, that her eyes were full of tears. He wasn't wrong: a tear rolled down her cheek, right to the heart of that little round daub of pink powder she'd put on her cheek. She was making herself cry. He didn't realise this. Such a degree of duplicity was unthinkable for him. She was pretty much devastated, but she still wouldn't have wept unless she'd forced herself. She was dead set on having a cry. Because a woman's tears always hit home: or so she believed. What would he have thought if she hadn't started crying at his accusations? It was him she was crying for. But since he took no notice, she let her rage rip loose. Bastard! Bastard! Bastard! she shouted at him. He drove on, unperturbed. Bastard! she said. I hate you! She thumped him on the upper arm. He yelled with surprise and anger. Not in the car! Don't you ever hit me when I'm driving! He was right. She was sheepish. I'm sorry, she grumbled. He said, firmly: You're fed up about this evening, fine, you're entitled, you don't have to come, so don't come. Just ring and say you're staying at home, and then stay at home. Whatever you do, just leave me in peace. He lost his temper. Leave me in peace. He was shouting louder than she ever could. Stop kicking me in the balls. There was not a shred of love left between them. She was sobbing convulsively now. Husband and wife, what a fine picture we make, he thought. His head was spinning with images of their early days, the treacherous details he couldn't forget. I'm not that good a catch, he jeered. She didn't know what he meant by that – nor did he. They sat there in silence. Get out, he said, I'm going to find somewhere to park. I can stay here with you, she said, in a tiny little voice. She was wiping the corners of her eyes with a handkerchief. Where did the tiny little voice come from? he wondered. It was horrible. No, he said, with his eyes still fixed on the road in front of him, hands on the wheel. I want to be on my own. So he watched her walk off towards the club, graceful enough, quite well dressed, her brown hair smooth against the back of her head, all her hardness hidden beneath its helmet. A trap. How had he managed to fall into this trap? The scene had exhausted him. And at that very moment, Gilles André was saying to his guest: What would you like to eat? The menu is excellent. Here, take a look.

9

The colours of the evening sky changed once you got out of town. While the centre was still aflame, the fire had left the suburbs. As the heat of the day seeped from the gardens, nature grew fresh and vigorous again. Melusine was enjoying the evening shade in the comfort of her lounge chair. Any moment now our future lovers would fall into step on the white-hot tarmac, while Sara, Louise and Marie were all trying to decide which dress to wear, and Eve was speaking coarse words to her husband. In the same fragment of time, each lived their separate intimacies. And even if their meandering paths did happen to cross, there could be only one person on each path: no swapping for a better one, no sharing. And when a man and a woman did throw in their lot together, was it clear what they were really doing? Wasn't one partner always the spectator of the other's life, his own life whittled down to nothing? This was the only question Melusine Tropp was capable of asking once she had a glass in her hand: What did you do with your talent? What did you do with your talent? The phone was ringing, but she didn't get up. What had she done? My God, she had no idea. She took a swig at her drink, which looked like lemonade. Let it ring, don't go dashing to the phone: you're free not to. The telephone's insistent peal rang out for Melusine's freedom.

Another awful day. Melusine hadn't left the kitchen since before lunch. She had drunk enough gin and tonic to achieve that languid state in which she was capable of doing nothing. She smiled beatifically as she listened to the radio back in the kitchen. In the silence of the empty house, voices were essential. Henri had always been happy living in this detached house in the outer suburbs. It was where the children had grown up, where he had his garden. But he had his office to go to; Melusine was completely isolated. Of course visits from friends had started to dry up just when she really needed friends. Nothing like heavy drinking for cutting you off. She had found herself increasingly alone. It was more practical for drinking. Drinking is an interesting activity. Melusine had heard some great philosopher say so on the television. And many very successful men were familiar with the benefits of alcohol. Instead of getting up to answer she took another swig. It was Henri, it couldn't be anyone else at this hour. He wanted to make arrangements with his wife for the coming evening at the tennis club. He must know Melusine was there. After four in the afternoon she was incapable of going anywhere. There, he'd hung up. She just had to be patient, to put up with the noise until he gave up. But he never gave up for long. He always rang back. One minute. Two. Sometimes a bit longer if he went off to get a coffee. The silence behind the voices on the radio continued. Three, four, five minutes went by. At last! Once again Melusine heard the stubborn ringing of the phone. Whoever it was calling knew that there was someone there to pick up. Melusine got up and walked with difficulty back into the house, pitching from side to side, like a boat.

Her hand shook as she picked up the receiver. Her ring finger was swollen up around her wedding ring and her nails were chewed away. Melusine, she said. Her voice was fluted and gentle, its timbre both sharp and mellow. A gift which had given cause only for regret. The source of my great guilt, she would say, is not to have sung. She said guilt rather than regret, as though she had actively failed to carry out some noble intention, as though she had been generally reproached for not carrying out a duty widely expected of her. The source of my great guilt. Of course no one gave a damn, she knew perfectly well, and she only spoke of it for her own comfort, to hear herself say something important. Why, after all, should other people get upset about the dreams we have left behind? My darling, Henri was saying. He was at the train station, in a phone box, he was about to get on the train. My darling, why didn't you answer? His tone was beseeching, the tone of a husband at the end of his tether, who has lapsed into petition and despair. She didn't answer. Darling, are you all right? he asked. He loved her in the way small children love their mothers: with no notion that they might ever disappear. But his adoration hadn't been enough. He had believed that to have a loving husband was all a woman needed in life, and consequently Melusine's life had lacked the thing love could not provide: a place in the world that you alone have created. He had protected her from the outside world. She had given herself over to him. He was so in love with her. How many times had Henri boasted of her voice? Oh Melusine's voice. It is, after all, much easier to boast and talk than it is to flourish and work. This is what she had taught her children: one must go through life like a donkey on a path, spurred by the stick, pulling now this way, now that, but plodding ever onwards from dawn till dusk. She had got stuck because no one had managed to make her understand this simple truth: you have to grab the stick and use it against yourself. My darling, my darling . . . He was saying it again: My darling, I'm coming back to pick you up. Melusine said nothing. Can you wait there for me? Would you rather come on your own? No answer. Would you rather we met at the club? He was doing the whole conversation solo. Darling, I'm so sorry I'm late, and she heard in his voice that he truly was, in fact he was worse than sorry, he was worried. She didn't answer, all puffy and touchy in her coffin of drunkenness. Melusine? he said. Can you hear me? Yes Henri, I can hear you, she said, at last. She was angry, he realised to his horror. Darling, he said, pleading once more, you're not cross with me, are you? She must really love him not to find his tearful tenderness completely maddening. I'll be there at half seven, he said. You're not cross? Big kiss, my darling. Darling, you're sure you're not angry with me? No, she said, infuriated by him. But I can tell there's something wrong, he said despairingly. I'm so sorry. I'll see you later, she said. Yes, see you later, darling. She hung up. He was stung. He looked at the receiver. He was one of those husbands who believed things would work themselves out if you didn't talk about them. Words just caused needless upset and were best avoided. What time was it? Melusine had sat down again. She would go to the club in what she already had on. In any case, she had nothing else left to wear.

The most important fact about Melusine Tropp was this thing she did: drinking. She would squeeze in between the table and the fridge, sitting down heavily in the early morning cool of the kitchen to pour the first golden droplets into her coffee. You could get drunk just from the smell of the whisky, the heat of the coffee brought it out. But she had always waited till she was alone before filling her nostrils with the familiar telltale smell: children at school, husband at the office and later, children gone altogether. A mother can find herself so terribly lonely. No one in the family ever picked up on it, since she only drank alone. But what had driven her to drink was the company of the washing machine, the laundry and the iron, the pots and pans. Right from the start, she had always come into the kitchen – my kitchen, she called it – to drink.

No one had noticed, not her husband, nor her children. It was her body that gave Melusine away. It had altered, had started to resemble an alcoholic's body. The skin of her face had taken on a coarser texture, the pores had dilated to the point where they were distinct little holes. Her stomach had begun to protrude, as though she were expecting another child. I used to be thin, Melusine would say, whenever, thanks to her state of drunkenness, she could bring herself to utter such a phrase. She had even been quite beautiful. These statements were so clearly true that she could kid herself that this was enough. Wasn't that what a woman's life was all about? Being looked at, smiling, being loved, loving back, basking in the happy state of constancy which fidelity between two people creates? Love was all she ever expected, and she believed that love would bring her everything else. But finally she had had to accept the obvious: even when you love someone, you feel alone. She had been abandoned, alone in her house, and even more abandoned in her head. What was she doing with her life? She was dying. She was living her life entirely for others. The awful fear of life, of death, clutched at her throat. She tried to express what she felt. Love answered her with smiles. Henri meant well. His tender little gestures were like tiny sparks – almost preposterously tiny in the face of the cold, of the void, of doubt. And yet such tender gestures were life's only consolations, it seemed. So what was there left to hope for? How could one hope to stay afloat? How did other people do it? To begin with, Melusine had wept. And after that, she drank.

And now she was a woman on the edge of slovenliness, drenched in sweat when she wasn't drinking. She could easily die, if her body would only let her. Death. She spoke the word out loud. I'm killing myself. That's what I'm really about! Sometimes her husband wept. He wouldn't look at her. He closed his eyes, the better to summon up the young girl she had once been. The lovely, dark-skinned Amazon, with her thick mane of hair. Strange how a person could just shatter, like crystal. Melusine was made of crystal. He'd always known that. It was her very transparency he had loved. Hadn't he noticed the flaw? He would watch her move slowly from kitchen to bed. How she had changed. She could hardly walk now. No more walks, no more travel, no more shopping. Fortunately, the train station was just next to the house. There was the noise of the trains to put up with, but at least Melusine could get into town.

10

Tell me how wallpaper gets made, he said, with determination. You've opened my eyes to a whole new profession, said Gilles André. The minute their conversation strayed from the subject of love, Pauline Arnoult felt a pang of regret. Her joy diminished. She liked it when he coaxed and wheedled, smiling and sly, when he focused just on what there was between them. She didn't want to talk about other things. But she could see he looked at her with genuine pleasure, and she was pleased, in turn, with the look. She responded with a smile. It's not really very complicated, she said. You won't learn anything new. Tell me all the same, he said. Everything to do with you interests me. And he added: You interest me. She didn't dare feel pleasure at his words – they were clearly so exaggerated. And so she began to tell him all about it.

II

Just as Gilles André was exclaiming, I don't know why they all start wanting divorces, God only knows, women aren't meant to live alone, Penelope Lepeintre was putting the key into the lock. Penelope Lepeintre had never married, and lived alone. She had never lived with a man, either. She felt that to live with another person without being bound to do so by oath was not possible. Penelope had not been short of suitors, but she had only enjoyed true, reciprocated, miraculous love once when she was twenty and then the young man had died. She had never replaced him. Every tender murmuring had fallen unheard, the door of her steadfast heart was shut, locked by the memory of those same words when uttered on the gentle breath of her first ever lover. That was nearly fifteen years ago. Her memories were the constant backcloth of her life, flapping like the empty garments of a ghost. It was, after all, quite possible not to die of loneliness and to open up to someone new, as though one were free, available, a normal, warm-hearted person.

Penelope had nearly gone straight to the club from work. She was already late. Upset by what could only be described as the shock of love, she gauged her feelings as she walked along, trying to rein back her taste for solitude, her pointless commemoration of the dead, to make room, at last, for another man's desire. She wished she could just remain tucked away inside this little fold of life. But she had promised Marie she would come to the party. The women wouldn't watch the fight. Penelope loathed the sight of blood. Back then her fiancé had died of blood poisoning in a matter of hours. If she hadn't said yes to Marie, she'd have stayed at home. All these words, swirling about us, words we hear, repeat, words we dismiss, words that deeply wound us. Imagine, a man had just asked her to marry him. It was like being punched in the chest when you least expected it. She was stunned because she'd just realised she was about to slip her hand into the hand that was stretched out towards her.

He would soon be, quite simply, an old man. She would never have believed she'd fall in love with a man older than her own father. That was why she'd been able to go out with him so often, and so naturally. Friendship was a bonus granted to them, because of the difference in their ages. She'd been caught off guard. Together they'd seen dozens of films, plays, operas, exhibitions and even ballets. He'd always been available. She'd thought this was because he was a widow and retired. They'd dined together, just the two of them, on numerous occasions, trying out new restaurants. Fish restaurants, North African, or Japanese. Penelope didn't eat meat. She told her friends: We make complete pigs of ourselves! Her friends were amazed at how well they got on, despite the age gap. But they had so much to talk about. They discussed politics, economics, literature. How old are you? he murmured one evening, shaking his head as though in disbelief or regret when she said she was thirty-six, and he immediately figured that as he was seventy-two he was all too exactly twice her age. How could he feel so drawn to her by desire, but so distanced by implacable chronology? The law of love was pitched against the law of nature. He'd be dead by the time she was just reaching middle age. In the grip of his emotion, Paul Jade felt young again, happy, lost for words. Penelope too, perhaps because of his sense of rejuvenation, felt pleasure at the meeting of their minds.

And so things progressed, as though, in the end, their bodies had no choice but to comply with the inclinations of their hearts. One evening as they were walking along together after the theatre, she noticed the atmosphere between them had changed. Paul was somehow different: there was a physical attraction there, a new kind of virile interest in her. He walked much closer than he ever had before. She was quite shaken. She was aware of a force driving him towards her, ever closer, as though he wished to reach out and catch her. Her pace quickened. She was trying to run from him. He paid her flattering, seductive compliments, as he never had before. It had irritated her, to find herself pushed into the classic role of a woman pursued. Yet in some way, without quite realising it, she was touched. And as time went by, the innocence of their words and their gestures was restored.

His letters to her changed. He didn't declare his feelings directly, but they were clear to her anyway. She was moved. Their relationship mystified her. They had had an immediate affinity. She remembered it perfectly. They were in a café. It was raining. When he said goodbye in the metro he kept hold of her hand. She felt somehow that she had met a real person. The man had charmed her. In fact, she thought, the reason she hadn't seen what was coming was because she hadn't wanted it to happen. Her love for him was a reality, but she had not yet admitted it to herself. A newborn emotion is so very vulnerable. She had allowed the attachment to grow, as though nothing was happening. She wrote. She wrote that the affinity between two people takes no account of their ages, that she'd previously not known this, but now was absolutely convinced that it was so. He had taken her in his arms and held her, as they stood there on the pavement, like two adolescents, reluctant to go home to their parents. They'd been to the cinema. Gone were the days when taking a woman to the cinema meant commitment, but Paul, being of a different generation, had popped the question all the same.

Penelope Lepeintre wrapped a golden scarf around her shoulders and went to the club, warmed by the sparkling fabric and by the glorious inner glow which comes from the knowledge that one is loved.

II

The Meeting

I

He had first seen her at school, in front of the coat pegs by the entrance to the infant classrooms. That was where the enchantment had begun. There, surrounded by children, chirruping in the early morning as they wriggled out of their coats, he stood in rapt silence: a woman took hold of a man. An image burned into his gaze.

They were busy doing the same as every other parent there: each kneeling down in front of their child, unbuttoning the coat and then the jersey, straightening up as they pulled on a sleeve to remove the garment, hanging it up on the hook under the name of their little boy or girl, hugging the child close, then taking them by the hand and leading them into the classroom, getting him or her to say good morning to the teacher, and sit down with the others, one more kiss, then waving goodbye and leaving. It was just as he was hanging up the coat and jersey that he saw her.

Pauline Arnoult was wearing a long red coat, belted at the waist and flared in the skirt, with two rows of gold buttons, as on old military uniforms. Gilles André was busy with his daughter. A splash of colour crossed his field of vision. He was on his knees. A pair of finely shaped ankles rising gracefully from a pretty pair of shoes, with the generous fabric flowing all around. A man on his knees before his daughter was well placed to spot a pair of nice legs under the pale stockings. He glanced up to get a look at the face that went with the legs. It was then he fell into hopeless fantasy. He was hooked. A pale face, talking and smiling sweetly. He couldn't take his eyes off her smile. He couldn't understand it – there were other fathers there who were not swept up in this vision. Was it something he'd seen before, lost, and found, something he'd been waiting for all this time? He felt himself transported by the joyous torment of desire. Blonde hair swept back behind her head, her lips planting a kiss on the little boy's white head of hair. She was whispering endearments in his ear, and the child's laugh rang out like crystal above the general hubbub. Gilles André stood there foolishly. All he could hear was the child's laughter. He wished he could swap places with that little boy. She only had eyes for him. Pauline Arnoult was both youthful and motherly, so that the impression she gave was of a young *femme fatale* crossed with a mature woman whose seducing days are over. She was devoted to her child, but she herself was not yet quite complete, nor entirely sure who she was. She still needed to be found attractive. Did he sense this?

Just at this moment she was entirely focused on her son. It was precisely her graceful disregard which enchanted him, that and nothing else. He was unmanned by this brief glimpse of the tenderness of a woman as mother. He was struck, as a man, by the charm and calm with which a woman handles her child, and it led him to think too of the delicious sensual warmth with which she welcomes a lover, parting her velvet thighs, head dropped back, face closed off. He wished to be that lover. Why? Only much later would he ask himself this. He would try to understand the weave of this attraction, how it had first come to him and then unfolded wide before him. Was there something in her which had stirred up this desire in him? Did the key lie with him or with her? He wanted immediately to be loved by her. It was as violent as it was mysterious. But it was also the most interesting thing that had ever happened to him. He was neither too foolish nor too young not to recognise that. So he did not hold back but went right ahead and gazed at her, lusted for her. She looked like no other woman he had ever loved, she carried no echo of the past. But she was so pretty, he couldn't not look at her. The outline of her form, the features of her face, her look of tenderness, her indifference to him – these were what generated the spark of his attraction.

And so he got hopelessly tangled up in the web of words and scorching silences that come from desire. He was torn from his true self, ripped open by an emotion he welcomed to his heart. Delirium seeped through him. I am the ghost of a rose you wore at last night's ball. I know you already, you are a sister to me, we were children together, I know no other woman as I know you, here you are, at last, in you I find my mother's tenderness, and my desire, the perfect image of the need in me I cannot name, all I can do is gaze on you, woman of my dreams, I will put my life in the service of your pleasure, to enchant you, to shelter you under the wing of my desire. How foolish I must look, ravaged by this sudden torment, I, an innocent man, whom nothing and no one have made a fool of until now – no, not even love.

The woman was kissing her son. The man watched her, speechless, rooted to the spot. Some of the children saw him standing there, captive, and tried to work out what he was staring at. They could see nothing to account for his air of stupefaction. All they could see was this man standing there alone, frozen in solitary bliss. His daughter grew impatient. Papa, she said, tugging at his jacket, come and see my teacher. Still wrapped in an aura of ecstasy, he was dragged forward by the girl's tiny hand, seized twice over by the sweetest of captors, he liked to think – he who (so he said) had always been bound to life by the hands of women. What secret knowledge did they have, these sweet princesses, that they could so lift him out of himself? As he greeted the teacher under the proud gaze of his daughter, he came to his senses, back to the real world, back to his awareness of himself fixed in time and space. For a moment he stayed with the child as she burbled sweetly, trying to stop him leaving. She showed him her books, her drawings, but he couldn't concentrate on what he saw. From time to time he placed his hands on her head, winding his fingers in her curly hair, kissing her. Pauline Arnoult pushed her son into the classroom. The little lad walked between his mother's legs and together they laughed as she tried to move him forward against his will. Her child was the sole object of her attention. Her indifference struck Gilles André as though it had been a real rebuff. He enfolded her in a gaze he could not control.

Only then did she notice him: a man fixing her with a rigid stare. And at once she recognised that the look sprang from a landscape of desire: in accepting it she redrew that landscape with harmonious, feminine contours. He sank deeper into that state of sexual wonder which men experience more frequently than women, since their desire responds more readily to what they see. She gave an embarrassed smile, and he knew he had been found out. The expectation had begun. We never know what route desire will take to achieve its ends. We never know why some dreams will be realised and others fall away. An invisible net was closing in on them. If they wanted to run for safety, now was their last chance. They were entering the gates of a prison, lit up like a palace. Till death comes to still your last caress, you shall desire one another. Till death do us part, your bodies will be drawn together, and even after, till all flesh is gone, and so on dust to dust. . . .

They had to leave the classroom. Come on, parents out! said the teacher. All parents outside! The children laughed. The woman was on her knees again, prattling away with her son. Outside, the male world waited, ugly, iced over, it seemed to him, cancelled out by the immemorial hunger which had taken hold of him. He hugged his daughter tight. I'll fetch you this evening, he murmured. Today was the precious day when he looked after her. His lot as a father was a bitter one. So at the decisive moment when they met, Gilles André was a man flooded with a sense of failure, failure in love. Coming home each evening to find the child's room empty and quiet, he felt afresh the pain of not living under the same roof as his little girl.

Pauline Arnoult waved to the teacher and blew kisses to her son. She was mother to his happiness, to this state of filial bliss, and as she left the room this aura of happiness lay upon her like a magic charm. The little boy was laughing. Every last cell of his body was in harmony. Gilles André saw this, and it was as though some secret part of him were being crushed and ground to dust. He held his daughter tight again. Some of the mothers were having a little chat. Divorcing mothers, child-keeping mothers, he thought. He looked at them, feeding on their children's flesh and blood. Did they own the children, then? That appeared to be the general view of the world: of mothers and grandmothers, lawyers and judges, and even of fathers themselves. They had to go off and have new children with a second wife. . . .

Gilles André turned back and kissed his daughter one last time. Just like a mother, he thought. But just then he heard a voice say the name of the bewitching image: Pauline. A woman was calling to her. Why was he suddenly so moved? He was, he was truly moved. His whole mood was lifted, simply at hearing her name. Ridiculous. Pauline, the voice called again. The head of blonde hair stopped walking. I'll pick up your son at lunchtime, the other mother said. Are you sure it's no trouble? said the bewitching blonde vision. No, no trouble at all. Thank you, exclaimed pretty Pauline as she walked away, wrapped up in her big red coat. Where was she off to? He could quite happily have followed her, not to find out, just to look at her. See you this evening, she called. Thanks! She waved her hand above her head, her arm delicately arched, her hip swung slightly outwards as she turned. Desire possessed and obsessed him. The entrancing vision had a name. Pauline. He murmured it between closed lips, like a precious line of verse. Pauline.

Of course there were no further developments that day, beyond the silent ensnarement of a man by a woman, and of a woman by a look. There was simply this silence, heavy with knowledge, with the ambiguous expression of what was in fact clear as day, a language of flashes, of water and light, a language spoken not by the mouth but by the eyes, the lingua franca of desire, whose only mystery lies in what remains unsaid, a fake mystery, in fact, since no words are needed to acknowledge attraction. Gilles André had found himself a fetish. Pauline Arnoult was in that happy state of being vaguely disturbed, quite common among women when they find themselves being sexually admired. It was a state of primordial and intense pleasure: a sensual spasm of vanity. She existed as a woman. She had felt a prick of interest in this man the moment he looked at her. Might one not say that women can fall in love through a simple act of mimicry?

Gilles André got into his car. The young woman was leaving on foot. He watched as her figure receded in the rear mirror. She vanished. Abruptly, he re-entered real time, flat ordinary time, that time in which he found himself separated from his wife. His new infatuation had risen out of the silt of his dead love. He was completely free. But could he allow himself to follow his feelings? He sensed that the woman was not available. Indeed she wasn't. And yet he would somehow make her available, without understanding what he was doing, or how to go about it.

At that same moment, in her hour of victory, she ceased to think about their encounter, which had been no more than a slight aggravation at being stared at. She walked quickly, but still in the wake of that feminine pleasure – as simple as it is dangerous – of being found attractive by a man.

2

Both of them were married. They had bound themselves by oath, according to the laws of church and state. They had lived through many days and nights of married life. They had spoken words of love. They had reached the high slopes of intimacy, that point at which one believes, preposterously, that one actually knows another person; they had also reached the point of bitter recognition that this can never be; they had gone on, despite this, to form a single tight sheaf out of their separate, naked stalks, to the point where each was visible, then invisible, then visible again to the other, where they were blind and set in their ways, where the body and mind of the other had vanished from sight. They had reached that point in a shared existence where, in the inexorable routine of daily life, in the poverty of a desire that has fled, you somehow find the necessary strength to go on putting back into your love what the years have taken out of it, the strength to add a spark to the good things time brings.

They were not blank sheets of paper. They were both married to other people. They had produced offspring. She was expecting another child. They knew the language of love. They had heard and repeated words of love, endless compliments, petitions and requests, low murmurs of ecstasy, before (at least in his case) they got to the words which cut for ever the ties that bind, or which even suggest that those ties have never existed, that the only thing that binds you together are chains. She had used those words more rarely than he, words that break people, even as they break the bonds between them. I love you. Do you love me? Are these words a magic formula, or the source of all doubt? I love you. Do you love me? An injunction, a petition, a never-ending, softly-spoken clamour: Pauline said these words every night before she slept, in the half-light, when their bodies were entwined. Gilles André had pretty much given up saying them. He got the feeling he was no longer loved.

They were both married to people with whom they were somehow out of tune. I'm sick of this, Blanche said, that same Blanche who once had said to Gilles: Do you love me? Marc would say to Pauline: You look lovely in that dress. Come here. Let me kiss you. Kiss me. Do you love me? And held her close in his embrace.

Gilles had kissed Blanche too, in the passionate, joyful way that succeeds straightforward passion. In another age. There had been no great fall, no explosion to mark the end. And yet the end had come, and they were now apart. And because she was the one who had asked for the separation, he felt as though he was the one who had lost her. Who had lost whom? It was the wrong question. Neither had possessed the other in the first place. They had lacked the courage to talk when they should have. Why had he not dared? Was it because, though he couldn't admit it, he had already accepted the loss of a love which had been unique in all his life? Had he actually always preferred infidelity, the fever of new relationships, the multi-layering of lives? Or had he failed right at the start and from then on chosen to wander and stray? He couldn't say. And so the split had happened: Blanche had recovered her complete emotional independence. The day it had happened she had spoken almost vulgarly: I'm sick of this. Those were the words she had used to say that it was all finished, all the passion, love, suffering and tears. I'm sick of this. Just that. He'd had enough by then too, he wasn't happy, but he hadn't done with living in this state of unhappiness. 'I'm sick of this' meant something different for him. If the truth be told, he had found a way to deal with the unhappiness of their marriage. He had a refuge Blanche did not have: he was unfaithful. Women chased after him. Since he was a very charming man there were plenty of them and they were young, since he didn't respond to those who weren't. They offered themselves to him because he seemed to ask for it, and he made the most of it. Strange as it may seem, his flightiness actually brought him closer to his wife. She was the constant flame to which he always returned. She was his harbour, the guardian of his faith in love, the only woman for whom he did feel love. It was all very simple.

And this was how he explained his own behaviour: he was unfaithful because Blanche rejected him. Deep down he was a naturally faithful man. He was happy loving just one woman, as long as that woman loved him back. But the one woman in his life had been unresponsive. Whenever he moved towards her in the intimacy of their bed, she would sigh, she wanted to sleep, he left her to sleep, she slept. She slept for ever, he thought, she slept away their love. Sensually, she never woke again. He pointed this out to her. I know, she murmured, I don't know what's happened (she meant since Sarah was born). He didn't get angry. He tried to talk about it. You can't push me away and then tell me I can't go elsewhere, he'd say. He was a man to whom fidelity did not come easily. In the end she said, angrily, You really think I'm rejecting you? You think that's fair? She wasn't prepared to accept it, since they did still occasionally make love. In the end he lost his temper too. Yes, he said, I do think it's fair. Their disagreement made an accountant of him: he felt the need to prove what he had said. If she had only been willing, he would have made love every day. She hardly ever wanted to. It was a simple enough calculation: if you counted all the years, all the days when they might have made love, all the days she'd refused, it came to almost three thousand noes. Blanche André had to accept this was true. At this her eyes filled with tears. She loved her husband, but she had lost her desire, and she didn't feel like forcing it. You should go and see someone, he said. He meant a doctor. What would I say to him? answered Blanche. There's nothing to say, she cried. She believed there was no one who could help her. The truth is, he said, you just don't care. She mumbled, as though the risk was reduced by saying it very quietly: I do care, because one day you'll fall in love with someone else. You're wrong there, he said. You're the one I love. And it was true.

And now someone else had come along: Pauline. He still didn't know her full name. But that was later, after Gilles and Blanche had separated. He hadn't fallen in love so long as Blanche and he were together. He had just run through a string of fair-skinned young bodies. Once Blanche found out she didn't put up with it for long. I'm sick of this. I've called a lawyer. If it's all right by you we can use the same lawyer, it's simpler and less expensive. She spoke calmly, and he realised she really had done it. He didn't sleep a wink that night. Blanche was actually capable of doing, thinking, saying these things: one thing was clear, they really weren't at all alike. He could never have broken off their precious pact unilaterally. Because if you wanted to believe in love you needed that pact to be a permanent one. A living feeling can't die, he thought, it changes, but it never actually dies. He himself was proof of that: he still felt great tenderness for Blanche. He told her this. He lay next to her in bed in the semi-darkness of their room (she had wanted to sleep on the sofa in the living room but he had begged her not to). What's happened to us? he murmured. How did we get to this point? You know how much I love you. He was using the intimate voice, but it no longer worked on Blanche. No, I don't know, she said, icily, for fear of showing weakness. His wife's capacity for firmness was staggering. I still have this great tenderness for you in the depth of my heart, he said. Give it a rest, she said, it's too late, you kept it too well hidden. They're just words, she said. He looked astonished. You really mean you hadn't noticed? she said. It's ages since you've shown me any tenderness. That's because you always push me away, he said. I'm not talking about that, she said (meaning sex). I'm talking about tenderness. And I'm trying to explain, he said. I'm trying to explain why I'm scared of showing you I love you. You, scared? she exclaimed. You're such a liar. You even believe your own lies.

As is almost always the case, they were both right. Blanche was all shaken up with laughter, anger and despair. She still believed she could get him to admit his faults. It's you who've driven me away, she said. You're the one responsible. Maybe just by not having the courage to walk away yourself, she said, thoughtfully. At this he exploded: Don't you dare accuse me of words and thoughts I never had! That really is rich, he said, making out I'm to blame for the very thing that's destroying me. But you are, she said. It's all your fault. It's never all one person's fault, he said. All right then, she said, but tell me what I'm supposed to have done. Immediately he answered: You know perfectly well. She pulled a face. He spelled it out: What you've done is, you've stopped wanting to be my wife in the full sense of the word. You've rejected me. Oh, my poor darling, she sneered, he wanted to fuck but he didn't know how to turn his wife on. Poor darling, he mimicked back, he wanted to make love to his wife, but she was frigid. You're pathetic, she said. She looked at him in silence. And he could see from her face that he was history. Maybe she had met somebody else already. It was the first time the idea had occurred to him. He had been her lover and her husband, and now he was neither, she was no longer interested in or attracted by him. You don't love me any more, he said. Blanche said nothing. Gilles let his eyes roam over shadows of things in the evening light. No matter that the apartment brimmed with objects which had come to them through their love, their shared past, their travels, all that was dead now, everything would have to be divided up. They would have to sort out what belonged to him and what belonged to her, to go through that strange and dreadful rigmarole of separating what once had been joined. And what about their daughter? Would they cut her in half as well? It was enough to make him weep. Instead of which he got up and went to look in on the child as she slept. She had no idea, poor little thing, that the roof she slept under was about to be blown away.

Since Gilles had left the apartment to his wife and child, it had become a well-ordered place, containing only feminine things. The day he came to fetch his possessions, Blanche had wept. She had found the hanging cupboards empty, no more shirts, no more suits. She had phoned him at once. You fetched your stuff? she asked, as though she was surprised. I'm so unhappy, she murmured. Me too, Gilles said, but you shouldn't be saying that to me. She knew what she wanted, but it didn't stop her suffering. True, she no longer loved Gilles (or so she believed); he had never appreciated, as long as she'd been his wife, what it meant to have a wife and family, he'd gone his own sweet way, got on with his work as he pleased, while she'd been left alone with the little girl. One evening it had suddenly hit home. Blanche said to herself: if I'm going to be alone I might as well be properly alone. She said this to Gilles and instead of making a sensible reply he had simply said he didn't want to lose her. All of a sudden, just because she wanted to leave, he didn't want to lose her! He'd even made a mess of their separation. He wasn't prepared to make it easy for her. He'd wept on Sarah's shoulder. She was only four. He rang every evening. It made the little girl cry. Blanche would switch on the loudspeaker. Do you miss me? he'd ask his daughter. Did you cry when I left on Sunday? Did you? Did you cry? Blanche put Sarah to bed and then rang him back. You bloody idiot! she'd yell into the receiver. I never thought you could be such an idiot. What she didn't realise was that this was what he thought about himself too. How can anyone be so stupid? she screamed. When they're miserable, he cried. When they can't see their kid. You can see her whenever you want, said Blanche. I want her to sleep under my roof, he said. You should have thought about that earlier, she said, tired now. Frequently she hung up on him. It'll sort itself out, her friends told her, just give him time to get used to it.

The meeting at the school had put an end to the harassment. Love had flowered from despair. I've met a woman, he'd told Blanche. I'm very happy for you, she said. She was both relieved and perturbed to find that her place in a heart, which until so recently had belonged to her, had suddenly been taken, that an era was now over, that they could never go back. But she kept control of herself. Do I know her? she asked. You might, he said, you must have seen her at school, and her husband plays tennis at the club. She's married? Blanche said, in surprise. I'll tell you about it, he said. Give Sarah a kiss from me. He hadn't asked to speak to her. Incredible, thought Blanche. She thought of the woman, thanks to whom she might perhaps be left alone, and be able to enjoy a reasonable relationship with her ex-husband. It pained to her to think that the woman might meet her daughter, spend time with her. And since she couldn't get her head round that idea, Blanche took comfort from the fact that the woman was married.

3

One morning, at school, he came up and spoke to her. I think we must know each other, he said. I play tennis at the same club as your husband. That was what he'd said. It was perfectly idiotic. Pauline thought this at the time – how perfectly idiotic. And yet his words made her tremble. And she had responded. She said: Quite possibly. Which club do you play at? And then (when he had told her): Yes, that's the one. They stood there facing each other foolishly with nothing more to say. And then she said: I think I know your wife. She often brings your daughter to school. He agreed that she did. (Pauline and Blanche said hello, as mothers do who see each other every day at the school gate.) And so, as though seeking to punish him for his silence, Pauline Arnoult gave a little mocking smile, as though to say: Goodbye. As she turned on her heels her heart was pounding, but of course he didn't know that. This first exchange had served to convince her that it would never come to anything because everything, right from the start, was pure artifice. Someone had had to make the first move, but what possible first move could there be when there was no natural direction for them to take?

He was trying to think of a first move that wouldn't be too heavy. Do you like that little boy? he asked his daughter. As fate would have it the little girl indicated that no, she didn't. Do you know him? went on her father, undeterred. What's his name? Theodore, she answered. Sarah couldn't care less about Theodore. No, she didn't want to invite him home to play. At her age, friendship did not involve the opposite sex. So he abandoned the idea of an invitation to the little boy, which would have been the most discreet way of setting something up. After that he considered all possible options for a first move.

A few days went by. Hello. Neither of the two lovers seemed to be able to say anything beyond this. Hello, hello, hello. But the word was murmured, whispered, accompanied by a look of reverence, a lingering look, as though searching for something. Beseeching looks, sometimes, or encouraging looks or intimate looks, fleeting looks or ones which suggested it was all hopeless. Increasingly Pauline Arnoult enjoyed being looked at. She answered with a smile, and couldn't help lowering her gaze before turning away. In the end he managed to create an opportunity. Do you fancy a coffee? Would you like to join me for a coffee? He brimmed with conviviality. They had left the classroom at the same time that morning. It was simplicity itself. She reddened slightly, but said: Why not? That would be nice. They walked as far as the end of the street, discussing the weather, the children, the teacher. In the café, she declined to sit down, preferring to stay at the counter. They found themselves standing side by side, embarrassed, stirring little spoons in little cups, talking once more about the weather, the children, the teacher and the school. Then she made her excuses: I must be going. And that was how he found out she had a job. Probably. Goodbye, he said, making his voice bend down before her, looking for warmth in her blue eyes. Goodbye. Thanks for the coffee. And that was it. Were they still as much strangers as they'd ever been? He tried to tell himself they weren't. This woman was not available. Did she even notice he was there? Sometimes he got the feeling she looked right through him.

He had to keep at it. Find the right words for the right moment: create a sense of easy familiarity. Hello. Hello. He was back to square one again. And yet she knew perfectly well what his looks meant. He was positive she knew. There are some things it would be perfectly easy to explain but because they can't be said, everything gets complicated. And ridiculous, he thought. Was that why he leapt in at the deep end? At any rate, that was what he did. It was almost the end of the school year. He said: We should have dinner together. It would give me great pleasure to take you out to dinner somewhere, wherever you'd like to go. He was completely exposing his hand. He had to, in order to move his plan forward. Life wasn't going to offer him an opportunity on a plate. If he wanted to get to know this woman, he had to ask her. How could he possibly have had the nerve to ask, unless under the effect of some magic spell? He had put the question to her twenty times, in his head, and so it came out sounding very rehearsed. It would give me great pleasure to take you to dinner somewhere. It sounded false too, absurd almost. How could he say it would give him great pleasure when he didn't even know her, and why should he take her anywhere, since they weren't even friends? But what could he say to avoid sounding false? It would give me great pleasure to take you to dinner somewhere, was so obviously phoney that it revealed what he really meant: I fancy you. And of course it was the intimate voice speaking, wherever you'd like to go, he'd murmured, as though it was all almost too much for him. He was aching to get to know her, to be with her. Unfortunately, in order to achieve this, he had to come out with this platitude. Even as he said it he felt as though he were both exposing himself and playing a little game. Wherever you'd like to go, sounded to the woman opposite like an indecent proposal. But she was jubilant. Life was shaking itself awake, something was about to happen, a swell and a roar; seized by a wave of desire, she could almost have danced. She seemed to be in a dream.

He had thought that perhaps she wasn't indifferent to him, but as the silence continued he thought he must have got it wrong. He melted his voice down to nothing and asked: Might that be possible? I'm afraid not, said Pauline Arnoult, with pinched lips. She couldn't believe it. How dare he? It was so clumsy. What could she do but refuse? It was the same old story yet again. A man notices you, watches you, you don't know him, he comes up to you, starts chatting you up, and then asks you out to dinner. What a pity, he said. And, in fact, Pauline was beginning to feel a pinch of regret. As luck would have it, he gave her a second chance, and she quickly seized it. What about a drink? he asked. One evening, when you finish work. Might that be possible? Yes, that would be fine, she said, quite breathless with confusion. Ah, he said. Then he laughed. I promise to be most amusing, he said. For the first time, she looked him in the eye and said: I should like that very much. She had not had a chance to prepare this response in advance, she had no more excuse than he did, and no less desire. Her phrase seemed as trite and false to her as his initial question. Only her eyes conveyed the unadorned truth. So that would be possible? he said again, as though greatly surprised. Of course, she said, why not? They were both thinking of her husband, of what he would or wouldn't say. She dealt with her unease by saying: My husband won't object, if that's what you're wondering. She was conscious of how absurd the whole thing would have been if they hadn't both been so caught up in the moment. She wasn't sure she wished to expose herself to quite this extent. And so she found herself bizarrely moved to ask: And will your wife be there? Suddenly she'd had a pang of doubt: perhaps he was suggesting the four of them meet for dinner, and she had got the wrong idea (she had been quite sure he had meant just the two of them). Without turning a hair he replied: My wife won't be there, but you're welcome to ask your husband. What a liar he was, they both thought. She shook her head. Words would have spelled out too plainly that she would be coming alone, with her freedom in hand. I'll come on my own: she couldn't even bring herself to say this simple phrase. It seemed too suggestive. Aware of how much their little game of pretence was actually revealing, she blushed, and bid him a brusque goodbye. He scarcely had time to reply before she'd gone. I'll see you very soon, then, said the intimate voice softly. He couldn't even be quite sure she'd heard. The hem of her skirt was already fluttering down the steps. He followed calmly in her wake. He was in a state of extraordinarily heightened perception. Just to be alive in the world was a fine and overpowering thing. For the first time in ages he thought of Blanche and Sarah without the feeling that his heart had been beaten to a pulp.

The mere thought of what was happening inside her made Pauline Arnoult blush: she was falling in love with the way a man looked at her. But this time she was opening her heart to a man in the knowledge that she couldn't offer him her life – since her life had been offered and accepted elsewhere. When her husband kissed her she responded to his kiss. Their love was tender and strong. This other thing was uncertain and rash. However pure, their love would still be illicit. Even if it was never found out, it would still be illicit. It would have to be secret because it was illicit, untimely, perhaps even tragic. She didn't say to her husband: I'm going to meet a man who looks at me at school. She could never say to him: I've met a man who makes my heart pound. All she could do was conceal it from him. Would any man be willing to hear such things from the lips of the woman who shares his bed, who is carrying his future child? And yet her love for her husband was in no way affected. It wasn't a weakness in their marriage that had set this other man in her path. She was quite sure it wasn't that.

To love and to cherish. Forsaking all others . . . as long as you both shall live. Pauline Arnoult had been brought up on these words. And yet here she was, in love with two men. She lived with one and dreamed of the other. Almost every evening, from within her cocoon of domestic bliss, she would conjure up his face and hear his voice. It would give me great pleasure. Wherever you'd like to go. She would drift off to sleep to the memory of his murmuring voice, his admiring eyes. It gnawed at her. Yet it wasn't remorse that was eating her, but desire. She tossed and turned between the sheets. Are you still awake? said her husband. Yes, she replied. And if he asked, What are you thinking about? she found herself having to lie. Nothing, she'd answer. And perhaps then he would know she was lying. They were lying on their backs. Their bodies made humps in the bedclothes, like two draped figures lying side by side on a tomb. Sometimes she would stroke Marc's face. He didn't move. She looked at him. This was how he would look when he was dead. The very idea turned her thoughts to love. I love you, she told him. I love you too, he'd say. He drew close, his lips brushing his wife's body as he spoke. As she lay there, she accepted his faithful love, her body alive to the touch but her mind wandering, thinking of the other man as she lay in this man's arms. Marc would say: You are so beautiful, so gentle. She knew this to be true, thanks to the love of men. No one but me knows how gentle you are, Marc would say. She would have liked the other man to find out. She delighted in having a secret which posed no threat to what she loved. There was nothing ugly here. Why cause a break-up, when she could simply lie?

4

Thus she lived with her husband, who loved her dearly. On the morning of the day she dined in secret with a man she found attractive, she had got up and dressed alongside her husband. Don't forget this evening at the club, said her husband. I haven't forgotten, said Pauline, but I'm not coming with you, remember. I told you before, I've got this dinner to go to, she said. Her pleasure at the prospect exceeded her embarrassment at telling him. A dinner? he echoed. He may have been hoping she would elaborate, but he didn't ask her to. But he did say, just to make sure: So you won't be coming at all? Not even after your dinner? I don't know what time it'll finish, she said. She laid her hand on his neck. You don't mind me leaving you all on your own? She could be sweet when she wanted. No, he said, I'm glad you're going to do something you want to do. He was such a nice man, she thought. Should she feel more guilty because he was so nice? She touched his lips with hers, fleetingly at first, and then, as he slipped his hand round her waist, with more insistence. She broke away. You don't like kissing me, he said, with a smile. It's just a meeting of minds, our relationship. She shook her head. That can't be right, she said. What do you mean? he asked. Don't you remember, she said, how I used to say you were good-looking but dumb? They both laughed. They never tired of recalling their tempestuous early days. Not for long, though, she said. I soon realised you were clever but crazy. And I thought you were an angel, he said, I wanted to creep in and sleep under your wings. Ah. Ah, she said, out loud. He was so close he could make out the pores of her skin and the tiny blonde hairs on her face. She didn't like to be scrutinised so closely, even by him. She tried to slip out of his embrace but he tightened his arms around her. I've got you now, he said. Can't be much fun to be the weaker one. I woudn't like to be so dependent on someone else's good will. He kissed her on each cheek, then released her, like a bird.

And off she flew. At that very moment, she was sitting grinning at a café table in her little yellow dress and saying: You can't exactly call me Madame! Thanks to one look at the school gate, Marc Arnoult was spending the evening without his wife. Without their little boy too – he was away at his grandmother's. Marc came home to an empty apartment. Darkness and silence folded around him. You forget what it's like to be alone in the silence of your own home. Someone had drawn down all the shutters to keep the heat out. Pauline must have dropped back home before going out again. What was she doing? he wondered. She had said nothing about this dinner. At least if she'd said where it was, and who she was seeing, he could have pictured her. But he knew nothing about it. He could have no idea that had he known what his wife was doing that evening, his entire pattern of thought, his certainties and his life would have been changed by the knowledge. He missed his wife. He didn't particularly want to go out alone. Without someone at your side, laughing, talking, learning, singing are pretty much meaningless. How sad the flat was when it was empty. The space belonged to that tall, graceful figure who moved between kitchen, lounge and bedroom. He did the things he had to do mechanically, thinking about Pauline. He undressed, threw his things into a large basket, showered, ran the electric shaver over his face and chin, had a quick look in the mirror to check he looked okay, stroked his chin, then put on some casual clothes. He loved her so much. He saw the clothes she'd put on that morning, lying on the bed, so he knew that she must have changed for her dinner. But he had not been there to see how carefully, how thoughtfully she had done so: making herself ready for a lover. If he had seen her, he would have guessed that she was having dinner with a man, that she wanted to please him, that he was no ordinary man. But since all this had been kept secret from him, Marc Arnoult was happy.

I don't get jealous, he often said to his wife. It was true enough. Pauline would protest, though. Liar, she'd say, laughing. He did get jealous in a way, she thought, but it was camouflaged jealousy of an entirely respectable kind. His subtle air of indifference, the lugubrious, closed-off look he would adopt to frighten off those of her friends who had somehow aroused his jealousy – none of this had escaped her. After dinner, when her friends had gone home (no doubt wondering what kind of a boor poor Pauline had gone and married) he would subject them to a piercing, accurate critique. At this she would chuckle and say: You're jealous. If that's what you want to think, he'd reply.

I'm jealous of the past, I'll admit. I know it's stupid, but I can't help it, he'd say. He particularly hated the vulgar way certain women disclosed the intimate details of their past love lives to strangers in the presence of their husbands. Pauline agreed with him about this: it lacked delicacy. There were, you see, many areas in which they understood one another very well. They were a lively couple, and the vitality of their love was plain to see, in their complicity as well as in their fallings out.

I'm really not jealous, Marc said that morning, I hope you realise that. I'm going to be spending the evening without you and I don't even know what you're doing. It was his way of getting his wife to tell him what she would be doing, but on this occasion she didn't want to say. Perhaps he would notice that, unusually for her, she didn't reassure him by murmuring, Don't worry, I'm just going out with such and such a girlfriend or colleague. Instead she had burst out laughing, like a child delighted by a practical joke. He continued to make his case: I'm not jealous, he said, I know nothing about how you spend your day. You say: I design all day, but how do I really know if that's what you do? I never see any of your work. I don't ask you who you see, or who writes to you, or where you go, or who you go out with. If you think that's jealousy . . . She smiled. His little speech unsettled her: that he should come out with it just on the morning when she was planning to deceive him. Deceive him? Yes, that was what it was, whatever she liked to think. For the first time she understood the real meaning of the word. She could have said to herself: I'm not doing anything wrong, which was in fact what she thought. But she couldn't actually put it into words. It would have been ridiculous to say such a thing, whereas to believe it somewhere deep inside her, without needing to formulate it exactly, was not ridiculous at all. Don't stay out too late, he said. It worries me if you're out alone at night. You're so lovely, he said, laughing. I promise, said his lovely wife, I'll try to get back early. You could get a taxi to the club and we could come home together, he said. What could she say? A silence would just make him wonder. I'll try, she said.

III

Time to Eat

I

They managed to find somewhere to eat and organised it so that no one could overhear their conversation, even if they didn't know themselves how far their conversation might take them, being more sure of their desire than of their audacity. They sat opposite each other at a round table for two. It was so small that they could have touched knees beneath the table, but they didn't. All embarrassment had vanished. At least the kind of embarrassment felt when a situation is odd but no one is admitting why. They had become used to what is in fact quite rare: a close physical proximity with someone one doesn't know well. They were not friends. That was the point – they would never be friends. Did they have work to do? No, not that either. A business deal? Certainly not. So why were they sitting there, getting to know one another, even laughing? It was quite plain to see: the expression of rapt attention on their faces gave the game away. By now it was open knowledge to them both: they were both totally committed to this encounter.

The harmony between them was based on a shared secret, a reward for discretion, which made the radiance of her smile all the more delicious. The attraction was beginning to have an effect, and their easy chatter moved on to less conventional topics. The charm which singles out lovers in a crowd made them conspicuous to others, to the waiter (we'd like a quiet table, Gilles had said while Pauline looked at her feet), to the strangers at other tables who had been watching them (two faces oblivious to the outside world), and to themselves. He gave himself away through his laughter and the dogged insistence of his gaze; she, by smiling too much, too often, and by certain specific little gestures women adopt when they are being admired. There was also the way she arched her bosom over the tabletop: angled towards her companion, as though pulled by a magnetic force. Every facet of his intimate voice was brought into play, courtly devotion blending with sexual interest. And with each new onslaught from his lips, Pauline Arnoult felt herself led further astray.

She was more forthcoming than she had been at the start of the evening. He discovered that this pretty thing under his spell expressed herself with some discernment. She was sensitive. In short, his blonde Venus had things to say, was not without wit. This made her more attractive still to Gilles André, for he was one of those men for whom intelligence is an erotic quality. Her words obliged him to stop imagining he could woo her simply by dominating her, seeing her merely as a toy he could manipulate, until she yielded up her secret. No, unless he was much mistaken, she was flirting back at him, and rather subtly. She was gratified by his desire. And she was waiting.

Do you believe in angels? he asked her. I think some people have an angel within them, she said, and sometimes I can see it. They laughed. You're a dangerous woman, he said. Can you see my angel? No, she admitted, I can't see any wings on you. They laughed again. I'm not surprised, he said, I'm not much of an angel really. She didn't take him up on this. I tend to see it more often with women, she said. I can't have been looking at them properly then, he said. I seem to have met more she-devils than angels. He became thoughtful all of a sudden. Tell me about your wife, she said. What's her name? Blanche, he said. Does she work? She's a paediatrician, he said. She's very beautiful, said Pauline. She is indeed, he said, smiling. (It was such a feminine remark.) He said: She used to be ravishing. She's a bit less so these days, she's aged. Don't say that, she said. Tell me some more about her. He didn't want to talk about his wife. She was naturally curious about Blanche, as one woman often is about another, particularly when the other is much loved. Did she work long hours? Was she intelligent, dedicated, maternal, loving, sweet-natured? How much did he love her? Pauline would have liked hear it from the lips of the future lover and former husband. He must be prepared to betray one love to another. How long were you married for? asked Pauline. He'd stopped answering her questions. She asked again, wheedling, this time: Tell me more. But no, he quite clearly didn't wish to talk about Blanche. Lovely Pauline would get no more out of him. No, he said, looking straight at her, I'm not going to talk about her with you. Besides, she's not really my wife any more. If I talked about her to you, he said, I mean in a way that was at all interesting (he didn't dare say: intimate) you would think – with good reason – that I might talk about you in the same way one day to another woman. But I'm not your wife, the young woman objected. He smiled. I know you're not, he said, but I think you know what I mean. Once you start to know someone really intimately, you forfeit the right to talk about them. Otherwise, he said, real closeness is out of the question. He stopped the conversation there: I'm not going to talk about my wife. I love her, that's all I can tell you about her, said the intimate voice. And yet you're getting divorced.

Jealousy had wormed its way into her amazingly quickly. It was all very well to tell herself, It's his wife we're talking about, I can't be jealous of his wife, this did nothing to stifle her jealousy or her sudden wish that he would talk about her with the same degree of gentleness and secrecy in his voice. No doubt I will get divorced, once and for all, he began to say. He broke off, thoughtful suddenly, then said, as though speaking to himself: And yet I never wanted that to happen. I still can't get my head round the idea. Then he looked at her and said: My wife thinks living with me has become intolerable, but I really don't think it's all over yet. Are you happy with your husband? he asked. Very, she said. And when he smiled she protested, saying: It's true! No, I believe you, he said. Why did you marry him? he asked in one of those conversational twists so typical of him. She replied without hesitation: I married him because I was sure that he would stop me taking a direction in life that I'd later regret. I wanted to achieve something in life, and I knew he'd help me do it. And what are you in the process of achieving? he asked, amused. She said fervently: Well, my designs, you know – it is a kind of art form. And I know it won't stop there, there's lots more I want to do. And I'm sure you will, he murmured. Her tone was slightly offhand because she was revealing something of herself while he – since her admission gave substance to their relationship – was enjoying himself. What about you? she asked. Why did you marry your wife? He said with a wicked look, Because I loved her. That's cheating, she said. What do you mean, cheating? It's the simple truth. She objected: We love lots of people, but we don't marry them all. She went on: Loving and marrying are two separate things. It's not enough to love someone. He didn't comment on such a self-evident remark. He smiled, and looked at her, feeling his desire return, captivated by the image of what he saw in her (an image which was strong enough to override the banality of what she said). He took her hand between his: I like your ring, he said, looking carefully at it. He stayed like that, bent forward over her hand and forearm. He was too close for her comfort. If she had wanted she could have smelled the scent of his sweat and felt the warmth of his breath. The idea made her extremely uncomfortable. She was one of those physically shy women, for whom growing used to a new body is a slow and far from spontaneous process. He saw she had grown quite pink, and little beads of sweat appeared at her temples as she withdrew her hand. She wasn't yet ready to let herself be touched, he realised, frustrated in the intensity of his desire – more intense at this moment than it would ever be again. (Later he would say to her: I could tell you weren't ready. Why was that? And she didn't know how to answer him. She would say, as though putting forward a hypothesis: I think I thought I couldn't sleep with you as long as I was pregnant. He was astonished: Why ever not? Did you think I didn't like pregnant women?)

Didn't you love your husband? he asked, mischievously. Of course I did, of course I love him. Then, before she could continue, he suddenly asked: Was your husband your first lover? He wasn't trying to be offensive or to harass her, he was just being himself. She wasn't shocked. She answered openly. He felt very close to her. She seemed unspoiled; he thought he might have upset her, or at least made her blush again. But ideas didn't make her blush, only concrete, prosaic things. No, she said, resolutely, I didn't marry the first man I loved. But I haven't loved very many men, she said. And smiling broadly, she said: I've never been cut out for love affairs. Is that about to change? he asked, laughing. I don't suppose so, she said. She was laughing. She was reacting to all the right prompts. This woman's got spring fever, he thought, and he was the one who would bring the garden into flower. He couldn't take his eyes off her and yet she stood firm under fire, as pretty women know how to do. And the rising sap brought colour to her cheeks.

Have you cheated on your wife before? she said, swept back onto the offensive by the surge of complicity between them, astonished by the things being found attractive made her say. But he wasn't shocked. They could say anything to each other. They spoke precisely about those things people never talk about. Cheated? he repeated, pulling a face. It's not really the word I'd use. Which would you prefer? she asked immediately. But instead of giving her an answer, he said: What about you? Do you cheat on your husband? He had deliberately used the present tense. Why do you say it like that? she said, indignant at the asymmetry he was setting up between them. Because you seem to think it's the right word, he said. You'd 'cheat on' your husband. She laughed. No one's ever spoken to me like that before. Well? he insisted. Have you ever cheated on him, poor guy? I never answer that question, she said. I see, he said. So you do have secrets? His eyes had become expressive again, speaking to her in long sparkling phrases. How could I keep it a secret from him but then tell someone else? she asked. That really would be a betrayal. He said: Aaaaah. And she added: For that kind of freedom, you have to make sure the other person doesn't find out. At least one other person would know anyway, said Gilles André. That's why you have to choose carefully, she said. You need someone who is happy and is going to keep quiet. You seem to have given the matter considerable thought, he said. Their conversation was full of laughter, collusion, embarrassment, fun and mischief. I suppose I have, she said. I've always found the question moving.

Moving? he repeated, indicating that he found the word somehow inappropriate. Yes, she said, because we all suffer from it to some degree. But isn't it just a problem we've invented for ourselves? He tipped his head, implying that he wasn't entirely sure about that. She said: We've made it up out of nothing. But we could approach the whole question of fidelity quite differently. I'm impressed, he said. And what does your husband think about all this? he asked. Stop poking fun, she said. My husband thinks the same as me, she said, I'm just saying what he says to me. Ah-ah, he said. So, after all that, he said, what kind of lover would you choose? With this, he believed, the decisive word had been spoken. Why was he so light-hearted with it? No doubt because he was happy. She said: I would choose a lover who has an interest in keeping quiet. And who has an interest in keeping quiet, in your book? he asked. A safely married man, who loves his wife and is happy, she said. You're a sly one, he conceded, anyone one would think you'd been doing it all your life! Not only did she not reply, she suddenly felt that this was going too far. What a subject for a dinner like this, she said, but could not stop herself there. You haven't answered my first question, she said. He had quite forgotten what the question was. Have you cheated on your wife before? she asked again. He smiled. His smile was an answer in itself. Have you had many mistresses? she said softly. She didn't like to hear herself asking him this. She'd never said anything like it in her life. This man was turning her into quite a different woman, and it bothered her, and yet she was unable to do anything to stop him. Yes, he said. He said it simply, and without a trace of masculine vanity. He clearly considered these women to be his equals. They weren't conquests, in any sense of the word.

He explained: Women seem to like me. At a certain point in my life I took advantage of the fact. She was chilled by his reply. She actually felt jealous. How could that possibly be? She was vexed that he hadn't yet made her his mistress. She thought of her husband. How come married men don't scare their victims off? Marc often used to wonder. Why are women such little fools? And here she was, one more little fool. How ridiculous, thought Pauline Arnoult. Here he was, saying I'm a faithless, a passionate man, and she was longing to be his mistress. So how would he go about it?

Does your wife know? she asked. Never, he said, with a gravity which seemed to suggest both love for his wife and the seriousness of his intent (though in this he was lying to himself). Pauline Arnoult felt another twinge of jealousy, a sudden burning sting, to hear him speaking so tenderly of his wife. She didn't register that Blanche André was a woman deceived, she registered that Blanche André was loved. Anyway, she thought, how was it that everyone else seemed to fail to keep things secret, and not him? She tried to untangle what was true and what was false. What was his love life really like? The thought of all these experiences of his, secret but so real, made her feel dizzy and unsure. She wondered if she was already included in his band of women. She wanted to be unique, and of course she wasn't. And now? she asked. Now, he said, I'm in a different life. I've paid for all that. And, lying once more to himself, he said: I stopped because I was making all these women unhappy. They wanted to see me all the time, I wasn't free, I loved my wife, I'd tell them I loved her, they didn't listen, it was stupid. She said nothing, thinking perhaps of a kind of extreme sensuality of temperament, a degree of infidelity which could not be pardoned: a cocktail of sexual pleasure and misfortune that spelled disaster. Despite the dread prospect of heartache, she still hoped he would make her his mistress. Ensnared by her very specific brand of charm, he would fall more heavily than usual: so she hoped. She would be unique, irreplaceable, because that was what, in fact, she was. He considered her as one might consider an object, not speaking to her, just smiling. So she said: You're lucky to have met me without my husband. Really? he said. And once again, they both laughed.

It couldn't all be fun and games. He began to speak seriously. Why do you think people don't respect the rule of exclusivity in marriage? he said. Do you think it's a bad thing? He put these questions methodically. He wanted to have an intelligent discussion with this woman, even as he seduced her. To make sure everything was quite clear from the start, by letting her know his own position. He already had all the answers, precisely formulated, and without taint of convention. He embarked on a long explanation. Of course not, she was about to say, but he left her no time to reply. You see, he said, you'll find some people who think that deception, say an adulterous love affair, is proof that a couple have problems. Nothing more than that, he said. He suggested the idea with a graceful movement of his hand. I've never believed that myself, he said. People fall in love with someone else not because their marriage is going badly but because we all need a secret garden. He said: Sometimes I think that that was the only reason I got married. So I could have secrets. The explanations he gave his wife for his infidelities were quite different to the ones he was giving now. Pauline was not to know this, and since he believed what he was saying, she believed it too. Since she was not sure she agreed with his theories, she said nothing.

He said: I'm not a husband, I'm a lover. I completely adore women. His voice as he said this was like a caress. He sounded not absurd, but determinedly sensual. He added, as though this particular quality of his might have escaped her: Not all men are like that. Lots of men have funny fads. A guy might leave his mistress because he can't stand the sight of her feet. Or another might not like women with pale skin. I've got a friend who can't stand women with dyed hair. The truth of it is, they're just excuses. She laughed. Is your husband a husband or a lover? Both, she said. You can't be both at once, he said. It's a question of what kind of person you are. Which is it? She admitted: I suppose he's more of a husband. I thought so, he said. She didn't like the way he was so sure of himself when talking about someone he'd never met. But he was just playing the courtship game, a cruel, manipulative game in which many are sacrificed for the benefit of one. I'm sure you're a very gentle woman, he said suddenly. People probably think you're not, but you are. The intimate voice had crept back in to say this. And at that moment – it was truly somehow moving – she blushed like a tomato in the sun. For a fraction of a second her face flared with colour. He wasn't drunk or even tipsy. He really meant what he said. Such sincerity is believable, understandable even, if one considers the immediate intimacy which is established when two people are deeply attracted to one another. They could say anything they pleased. They shared an exact affinity. It was beyond their control, anyway; she was lost in the spell, he was trying to pinpoint what he felt for this woman, to compare her to others, but she was not like any of the rest.

He rested his forearms on the table and sent across a smile to meet hers. Tell me about something really good in your life, he said. What really helps you? She smiled. My son, she said, without hesitation. And, since he didn't take her up on this, and being a little afraid of silences, she said: When I hold him in my arms, when I dress him, I feel as though I'm holding life itself in my hands. She noticed he was distracted. It was tactless to talk to him about having children in the house. She changed the subject. Music too. Music really affects me, she said. I don't know if I could live without music. Sometimes I think when I die there'll be no more music. That would be the worst thing about it. She blushed. Why was she telling him this? She didn't know why she was telling him things she had never told anyone, but she went on. Do you think death puts an end to music too? she asked. I love having ears, she murmured, laughing. He didn't seem to understand what she was talking about. Her tone had changed. Oh, she was so much younger than him! At times the age difference was very apparent. He studied her blue eyes. No, she wasn't naïve, she was simply young, he thought. She stopped laughing: You know people often say music summons the angels? Do you think that's true? Do you think the dead are here among us, but invisible, like secrets, and that they can hear music too? Do you think we'll turn into angels? She spoke seriously, but he had to laugh. I'm sure you will, he said. But she didn't laugh.

She said: I'm really afraid of dying. I sometimes think I'll never manage it. Life is so delicious. I just can't accept it's going to end one day. Even if we have immortal souls, I like having a body. Life is all about having a body, because that's what we lose when we die. You're very sententious, he said. I won't be able to look at you like this when I'm dead, she said, mischievously. And our hair will get wet in the rain, he said, deliberately picking up on her rather dramatic tone. But she didn't realise he was teasing her, gently. I find it so hard to imagine, she said. And yet it's the one thing we can be sure of in this life, he said, flatly. There will be an end to us, and personally I believe that's it, nothing left but the memories we leave for a short time with the people who knew us. Which is why, he concluded, we have to live simply and intensely while we can. Do something if it's what we feel we have to do. Be happy, if that's enough for us. And love, he said. My husband would hate it if he heard you talking like that, said Pauline Arnoult. He believes in reincarnation. She laughed, as though she had just said something really stupid. He thinks we'll find each other again in all our future lives. That's because he can't accept that one day you'll lose each other, he said, without really thinking about what he was saying. He was too preoccupied with the lovely face opposite. No it's not, she said. He's quite convinced that love is stronger than death. What about you? said Gilles André. What do you think? She didn't answer. Her eyes, which were a very pale blue, were not her best feature, and at that moment they looked rather stupid. Any woman who talks mockingly of her husband's love is surely bound to look idiotic. He could easily have thought this. It was pretty much what he would have thought normally. But he was smitten with her, her face, her complexion, her slender, graceful neck, her Nordic blondeness, everything about her, from her coldness, which melted whenever she laughed, to the childlike teeth. He would never have admitted to himself: She's got the kind of blue eyes that never seem very alert. So he noticed nothing. He said: It would seem that love ends when our bodies die, even according to Catholics. She didn't reply, so he recited in a learned fashion: 'Ye do err, not knowing the scriptures or the power of God. For in the resurrection they neither marry, nor are given in marriage, but are as the angels of God in heaven.' Don't you know the words of Christ to the Pharisees? he said, with a weary smile, as though his profane use of the quotation filled him with sadness. She murmured: Maybe if I could really believe that it would give me some peace.

He looked at her again. She smiled at him. He took her white hands between his, squeezed them gently for a moment, all tangled up in his desire, his ardour, the obstacles before him, placed them tenderly back on the table and said: Take it easy. What's the matter with you? Look at you, you're blazing with happiness. He laughed with an impudence which was entirely natural in him. But she didn't like him making fun, she wanted him to love her. And in the madness of the moment, trapped in the shop-girl mentality this man seemed to induce in her, she heard him say, despite herself: Take it easy, I love you and cherish you and will protect you. It was all she wanted to hear. So why didn't he say it?

He didn't say it because he didn't think it. And had she known he didn't think it, she would have wondered: Why doesn't he think it? Because that was what she wanted: she wanted him to love her, to cherish and protect her. When women demand love, they demand adoration, and she wanted his adoration spelled out for her. She wanted to be loved, to have it affirmed with the right words and without having to ask for it. And if she heard the words, she could then repeat them after him, she could be the echo in their love duet. She could happily repeat them back, but she could not be the first to say them, because she still hoped to hear him say them first. In short, she was extremely exacting, a quality both hard-faced and shamefaced which revealed the depth of her feeling for him, exposing it as both absurd and proud, courtly and romantic.

But Gilles André said none of the things he was supposed to. And since she didn't hear what she wanted to hear, Pauline Arnoult was annoyed. The words which refused to come brought out the angry coquette in her. Why didn't he want to say it, since it was what he thought? She couldn't admit to herself that he just didn't think it and she wasn't prepared to tell him what she expected of him. I would like you to love me, cherish me and protect me. If she'd simply said that, he would have known perfectly well how to respond. He would have said: That's what your husband's for. Why would you want me to do that? But she didn't ask him. It was still too early to ask him to say the right words. Later on she would beg him. No, she didn't ask, and since it was quite clear he would say none of the things she wanted to hear, she concluded he must be calculating, not admitting his feelings for her so as not to give her power. She was just a little suspicious of him. Had she suspected other men of having strategies, of being manipulative? Clearly, she thought, he was playing with her a little, with the sly cunning of a lover. But she was wrong. All he was doing (all he would ever do) was following his inclinations, enjoying the simple beauty of an undeniable affinity. So no, he uttered not one of those sacramental words. He began to talk of something else entirely.

He said: Your husband must have met up with his friends by now. Why do you say that? she asked. The thought of her husband swooped back down on her through a cloud of illicit dreams. Because I was thinking about him, he said. At this, a silence settled between them. I was thinking that he doesn't know where you are, he said with laughter in his eyes. She didn't find it all that funny. So he said, in a serious voice: I wish I didn't know your husband. Well then, she said (impatiently), you don't know him, so that's all right. No, he said, I know what he looks like, I've heard his voice, I remember his body, I've seen him naked in the shower at the club. Can you imagine that? he said. There's something grotesque in that. I don't see why, she said. And she was quite right. He was exaggerating a problem that didn't exist. He was having fun. When you find a woman this attractive, things are really very easy. But he wanted to get a rise out of her, and he loved it when she got annoyed. How long ago was that? she asked. Ages ago. Is there a time limit on it? he asked (with irony). She didn't know what to say to that, and another silence fell. I was joking, he said. I don't know your husband. But let me give you a piece of advice. If ever you're unfaithful to him, don't tell him. It's the most wounding, selfish thing you can do. She said nothing. He had an incredible cheek to say such a thing. She looked at him. Their love would be illicit, she knew that. Who can foresee whether the other person will agree to break their sacred vows? What does a lover really think of an adulterous woman? She asked him this. What would you think of me if I was unfaithful? He smiled. I'd think you needed to have a secret. You always say the same thing, she said. Yes, he said, I'm straightforward, I tell you what I think and I don't change my view every five minutes. This of course took her breath away, since it was quite clear that what he was saying was true. He wasn't playing games, whereas she was actually cheating a little bit to make him like her. That was it in a nutshell: she wanted to make him like her, even if it meant she had to invent and lie.

Why was she so determined to seduce him? Because he'd looked at her and desired her and that had been enough to seduce her. He had guessed she was a woman who could be a lover. He had fixed his eyes on her face. And because a woman's attachments are always governed by the principle of imitation, she would henceforth be in thrall to whatever face he showed her. This she knew, and was secretly rather ashamed, but she still accepted it as a fact and was prepared for the consequences. He wanted to decide for her? Then let him. How was it that she followed so readily where he beckoned when she already had a husband, already had a love in her life? She desired him simply because he had desired her first, looked at him because he'd looked at her first. Surely there was something odd going on? He'd had the nerve to approach her. He'd stood there before her like some great conqueror, driven by a force she recognised, despite all the barriers of human flesh and words. She had been conquered, like a foreign country, a treasure, an object. It was, she found, quite delightful to be wanted as though one were an object. In any case, she told herself, as though it were some kind of conclusion, it's not your place to talk to me about my husband. Oh no? he said. No, she said. He remarked, with irony: You're very strict. The waiter came up to their table to fill up their glasses. He arranged the napkin around the neck of the bottle. He was wary, not wishing to disturb them. But he could tell the atmosphere between them had relaxed.

2

By now the women had all met up: Louise, Marie, Sara, Eve, Melusine, Penelope. Some of them were friends with Pauline. Pauline had been invited to the dinner. They were chatting away animatedly in the club dining room, where the tables had been pushed against the walls as though in preparation for dancing. There was something almost frivolous about the expression on their faces, a look of celebration and exuberance. The all too rare prospect of a girls' night out had them chattering excitedly. We don't do this often enough, said

Penelope. She often got particularly lonely, because the others never did anything without their husbands. I agree, said Melusine, I don't know why we're always glued to our husbands. Speak for yourself, Melu, said Sara. Mine's only half a husband, I can never get hold of him, so the idea of never leaving his side – he'd think I was trying to bury him alive. She gave a half-hearted laugh. The others knew she was close to tears. I'm really happy to be here tonight, said Melusine, at the thought of all the many reasons they had for tears. Only Blanche and Pauline were missing. It's not like Pauline to be late, said Sara. She's not coming, said Eve. Blanche'll be late, said Louise. It's Wednesday, she always has more patients when there's no school, said Melusine. Have Pauline and Blanche met? asked Eve. Their children go to the same school, said Marie, they must have bumped into each other there. It was Melu's idea to introduce them. I've decided to invite the young ones along with the oldies, said Melusine. Yuck! Oldies all of a sudden! said Marie. Old? said Louise. Don't know the meaning of the word.

Their friendships were organised by age. Sara, Eve, Pauline and Penelope often played doubles together. Melusine, Louise and Blanche were more often to be found chatting by the pool than on the tennis courts. Eve said, What a life, being a paediatrician. While your own children are at home you're out looking after other people's. It's true, whatever you might think, it's not really a job for a woman, said Louise. Too many emergencies, said Marie. The waiter stood stiffly in his white jacket behind the little buffet table, listening to the colourful, noisy little party. None of them took any notice of him. He would tell his girlfriend he'd served dinner to a group of women and my God, they hadn't half talked! It was all rather tiring after a bit, he would say. Who are we waiting for, apart from Blanche? asked Louise. As she spoke she moved towards the buffet, inspecting what was on offer. What would you like to drink, she asked, wine or champagne? Who wants some nuts? said Melusine. What time does the fight start? said Louise. Half nine, said Eve. Do you know what Pauline's doing tonight? said Marie. No idea, said Louise, I just know she's had this evening booked for ages. The buffet's an excellent idea, said Marie. Yes, said Louise, it's really good, you help yourself to what you want, then go and sit down, and you don't have to spend the whole evening sitting next to the same person. Have the men got something to eat in front of the television? Don't you worry, said Louise, your Jean's got everything he needs.

Louise said: They're like little kids, all excited at the prospect of watching two men beat each other up. Boxing is a noble sport, said Marie. It's a fight with rules, almost like a dance. It's not just violence. Come off it, said Louise, that's Jean talking. A knockout's like a mini coma. I've seen enough fights. There's blood pouring down along with all the sweat and then the brain switches off and the guy collapses, for a second you think he's dead and then – I promise you – you feel like yelling abuse at these men for heaping one more horror on top of all those that already exist. Marie said: It makes them happy, that's what matters. Holy mother! said Eve. I've never been able to take love or happiness to the point where I'm happy just because my man is. No, said Sara, it's true, not everyone's capable. Louise had begun to pass round the wine, and Melusine was going round with a tray of sandwiches with different fillings. She moved slowly and carefully, swaying among the other guests, with a smile that nestled deep in the crevices of her puffy face, and was quite unaware of what she looked like at that moment, a hefty woman in a floppy shirt. If she had been, she would have stopped handing round the savouries that instant, and quite possibly have gone home to hide. But she was a little drunk and was quivering on the verge of an outburst of emotion provoked by their words, by things seen but not mentioned, by celebration and human warmth. She was not alone. It was so nice not to have to think. Not far from Melusine, Louise went on filling up the glasses on the counter. She was so slim you might have thought she was ill. She had heard Eve and Penelope talking in quiet voices together. Eve said, Three months, nodding her head and touching her belly with her hand. Her evening was ruined. It was stupid, but she couldn't stand the thought of another woman's pregnant stomach. Do other people's lives always have to trample over our own? thought Louise. Why couldn't she just shrug off what was happening to Eve, be happy for her and live out her own life without always comparing herself to others? Of course that was what she ought to do, but that wasn't what women were taught. There was a pecking order between them, established by the dark forces of envy and jealousy. Am I prettier than . . . ? Do I look younger than . . . ? How many times she had heard her grandmother ask her these stupid questions. Louise thought: Women get set up in competition for the males, and they fall into the trap without thinking, they take pleasure in the way men see them. This thought calmed her down, as though understanding could bring exorcism. But understanding didn't help and her face was contorted by her secret pain. All at once she was a million miles from the party, alone, surrounded by her friends. The idea of another woman's baby made her feel her own loneliness. She could have broken down and wept.

Melusine put down her tray and went over to Louise. What's the matter, Louise darling? she asked her friend. Is something wrong? It's a lovely evening. Don't you like it, just women together? said Melusine. Yes, sometimes, said Louise. Louise didn't feel the need to get rid of the men. It's fun, she said, we talk about different things. I should say so, said Melusine. But something's missing when they're not here, isn't it? said Melusine, laughing suddenly. I can't explain it, said Louise, but you're right. She reflected for a moment. Maybe it's just the sexual climate, she said, something to do with desire. I miss sex when there are only women around, she said firmly. It was her turn to burst out laughing. Did she really believe what she'd just said? She didn't know. But she knew what she meant. No question, she added. Absolutely, said Melusine. When it's all women, we can take a break from the whole game. Did I say it was a game? said Louise. Oh, said Melusine, don't tell me the sexual climate, as you call it, doesn't involve all sorts of little games. Louise conceded the point. That must be what I like, in the end, she said. But it's good not to play for once, don't you think? said Melusine. She was smiling. I've grown so hideous, she thought, I've managed to drive all desire out of my life. Louise's expression, *sexual climate*, had brought her thoughts back to her own life. There was nothing erotic about her relationship with men any more. She said: Anyway, you're a beautiful woman, I can imagine you miss men. But as for me . . . Louise said nothing. I could never undress in front of any man but Henri now, said Melusine, with disconcerting directness. So I'm happy with my female friends, she said. She tried to meet Louise's eye. If you didn't exist, if I didn't have female friends to confide in, who understood what my life was like, I'd kill myself. Don't say that, said Louise. But it's true, said Melusine. Without you I'd crack up. I wouldn't be able to get through. I can't really as it is, but it would be truly terrible without you. I wouldn't last a minute longer in this world of sorrows. She finished her glass of red wine and and filled it up again within seconds.

Women are what make life liveable for me. Louise smiled. But Melusine insisted. Some men know it for a fact; they'll even admit it, said Melusine, as though this proved her point irrefutably. The kind of men who only really care about women. Some of them have told me, she said. Then, wildly, she added: And if they do realise it and don't put anything back of what they take out, then they should be ashamed. So what have women got that men don't? asked Louise gently. I don't know, said Melusine, at first. But they've definitely got something. But what? said Louise, who was laughing by now. They know the meaning of suffering, said Melusine. They've got these incredible bodies, they bleed, give birth, I'm sorry, I shouldn't say that to you, they're gentle, they have this instinctive love for the sick and dying. At this point she corrected herself, seemed to reflect for a moment, then said: All the joy, all the sweetness in my life, has come from women and children. Do you really believe that? asked Louise, amused by Melusine's hyperbole. Melusine was adamant: Do you think a man can bring beauty or sweetness into your life? Of course, said Louise. It's not the same kind of sweetness, said Melusine, or the same kind of beauty. Her secret suffering made her stubborn. Look at the way little girls are all maternal with a small baby, she said. But little boys do that too, said Louise. There are some men who are really tender, after all. Oh yes, said Melusine sarcastically. But you know as well as I do what they're after. It's a kind of tenderness that bubbles up like milk and never quite spills over. She was thinking: it's a kind of alien tenderness. There's a part of the world men just know nothing about. How can we talk to them about it, when it's our whole existence? How would they know anything about the way other people's lives lie heavy upon your own, how could they possibly know, since they never take any notice of anything? Every time I've confided in a man, continued Melusine, it's been quite clear he hasn't understood what I'm talking about. I knew he was thinking: here's another pain in the butt. Her eyes filled with tears, as often happened when she was tipsy. Melu, said Louise, are you drunk? No, said Melusine, I'm just telling you what I think, and it makes me upset, and I know you don't think the same, but I'm not drunk (although she was). You're so young, said Melusine. Louise nodded, in a way which suggested she wasn't sure she was any more. Oh you are, said Melusine. I'm the old one. Every morning my face is kind enough to remind me of the fate that awaits us all. You're still young, you don't think about what's in store for us. Of course I do, said Louise. Grief, tears and the coffin and I don't even have a child to help me put the horror out of my mind. Forgive me, said Melusine. I'm sorry to make you think about that, I don't know why I talk this way, I'm so sorry.

Lovely conversation you're having, said Eve as she went past with a glass in her hand. She had just caught Louise's last words. Stupid, vicious cow, thought Louise, as she did every time she met Eve. Melusine didn't even break off what she was saying. You know, she said, children aren't really an answer. It's dreadful when they leave. I spent days and days weeping in our empty house. You try not to think about it, but they're not really ours. And now they're grown up, they live their own lives, and I've finished what I had to do. You've still got Henri, said Louise. Pah! said Melusine, he doesn't really need me. Sometimes I even think I'm ruining his life. In fact I know I am. They both laughed like little children. Melusine sank back into her daydream again. I'm so depressed, she said. Her swollen hand clutched the stem of the glass. Come on, don't let's start the evening off like that, said Louise. No, said Melusine, mustn't get weepy. Let's get drunk. And this evening Louise is generous. Let's drink then, she said to Melusine, who was already drunk.

3

The man sprawled on the sofa – Jean, Marie's husband – had begun to talk about Gilles' divorce, a subject he'd been thinking about all the way to the club in the car with his wife, who had just told him the news. Did you know about it? he asked Tom. Sara warned me, said Tom, so I wouldn't put my foot in it if I saw him. And there you have the state of modern marriage, said Jean. The women leave and they take the children with them. And the worst thing of all, he said, is that everyone thinks it's quite normal. Is that what it's going to be like from now on for us men? he said. Just a temporary role, siring the offspring? He was thinking of his own four boys. The thought of Marie disappearing with the four of them seemed unthinkable, and yet it happened to other people and they somehow managed to go on living. How times had changed. And had people changed too? He often wondered this. Do you think women in days gone by used to want to disappear and take the family with them, but couldn't, because they didn't have the means? he said. What, our grandmothers? said Tom. Do I think our grandmothers wished they could just fly away with their little flock? Tom had an image of a serene face next to the dried-up body of the man she loved, and he couldn't imagine the two separate from each other. And so he said: I can't imagine it.

The others had all heard Jean's question. To start with, said Tom, you have to give justice to women today, they don't all just hop off, and I know some who would have good reason. Your wife wouldn't, said Jean, whatever you did. Maybe that's because she couldn't afford to, suggested Guillaume. Shut up, that's a terrible thing to say, said Max, giving him a thump on the arm. He was still upset after his row with Eve, and he understood exactly what Guillaume had just said. He knew, in a confused way, that his own wife was not about to up and leave him, that his marriage wasn't an alliance but a contract in which he had become the provider. Modern love is all to do with women's economic independence, said Tom. It's a good thing, he said, that way we can be sure they love us for ourselves. Max was silent now. What would he have done if Eve had been independent? He would have had more freedom too. But she had given up work as soon as she'd found out she was pregnant. It occurred to him that he couldn't discuss his wife here. He remembered his own engagement all too vividly, the way his friends could scarcely hide their astonishment when he introduced them to Eve, the fiancée they'd heard so much about. Fiancée? Tom had mocked. Do they still exist? Eve had been furious. She'd wanted nothing more to do with Tom. Max hadn't bothered to try to explain at the time. In any case, what could he have said? He realised now that nothing he could have said would have convinced them. He'd got carried away, like a virgin. He'd been quite blind. Remembering this now, his face darkened. He still couldn't accept that he'd taken completely the wrong turning. The others interpreted his gloominess as tiredness. They were all tired, thought Tom, looking at Max. They all worked incredibly hard. We live stupid lives, Guillaume said. He really believed this. He was the only one who tried to protect himself. I'm taking eight weeks' holiday this year, he said. Yes, but you're the boss, Max said. We just work to pay our tax, said Jean.

Even so, his decision not to break up a marriage in which he was unhappy led Max to remark: What's changed in modern love is the sense of duty. People don't feel a sense of duty any more. He said this because he himself suffered from the fact that he did, and chose to stay in the marital mire despite believing that it would have been braver to go (because it would have been harder). Why did some people belong to the type who find the price of staying in a marriage too high, and manage to break free, and others to the type who find it impossible to leave? Was it perhaps, as with other choices in life, a simple question of mobility? Wasn't it always the same people who chose to change jobs, towns, countries, wives? He would have been hard pushed to even begin an analysis of the question. He was particularly unclear on whether it depended on the temperament of the person deciding, or on the situations they found themselves in. To put it another way, did the people who left their wives, in some cases remarrying, in others not, have worse marriages than his? Or were they less able to put up with unhappiness? In his heart of hearts he inclined towards the second of these ideas. And so he said again: People have no sense of duty. They get married, have children, and get divorced as though it was no big deal to destroy a relationship where there are children.

The others clearly did not agree. Guillaume said: It's accepted now that it's not a good thing to stay together for the sake of the children. Psychologists say that a couple who don't get along is more damaging for the children than an amicable divorce. An amicable divorce . . . , said Max with a sneer. He didn't believe in such a thing. Some people divorce without a fight, said Guillaume. Do you really believe that? said Max. The other man nodded. Well then, said Max, triumphantly, how do you explain that divorce comes out only just behind bereavement in the list of the most traumatic life experiences? But nothing would make Guillaume budge. That's a separate issue, said Guillaume. Why should breaking something up and being unhappy necessarily go hand in hand? He was vaguely aware that Max's view stemmed from the unhappiness of his own situation, but he couldn't stop himself saying: You see, I think our offspring know an awful lot about us. Obviously they pick up on harmony or dissent, but also revulsion, desire, they even know whether their parents still make love or not. I don't believe that, said Max. Children know nothing about that sort of thing: that's why they're always surprised when their parents split up. Or relieved, said Guillaume. His broad face was full of humour. Can we talk about this seriously? said Max. Can we have a laugh? replied Guillaume. What are you trying to say? Jean asked Max. I'm just trying to say that if a couple really love one another they're not going to make an effort out of a sense of duty when it looks like it's over, said Max. If they make an effort at all it's going to be because they love each other, because somewhere they feel there's still some love left. Isn't that a good thing? asked Guillaume. I'm not saying it's a good or a bad thing, said Max, I'm just saying that a sense of duty works to support your love, it carries you through those empty times. And if you give a lot to someone, he added, you love them all the more for it. It can also make you hate them, said Jean. How could Max accept that? He said: We used to be able to rely on a sort of virtuous circle, but that's gone now. What's the point of marriage? It's to make love last, pure and simple. And why is that a good thing? asked Tom.

Because we have to bring up our children, replied Max. And if there aren't any children? said Tom. Oh well, in that case, said Max, you can do what you like, you're free, you don't need marriage, it lasts as long as you want it to. What can we count on then? said Jean. On women, perhaps, murmured Tom, thinking of Sara. They have a strong sense of commitment. As if! said Guillaume. They're the ones who usually ask for a divorce. Look at Gilles, he's no wish to get divorced. What makes you think that? said Max. Because he still loves Blanche, said Guillaume. I expect he does, said Max, but that's not why. It's because he doesn't want to see his daughter only four days a month. Four days a month, can you imagine? Not much basis for a relationship with a child, he said sourly. Max continued: You get divorced because you've stopped loving your wife and all of a sudden your children don't live with you any more. So what can you do if your wife no longer makes you happy? You kick up a bit of a fuss, but basically you knuckle under and you stay put. But you don't have that choice any more either, because your wife realises she doesn't love you as she used to, and she divorces you and where does that leave you? Your own children end up living with some other man. Because in most cases she leaves you when she's found someone else. Why didn't he apply for custody? said Henri, referring to Gilles. What, refuse custody to a mother who's a paediatrician? said Max. Can you see a judge doing that? Why not? said Henri. Blanche is always working, she's not there much, she has to go out to emergencies. Gilles is more available than she is. I don't think he had the heart to take his daughter away from her mother, said Guillaume. Guillaume was visibly disturbed by this conversation. But he said nothing. He didn't mention his own situation, either to support the argument, or to point out the tactlessness of talking about these things in front of him, when his own three children had ended up hating him. Even given all that, said Henri, I still think Tom's right, they've got courage, common sense and commitment, and they'll drink every last drop if they have to. As long as there's enough money, said Guillaume. If there is, they'll stay put, they'll come to terms with a life without grand passion, with their children, their house, their female friends. But watch out – lose your job and you'll lose your wife as well.

They all fell silent. What were they doing, picking at their wounds like this? They would have liked to have wives like their mothers and grandmothers, maternal, feminine, upright women, instead of which they had these harpies who nagged them about sharing the housework. Jean and Henri had turned away to watch the television, though the sound was turned down. Ten minutes of adverts, said Henri. There must be a huge audience for this fight. Mark, who had said nothing till now, turned towards Guillaume: Is Gilles that smallish guy, tough looking, seems quite good fun? He's a very funny guy, said Guillaume. And his wife used to be gorgeous, said Tom, a true redhead, Junoesque. How long had they been married? asked Marc. And the conversation began again. How old was Gilles? Forty-nine. He met Blanche just when he was leaving university, they were twenty-five, so they've been together over twenty years. And they've got a five-year-old daughter? Yes, I think she was a surprise. Blanche had been told she couldn't have a child, then suddenly there it was. She wasn't happy about it, she thought it was too late, but of course the minute the child was born she was just like all the rest, her daughter was everything.

They discussed Blanche and Gilles's private life without really thinking about it. It was a way of protecting themselves against the feelings stirred up by the divorce. Elements of their past, their dreams, taboos, impossible desires were brought to the surface, simply because two of their friends were splitting up, friends they had seen love one another, of whom they had a strong sense as a couple, a couple that was now unexpectedly falling apart. They had to convince themselves that their own love lives were not mistakes or lies. They needed to recover their sense of emotional security.

Blanche told Eve a long time back that things weren't going well. I think things had gone wrong between them physically; I wouldn't be surprised if Gilles was unfaithful as a result. Did Gilles have affairs? Didn't you know? Everyone knew that. She said no to him, so he went out and found others who said yes. And she couldn't accept that. That wasn't how she was brought up. Nobody was. We've all been educated to expect sexual exclusivity, ownership, jealousy. But that's stupid. (This was Marc.) Why's it stupid? Because a healthy sexual climate, said Marc, needs to adjust in response to all sorts of different elements. Like what for instance? asked Tom, laughing. Scientific advances, hygiene and illness, people's temperament. Okay, people's temperament, I'll go along with that. You don't think, do you, that we might be a bit jealous? I think it's possible. Because deep down we all know you can have a sexual relationship which doesn't mean anything. Do you think so? Of course. So do you. The only problem is, those aren't the ones we really want. You just have to learn to keep them like that: pretty meaningless. We're the ones who decide if they're important or not. I could put it another way, said Marc. Some sexual relationships are more important than others, but the extra importance comes from precisely the bit that isn't sexual. It's women who place so much importance on sexual relationships. Yes, said Marc, but only because we've forced them to. We've taught women to consider them important. We've told them they mustn't be too easy. We've managed to convince them that they are giving or losing something really precious when they go to bed with a man. And the reason we've done that is because what we cared about most, in terms of morals, was feminine virtue. What makes promiscuous women unattractive is this idea we have – and which they subscribe to too – that they're committing a crime. And so what do we do? We try to reshape the way we love. And if it's deep in our guts? Then we rip out our guts, said Marc, laughing. If you love your partner, whatever makes them happy makes you happy. I fall a long way short of that. You are the guardian of your wife's freedom, said Marc. And if I'm jealous . . . ? Then don't get married. Oh great: if you're jealous, don't fall in love. Don't be a jerk. If you're jealous you need to examine what it is about your love for your wife that makes it special in your eyes and you'll find it's not your sex life with her. Even if your sex life is a sign of the intensity of your love. And if there are some things you just can't bear to imagine? Well then, don't let yourself imagine them, don't allow yourself to. Images like that aren't the cause of jealousy, they're the product of it, they're the invention of a jealous mind. Of course they are. How did we get round to talking about this? What's it got to do with Gilles and Blanche? I'll tell you, said Marc: if we were prepared to tolerate infidelity, Blanche would have rediscovered her libido with some other lover, for example, while Gilles kept himself happy with other women, and they'd still be together now. Gilles has always said he loved his wife. Basically you're saying infidelity cures all ills. And he's the one with the purest, least corruptible wife of all of us.

Jean and Tom had begun to pour out glasses of wine and hand out plates. There was a spread of cold meats, bread and red wine. Tom said: I find I desire women more and more, and I want more and more of them, I don't care how they live, I don't want to know who they are or who they think they are, all I want is to lay them down and slide their knickers down and touch their lovely thighs and slip in like a thief and have my wicked way and then do a runner. What about Sara? said Jean. What about Sara? said Tom. Jean gave up. You're so banal, said Max. What makes you say that? said Jean. Why do you get so irritated if I do? said Max. You're not irritating me, said Jean, but I don't understand why you're egging him on, making him think everyone thinks like him. I'm just getting him to say what I think, said Max (he stood up). I'm getting him to admit that he's like everyone else, that desire interests him, that he often gets turned on, that he looks at women, that he wishes he could go out and seduce the ones he likes whenever he chooses, touch their breasts, see how far they'll go, discover their hidden beauty, all their different guises. And he's wretched because every way he turns he's told he mustn't, he can't, and what's exquisite is made to look cheap. Have you quite finished? said Guillaume. Why? said Max, surprised. Because I want to say something. Sorry? asked Max. No, go on, you finish first, said Guillaume. So Max went on: Why should it not be possible to spend part of the night with another woman, without our wives automatically throwing a fit? Or without having to go home and lie to her? I want to be free to see who I want when I want, to do what I want, for her to confide in me, for me to console and caress her, to have a place in other people's hearts, and I can't, and what is it I do have? He suddenly broke off. Guillaume said: I like to go home and find my wife there and to know she's all mine and she's the only one I love. Remind me, how many wives have you had? asked Tom. Four, he said, without waiting for the reply. One every five years. Marriage! he said. You don't know what you're talking about. Now Tom, said Tom, thumping himself on the chest, Tom stayed with the same woman for twelve years. And now Tom's running around making Sara unhappy, said Jean. No, said Tom. Tom is trying to make his passion for Sara last.

Has anyone noticed, there's someone who's said nothing in all this? said Max. They all turn to look at Henri, who has been listening all along, but feels as though he belongs to a different age. He's mulling over what they've said with a kind of sad wonderment, as though he envies their fervour, but not their lust. I'm amazed, he said. That's all I can say. How do you mean, amazed? said Tom. I'm amazed you're all so inexperienced, said Henri. They waited for him to explain. Marc had turned down the sound on the television: it was still the adverts. Henri said: Making love with a new woman is no more a guarantee of pleasure than doing it with the woman who gets undressed every night in your bathroom. Tom and Max laughed quietly, while Jean nodded approvingly. Marc and Guillaume waited for him to go on. Is that it? said Tom. Yes, said Henri. People think it's exciting to be unfaithful simply because they themselves aren't, or because they're so burdened by fidelity they've forgotten all the good things about it. Novelty isn't everything, he said, it heightens emotions and problems, but it doesn't necessarily give you more pleasure. Because part of pleasure comes from practice. The man or woman you've grown tired of knows more about what you like and don't like than anyone else. That's not going to be true of the beautiful unknown woman you take to a hotel. And even if her knowing you so well isn't romantic, it's certainly effective. I'm amazed, he said, that with all your huge appetite you seem not to have discovered that. Habit's better than novelty when it comes to giving orgasms. Right, said Tom, it's starting. Look at him, what a good-looking guy. A black boxer was walking towards the ring in a haze of white smoke, hailed by shouts from the crowd. He slipped nimbly between the ropes. They all sat down. Henri, you're incredible! But the way I see it is . . . Ssshhh, said the others.

4

Was your fish good? he asked. Delicious, she replied. Madame, Monsieur, said the waiter, handing them menus. Would you care for a dessert? No thanks, I won't, said Pauline. Go on, said Gilles. Live a little. I love women who have dessert. I'll have the fruits of the forest with raspberry ice cream, he told the waiter. Pauline ordered the same. Good, he said. Do try to be a bit more submissive. I get the distinct feeling you just do what you please. She confirmed this with a proud little laugh. He said: I don't know why women always get such a kick out of getting control over a man, and refusing to be controlled by him. You like to get us pinned down where you want us, utterly devoted, and then tell us what to do. Why? She didn't know. She laughed. You look lovely when you laugh, he said. She seemed to doubt this. You can't see yourself, how would you know? he said. Trust me, he said, looking her straight in the eye, you are a pretty woman. He was about to add: And I find you very attractive. Instead of which he said: And I prefer you when you laugh. She wore rings on both hands. He took her hands between his. But he could feel her pulling them away, and he kept quiet. She knew. She knew already, he thought. And he let go of her hands. Ah, Pauline . . . he murmured, as if, in speaking her name, he summoned up a whole new world. What could she say? She was smiling. That's a nice thing to say, she said. I wasn't being nice, he said. Well anyway, she said, I'm very glad to have spent this evening with you. He started to laugh. When someone finds you attractive it's impossible to find them completely disagreeable or boring, don't you find? She gave a thoughtful little half smile. I'm very happy too, he murmured. He'd got back his intimate voice. Why are you happy? she said, restored to bliss by the sound of his voice. Ohh, he said, suggesting with a wave of the hand that one couldn't know these things. That's just the way it is, he said. She found this conversation, sincere and provocative at once, quite delicious. Has this happened to you often? she asked. What, this kind of affinity? he said, laughing. She confirmed with a look that that was what she'd meant. Never, he said, firmly. What about your wife? she asked. I can't remember now, he said. I don't believe you, she protested. No, he admitted, laughing, you're right. She was sensitive to the wisdom of his words: he would be discreet, he would not reveal everything. She could always be confident of his silence. It was wonderfully reassuring. To be the special secret of a man who won't tell.

You still haven't told me what you do for a living, she said. It was more interesting listening to you, he said. But I've got nothing to hide. It's quite simple, he said. I earn my living by writing TV movies. But they're dreadful, she exclaimed. I know, he said, his voice sharpened by a hint of humour. I make up dreadful stories and I get paid handsomely for it. It was precisely because he was so sure of himself that he never seemed to get annoyed. Don't try and talk about things you don't understand, murmured the intimate voice. What was it gave him this superiority over her? She felt like a little girl. He leaned over towards her, not speaking. People were looking at him. He could see they were looking at him. A high-minded-looking couple, well past the age of passion, appeared to be thinking: What's that guy doing with that young girl? It's disgusting. He sat back upright and said: You're so young and tender, people are looking at us. I hadn't even noticed, she said. That's because you only have eyes for me, he said. Exactly what I was going to say, she said. She had started to become playful, like him. They had achieved the harmony of courtly lovers. They both laughed. She had such lovely teeth, like a precious casket, he couldn't take his eyes off them. He leaned over towards her again and said very softly: Do you see that couple over there? She glanced across and nodded. They're thinking: he's too old for her. She began to laugh. She was flustered but happy. She said: You're not. She looked so serious, he had to laugh. Because once again, the truth was out. Pauline, he said very softly. Yes? Nothing, he said, I just like saying your name. She was enchanted, intoxicated with pleasure, that he liked her so much. But her pleasure was such that it almost made her mistrust the man who gave it. Is he making fun of me? she thought. Her fear was real, and persistent. She was not unaware that there was something horribly banal about what was happening between them. A man and a woman. Of course he must know the whole game by heart. He must be aware she was doing her graceful simpering act. Perhaps he found it amusing. He was working her up into a state of ecstasy and laughing inwardly to see her swooning at the sound of her own name. He must have seen hundreds of women smile at the idea that he adored them. Vain creatures. These brief moments of insight ruined Pauline Arnoult's pleasure. The banality of their intentions was somehow incredibly coarse.

She picked at the wild strawberries around the edge of her ice cream. He watched her thoughtfully. She looked up from her plate and smiled at him. This is the sweetest moment in a love affair, he thought. And he said: This is the sweetest moment, when lovers meet. Silence, a smile. She said nothing. He murmured: As for the future. . . . Pauline still didn't speak. He preferred it that way. Basically, he was feeling his way around her, handling her with care, stringing one word onto an other, and she was listening, smiling, showing her pretty teeth. The problem with this was that he now found it impossible to step off the carousel, to imagine something else. She was intensely present, he was very aware of her, and yet he found it increasingly difficult to see himself making a move. She was intimidating, as the ingenuous often can be. And yet she wasn't an *ingénue*. She just knew. Close your eyes, he said. He looked at her shuttered face, saying nothing. What wonderful skin she had. The blue eyes appeared again. Just checking you know how to obey, he said. Give me your hands, and don't pull them away. But he had gone too far. She shook her head vigorously. She was ashamed to be going along with such silly games. She said to him: Stop doing your routine on me. He laughed, but didn't deny it. You're terrible, he said, amused. No, you are, she replied. And I let you get away with it. Only because you like it, he said, in his suave voice. Quite probably, she conceded. Do you regret it? he asked. He seemed anxious, delicate in his concern. No, she said, I know perfectly well what I'm doing. I never doubted it for a moment, he said. Each word was weighted. Their meaning was distorted by the attraction between them. They laughed. There was no escaping the game.

5

Marc said: We lust after other women besides our wives, it's inevitable, and some of them respond, it's like a kind of an electricity. But we live our lives with one woman, and we can stick with the one relationship.

Without thinking about it, our children want us to go on loving each other. How can you reconcile two opposing forces? I wonder whether we don't simply need the whole sexual game, the feeling that a woman might just say yes. In which case, you can stop once you've got the message, he concluded. So you're suggesting we go out hunting unarmed, said Tom. That's pathetic. They're off, said Guillaume. The fight was starting. The two boxers were hopping about the ring. The crowd had grown quiet. Max settled down into his chair. He was still thinking about Eve.

Married men have a kind of stoicism. Conjugal love is a foreign country to them. They get things wrong, they have misunderstandings, sometimes they don't understand anything at all. Were it not for the desire they felt for their wives, they would find themselves set against them, always capable of blundering or giving unwitting offence. And so they end up miserable. It takes courage for husbands to keep their position, day in day out, alongside a person whose nature is fluid and fiery, rocked by moods and by blood.

And so husbands watch. To do so is a sign of love. If they ever stop watching and waiting it means they've run out of love. Husbands watch out nervously for a smile on the face of their wives: the smiles they give and the smiles they don't. And when there's no smile at all, when her face is shut off, men say nothing, they settle down patiently, sometimes secretly turning to find some other face. For the most part they choose to believe that what isn't spoken of doesn't exist. Until such time as the smile returns, they keep their worries hidden. But wives like to talk about things, they want to be understood, they kick up a fight, they make a big noise. This is how we fall into our respective roles.

I yelled at Eve in the car, said Max. In the ring, the first round had just finished. Two tall girls in miniskirts were moving towards the ropes, holding up a board bearing the words Second Round. In the hall, men were shouting. What had she done? asked Jean. The usual, said Max. She was fed up about something and she was complaining. Do you and Marie often row? he said. All the time, said Jean. I hate it, he added. It's really stupid, shouting at each other just makes people look ugly and ridiculous. But isn't it pretty inevitable? Two people with different rhythms living cheek by jowl are bound to fall out of step from time to time. How could they not? But I don't want to give in all the time, said Jean. Marie's a despot; she's got this incredible energy. She'd just turn me into a doormat. We always row about money, said Henri. I try to keep an eye on what we spend, Melusine lies to me, and I won't stand for it. She buys herself new clothes and then tells me they're old ones. He doesn't say she also buys bottles of whisky, but the others think it. Do you never lie to her? asked Guillaume. The mild look on his face amused Max. People are always very understanding of other people's problems in this sort of discussion, he observed, for the sake of saying something. And Henri said, No, I never lie. Liar, said Guillaume. I promise you, it's true! Tom said. The worst liars of all are the ones who say: I never lie. And then they tell these great big lies, and never get caught out.

I'll tell you the classic kind of row, said Jean. The others stopped talking and listened. The expectation of laughter to come moulded their features. Guillaume's big head had turned quite red. Max was focused again. Jean began: The guests have left. Marie shows the last ones to the lift. I stay in the sitting room. She locks the front door quietly, so as not to wake the children. Then she starts. She's more like a machine than a woman. She starts clearing up. She takes the glasses and dessert plates off the table, throws away the paper plates, puts the tablecloth in the laundry basket, stacks the dishwasher. I just need to do nothing for a moment, he says. Everyone laughs. I usually sit down for a moment at the computer. I put on some music. Marie is already busy in the kitchen. She's tired, but she forces herself to tidy the place up. I don't know why. We could clear up at leisure in the morning. But no, Madame says she doesn't like to wake up to a mess. I completely understand that she's tired. I say: You go to bed. It's after midnight, some people just don't function after midnight but Marie's worse than that, she turns into a monster. After midnight, says Jean, Marie bites. The men laugh again. She comes into the sitting room, says Jean, and starts barking. So I tell her again: Leave all that, I'm going to do it. She says: It's always, I'm *going* to do it. Maybe one day you'll tell me why you can't do it straight away. Surely it's more logical to clear up first and then turn on the computer. I stay calm. I say: You said a bit ago you were going to go and have a bath so I thought I had a bit of time before I had to clear up. Why don't you just do what you said? She's getting really mad at me now, I can feel it rising! She says: My bath's just running, and in the meantime I'm doing the clearing up. She starts explaining stuff to me, always the same stuff: I don't mind doing it myself, in fact I enjoy looking after everyone, but just don't pretend you want to help, do this, do that . . . that really irritates me. By this time I've had enough of the lecture. Perhaps you'll let me decide when I want to do something – or maybe you want to tell me exactly when to do what? I put my question clearly and simply. She doesn't answer. I go through to the kitchen and watch her tidy up. It's incredible, the speed she goes at. She's plugged in to some special voltage. She won't smile, of course. People look nice when they smile, so she looks pretty awful. I say: You should see yourself, a real sourpuss. She says: You don't have to tell me when I'm angry, thank you. In any case, I say, I'm not your granddad. I say that to annoy her. Her grandfather completely abdicated, just did everything her grandmother told him. Tom laughs. At that point, says Jean, I'm home and dry, that shuts her up nicely. Then I leave her alone in the kitchen. I shut the door on her, literally. It drives her crazy when I do that: shut up in the kitchen – imagine. She opens the door again. She goes back to scrubbing the cooker. She thinks how dreadful her lot is. I'm just the maid around here. I've gone back to the computer for good now, I've said my bit. She can't get to me. She knows she's lost. We go to bed, not speaking. She turns her back on me. The next day she's rested, it's all forgotten. We're like children, says Jean, summing up: when we're tired we get cross and angry. Guillaume says, We always make up before we go to sleep, but otherwise it's exactly the same.

They had great fun with their tales of marital rows. Max found himself slightly soothed by the shared experience. Everyone had their wounds. The mix of characters and emotions was the same for all of them, more so for them than for many groups: they were all men in the prime of life, busy worldly men, with power, money, wives and children, men who had always had these things, and would go on having them. I'm reassured, Max said. It's not just my family, then. But he was wrong: the love which existed in Jean's family had gone from his own. It's not always a sign of love, to quarrel. Yes, said Tom, in every household, there's always a controlling terror. That's why I got out of mine. But you gave up the good bits too, said Marc. What do you mean, I gave up the good bits? said Tom. Now I have nothing *but* the good bits!

6

Louise said: Do you know why I may never be able to have a child? Marie waited for her to go on. It's not because I'm sterile, or because I had an abortion when I was young, said Louise. It's because I'm old. Nature says I'm too old now to have children. And why have I never had children? Because I've spent my life in fear of having them, in fear of having to give something, having to be like other people: madly in love, almost stupidly so. And now I'm no longer fertile, and I'd have to be very lucky, I'd have to be absolutely sure I wanted a child for my luck to come good. But I'm not even certain I do. I'm still not sure I want this other flesh in my womb. There's no reason why I can't have a child, there's nothing wrong with my organs, nothing's wound down, except maybe my sex drive. And even now, when I desperately want it, there's still this hate and this fear, somewhere. Deep down, motherhood disgusts me, said Louise. Because somehow I know it brings this dreadful bond with it.

Don't say that, don't give up the fight. It may yet work out, said Marie. Oh, you're so sweet, said Louise. I heard Eve was pregnant and suddenly I got all anxious. It's stupid, Marie said: there's more to life than having children. When I think of my children I'm frightened for them, their problems overwhelm me, I worry about stupid little things. It's madness, she said. And it'll go on all my life. There's no end to it. Some days I feel exhausted just thinking about it. They both had to laugh. Then Marie went on, seriously: Some days I almost wish I'd broken the mould, not just obediently followed my instincts as I did. Our heart rules our lives, it jumps and we follow. And my parents . . . , she said. Already, just thinking about the fact that they're going to die makes me weep. When my father notices he's aged, I find it devastating. When in fact it's just natural, he's fine, and we're all very happy. But no, I have to go and get upset in advance, as though the thought of the end was somehow ruining my life. What about your husband? said Louise. Does he make you unhappy? It's funny, said Marie. Not in the same say. They both laughed. Don't tell anyone, whispered Marie, but if you don't have a child, you'll do something else with your life, you'll create something, discover something, sacrifice something, something just as important as having a child.

The most important thing for Louise was what she wasn't able to do: have a child. Her life was going to waste, mourning for this loss of continuity. She went from one hospital to another in pursuit of a love which could be created inside herself, which would impose no conditions on her. She was still so young, but she already felt as though she had left her youth behind her, as though this was what it meant to grow old without descendants: a rapid lonely slide, accelerating towards the grave. The ages of Louise's life were slipping by, and as they did so she became less and less fertile, of that she was evermore certain. Even the most sophisticated medical techniques would not succeed in planting a child in her womb. And since the body speaks out loud, her physical features had modelled themselves on this emptiness within. Her hands and wrists were bony, she was light and lithe with worry. Men are lucky not to age as we do, said Louise. All they need to do is find themselves a young wife and however old they are, they get to have children. Melusine was approaching. I see a dark cloud and I'm sure it's you, she told Louise. Louise smiled sadly. She murmured: I must look like I'm in mourning. Do you always wear black? said Eve. Always, answered Melusine. Placing her hands on

Louise's shoulders, she said: Open one of Louise's closets, everything's black: her stockings, her shoes, her clothes, all her flouncy bits and pieces, everything, the whole lot. Louise was laughing. She felt Melusine's ample bosom envelop her shoulder, she sensed that Melusine was supporting herself against her. But even so, she picked things up, she was the only one there who sensed how depressed Louise was. Louise kissed Melusine. Louise's skin was pale against the dark shroud of her dress. She looked wonderful. She looked incredibly fragile, and almost naked. Why are you so fond of black? asked Eve. Louise said: I don't know. Do we know why we do some things, why we like others? she said, uncomfortable with the sombre tone she had introduced. At any rate, she looks very good in black, said Melusine. The edges of Louise's irises were mauve and slightly faded. You look tired, said Melusine. I am, said Louise. She didn't say that she was constantly watching her blood, little honey-coloured strands, white cells. You wouldn't believe the things that are expelled from the womb of a woman who's trying to have a child. She chose not to mention the cause of her tiredness, which was not work, nor children waking up in the night, nor orgies of love-making, but just waiting by the phone when she got home from the hospital: no, she wasn't pregnant, the tests were negative. No one ever counts the tears a woman must fight back if she is to go on loving a man who cannot understand her desire, nor her exhaustion, who says: You'll ruin your health. They think it might even cause cancer. Why don't we just adopt?

Have you never thought of adoption? asked Eve. Louise shook her head. She couldn't love someone else's child. She wouldn't be able to offer a mother's total forgiveness. You can have my children, Guillaume sometimes said. She didn't even answer. How could he be so stupid? She wasn't even prepared to think about it, or she'd end up with neither child nor love. I don't have children, said Penelope. Her voice piped like that of a small girl. And I don't have a husband either, she said.

7

Louise never knew what to say to Penelope. So much bad luck, so much sadness and so much charm, all loaded onto one person. But all the men are in love with you, murmured Marie, giving Penelope a kiss (and whispering: I haven't even said hello). I'll second that, said Louise. Well of course, said Penelope. People tell them I'm inaccessible, so it's safe for them to fall in love with me. What about Paul? said Marie. Does he love you from a safe distance? No, said Penelope. Then her eyes seemed to drift off into a reverie and she said: He asked me to marry him this afternoon. Paul did? said Marie. And what did you say? said Louise. I said I'd think about it, said Penelope. That sounds just like you, said Marie. So, said Louise promptly, have you thought about it? I already had, said Penelope. Her face spread in a mischievous grin. And the answer's no, obviously, said Louise. Wrong, said Penelope. Really? exclaimed Louise. You mean you're going to marry Paul? She laughed happily. Yes, said Penelope, I think I really love him. In spite of everything, in spite of the age difference, I realised that when we were together we were somehow ageless. And I love him because he's old, because he'll die soon and I'm the light of his life, I'm good for him. I'm like a miracle to him, can you imagine, being someone's miracle? She broke off, her mind elsewhere again, awash with images. And I love him because we both mourn a loved one we've lost, she said. Her eyes filled with tears. Something about her tears fascinated Louise. A stream of never-ending tears. That was the thing that had really left its mark on her, but she had never mentioned it. It makes me cry, said Penelope, embarrassed by her emotion, but unable to hide it. Penelope said: I love him because he's old, and he's going to die, and sometimes he'll talk about it openly, and sometimes he pretends to believe he's got lots of time, so as not to scare me. It's wonderful news, said Marie. You should be really happy. I am, said Penelope, and as well as that I feel I'm being rather radical, you can imagine how much that pleases me. I'm thirty-eight and getting married to a man who'll soon be seventy-two. Some people won't understand how I've waited so long to end up doing this. They burst out laughing. It's a lovely way to end up, said Louise. I'm so amazed, said Penelope, that's why I'm laughing. She began to giggle uncontrollably, like a little girl. She said: People will say, just think, Penelope's marrying her aged lover. Then: I think I'll have a wedding list!

They all choked themselves laughing, Louise and Marie joining in a little later than the rest, a moment of delay reflecting their tact in first checking out Penelope's own reaction. In theory, said Penelope, we can have a church wedding, since he's a widower. But he doesn't want to. How long has he been in love with you? asked Louise. I don't know, said Penelope. He courted me without really thinking he had a chance, he just couldn't help himself. And he's patient, as people are when they've lived a long time. Was it really patience? It was more a kind of melancholic resignation to the rules of Time. I think I wanted to be able to offer him the tenderness of a young woman, she added. I was moved, I closed my eyes, I let him touch me, and he wept, and in the end so did I. That's how it all began. Sometimes I think that I'll live to see the world without him, that the flow of letters will eventually dry up. His presence will be gone from my life. And it makes me love him all the more. Does that surprise you? asked Penelope. Not at all, said Marie. Nothing surprises me, said Louise. Nothing shocks me. That's where curiosity gets you, said Marie. She said: You're lucky to have the experience of such a unique relationship. Don't go and spoil it. (She stroked Penelope's cheek with motherly tenderness. And in that moment that was almost entirely what she was – a mother.) It's the most wonderful time in your life, the beginning of love. Louise repeated the phrase in her head. Why was she uneasy with it? She realised suddenly that it was the use of the singular that bothered her. Marie had only known love once, and she spoke as though it was the same for everyone. At least, for me it was a wonderful time, said Marie. It was the first time I'd been in love – that feeling of loving and being loved in return, she murmured. Where did you and Jean meet? asked Louise. At a dinner party, said Marie. I remember it like yesterday, said Penelope. Were you there? said Marie. Of course I was, said Penelope. Remember, everyone thought you knew each other already. Yes, you're right, said Marie. What a moment: such happiness. Penelope turned to Louise and said: With Jean and Marie it was real love at first sight: you'd have thought they'd known each other all their lives. What's more, said Marie, Jean really believes that. That we'd known each other, but hadn't been able to be lovers. That we'd been brother and sister in a former life.

8

With a quick, animal gesture, Pauline Arnoult licked up a drop of coffee which was running down the outside of her cup. And since the dominant tone of the dinner was desire, the movement of her tongue carried a sensual charge. She was well aware of it. Well brought up women didn't go round licking the edge of their cups. She knew all this. But she had no idea of the effect she was having. Her tongue was quite red from the raspberry ice cream she'd just eaten. And this simple image exploded within him. She was so young, so fresh: was that what really bowled him over? Most probably. Do we really understand the power of a firm body, full but fine features, unspoilt lines, and the faultless luminosity of smooth, tight skin? And the effect of such perfection on a lover? Out came her little red tongue. . . . No man on earth could resist. His heart seemed to stop. Even in his hands he could feel the force driving him towards the young woman. Pauline Arnoult was aware for the first time – it was brutally obvious – that he wanted to get right up close to her, to grab hold of her. A sudden clarity came upon her. All at once she understood the fear of a small creature, squeezed between human hands, which trembles, shivers and goes suddenly slack. That was how she felt with this man, naked before his strength, with just enough time to withdraw the hands he'd grasped, to blush awkwardly, to feel wretched at finding herself caught up in the chase, to escape and thereby make him suffer. He looked at her, not speaking. Her pretty face had grown tense in just a fraction of a second. Faced with this disaster, he wondered, disconcerted, what had happened to ruin everything. He didn't understand her. Was it just his reaching out to take her hands? He couldn't imagine anyone could be so seduced and yet shrink away. He'd lost her, he thought. She had that instinct for flight which is never quite extinguished in a woman, or in any creature that lacks physical power. She had backed off, far away from him, in a flash she was gone, just when he'd yielded to the instinct to touch her. He guessed correctly: she was thinking of her husband. A phrase of Marc Arnoult's came back to her, as though the sight of this other man's virility brought back her husband's words. It's a sword, this thing, Marc used to say, meaning the male sexual organ.

She might have said: Don't touch me, it's bound to spoil it. A small inner voice told him anyway. They didn't know one another, and here he was, bearing down on her like an eagle. And she'd pretty much thrown herself at him. While she wished she hadn't flirted and played with him, she would carry on anyway, she knew, and the knowledge gave her great joy. She heard the intimate voice whisper: Don't shy away from me like that. He was making fun of her a little, hurt by her rejection of him. He'd been right to sense she wasn't ready, he thought. I'm not being shy, she said again. Fear had robbed her of all words.

They sat face to face. Now he was staring at her mouth, a slightly fanatical look in his eye, teasing her. His eyes never moved from her lips. She began to wonder if there was something wrong with her mouth. She felt trapped by his scrutiny, disconcerted by his gaze. She could sense how much he would have liked to kiss her. He was thinking of a long deep kiss, and somehow she could actually hear him thinking of it. But she wasn't ready. The thought of bodies touching dumbfounded her. And yet she was still affected by the irresistible attraction of the man. She didn't want to lose him. But she didn't want to win him quite this quickly. The hands on love's clock move more slowly for women than for men.

They had finished dinner. They could have got up and left but something held them back. It was more than simple pleasure in each other's company: it was a compulsion. It would have taken more willpower for them to part at this point in the evening than either of them possessed.

Would you like another coffee? he asked. Two more coffees, he said to the waiter. The intimacy created by the absence of words was more troubling for both of them than anything that had been said until now. He became serious. His face fell, with just a slight contraction of the muscles. He was about to tell her about the strength of his feeling. She immediately understood this, which was why she spoke. I know what you're going to say, she said. Because . . . She hesitated, then resolved to speak. Because I want to say the same thing. He'd begun looking at her mouth again, and she lowered her eyes. Please don't say it, she said. Don't say those words, because there's nothing I can do with them. She had the nerve to express her confusion. This was not exactly news to him, but he admired her sincerity, for such a pretty woman. It's quite rare, isn't it, to feel troubled like this, don't you think? His face pulled back into a smile, because she hadn't quite dared to mention sex, but he knew she was thinking about it. He said nothing, and she went on. I'd like you to carry on talking to me about it, but not with words, she whispered. He thought he must be dreaming. But no, she really had just said to him, as though to a callow admirer: Say nothing, but please don't stop admiring. Oh, she was typically feminine. But why should I go on? he said. His humour was still undented, despite all she'd said, and he was openly mocking her. She said: Because it's nice. At this he burst out laughing. How he despised this brand of fake lasciviousness, this dithering about that led you nowhere. Women who played for small stakes. It was shabby and mean. No, she couldn't be just one more little tease, she must be lying to herself as well as to him. He'd treat her roughly for a little, see who had the last laugh. How do you know what I was going to say to you? he asked. The question was intended as a quick slap in the face. But it seemed not to bother her at all. She was high on her new-found loyalty, and everyone knows how loyalty boosts our strength. Because I might have said the same thing to you, she said, blushing. She knew he was right to put himself on the line. She knew what it was that was torturing them both, and that while she'd been flirting with him she'd felt no fear of words or of desire. It was only now, when they were becoming a reality, that she felt afraid. Just at that moment he saw her as a perverse child. What will happen then? he asked. I don't know, she said. He looked into her eyes, and said nothing. At this their desire for romance brought cracks out on the surface. Everything's so complicated, she said. We have our separate lives already, and I'm expecting this baby. She couldn't think straight. Don't you think it's possible to love two people at once? he said. Yes, she said, I do, but it makes life impossible. Affairs are doomed from the start, they've got no space, no time to blossom in. So you can feel attracted, and not give in to it? he said. She nodded. You're a strong woman then, he said. Yes, she said, bowing her head. But you're wrong. You'll regret it one day, he said. In ten years, in twenty years, you'll wonder how someone can turn down love when it comes along. It's what we're made for, he said, it's what keeps us alive. It's the only thing.

He was dangerous. He was persuasive. He was preaching in his own interest. So she thought, as she listened to him. But she was wrong to be suspicious of him. He wasn't trying to lead her astray, he meant what he said quite sincerely, he was admitting what had led him to act in this way. He said again: One day you'll regret it. He began to laugh: And then you'll think of me, because I warned you. It occurred to her that he could have said: Because I tried to seduce you. They laughed again, and it was as though they found themselves once more back right where they'd started, where this enchanted evening had begun.

Oh! she was so happy with him, it was so simple, so delicious just to be there and feel this extraordinary renewal of desire. The thought that she would have to leave him cast a shadow on her pleasure. A butterfly fluttered, its wings beating in the little nest between her thighs. Her whole being cried out against what she had just said. The exact opposite of what she had just said was true: she wanted this man, she would find room for him, she would obey the imperious dictates of her body, she would have two loves in her life. I have a lover. Yes, that was the exultant cry of women down the ages. She was just like all the rest, sharing their shame, their *naïveté*, their delirium. Her silence camouflaged these thoughts.

He knew he could love her for her seriousness alone. He knew he would not let go until he had been to bed with her. He'd make her cry out loud. He could just picture it. What he felt was the force of desire, the violence of the hunt. She would have no inkling of the storm which was waiting to break. He'd make her cry out loud. The thought made him confident of victory. What was she like in bed? He could form an idea just by looking at her, listening to her. But why not ask her straight out? he thought mischievously. So he did. Are you good in bed? he asked, almost nastily. His face was divided – half straight, half joking. She hesitated. I don't know, she said, looking worried, attempting a little smile. Am I the best person to tell you that? She had blushed slightly. You're the one I've chosen, he said. Again, swayed by the delirium of a woman in love, she thought she heard him say that he'd picked her out as a woman he could love. She said: My husband says I'm too lascivious. He's your husband, he replied, with a mocking smile. I know you're not a cold woman, he said, looking into her eyes. She said: If I'm good in bed, it's because I think it's a serious matter, giving your body to someone. I can understand that, he said.

Once again, they had to laugh, because it was all rather strange, this new turn in the conversation. So he said: I said it to embarrass you. She didn't understand what he meant. It was a silly question, he said. It wasn't a silly question, she said. Of course it was, he said. There's no such thing as a woman who's bad in bed. She said: My husband – At this he reassumed his serious schoolmaster's face, and interrupted her: That simply means he doesn't know much about women. What about you? she asked playfully. I know a great deal, he said.

Isn't it quite late? she said, glancing at her watch. Are you cold? he asked. You look all hunched up. Are we done? he asked. Was that everything you wanted? Shall we go? And with these words, he stood up.

They were out in the street again. The lot of lovers. Walking behind her as they left the restaurant, he'd taken a good look at her. The boldness in her eyes excited him hugely, and he was gripped by desire. She could measure her own desire by how hard it was to leave him without knowing when she'd see him again. Was it him she really needed? Or did she just need lovers' talk, the admiring gaze of a man? You'll call me, she said, in a choked little voice. It was a plea. I promise, said the intimate voice. She was afloat, weightless with anguish. He no longer looked as though he wished to trap her; he just stood there calmly at her side. Strange as it might seem, she was unaware of how hard he was working to oppose his attraction towards her. She had no idea of the desire he felt at that moment just as he was unaware that she too was tormented by desire, as though by a monster.

They came to a small, local hotel, with two stone steps onto the street, a simple push door, narrow windows set in a grey façade and a neon sign saying 'Hotel'. She looked up to read the words beneath the neon letters: The Golden Lion. She thought: I could never go to a hotel with a lover. The thought occurred to her because it was what she actually wanted. Who could say what she was and wasn't capable of? He saw what she was looking at. The distance between them was greater than it had been at the start of the evening. A tangled knot of silence, desire, regret lay in the pit of her stomach. She realised that everything scared her: leaving him, touching him. She was scared of herself. She suddenly felt impure and sad, facing a black horizon where all was sadness and deprivation. He was thinking of taking her to a private room, a little further down the street, where no one would see them. Then he thought that she wasn't ready for that yet, and decided she wasn't the type of woman you took to a hotel. And so he looked at her, and said nothing. He could see the right hand side of her face and her small, rather authoritative chin. She walked along with a kind of smile fastened to her mouth: a smile of suffering, he thought. But he thought that because he himself was suffering. It's very mild, he murmured. Shall we walk for a little while?

9

The old black boxer was dancing around again on his slender legs. One metre seventy-two, fifty-seven kilos, said Guillaume. The others were settled in big armchairs, arranged in a semicircle round the television set. The boxer had one of those bodies whose perfection set it quite apart from other bodies. Its beauty – pure and dazzling – was exposed to view, content simply to be, displayed in every corner of the ring, as the angry fists rained down. The men were hypnotised by the ceaseless dancing of his legs. They were transfixed by his splendour.

Tom broke the spell. You know how this guy lives? The others indicated that they didn't. He works in a warehouse in Arceuil, he lives in a little three-room flat on a housing development with his wife and two daughters, and he's going to be world champion of his weight. The silence continued as they watched the boxer's graceful movements. Fighting was an art to him. His daring had won him the hearts of the fifteen thousand spectators in the stadium. Behind the commentator's voice could be heard cries, shouts of advice, the usual pulse of impotent emotion.

I wonder what the men are doing. You know what they're doing, said Sara. They're watching two guys beating each other up. Now leave your Jean in peace for a little while. He'll run off and leave you. No he won't, said Marie. You're very sure of yourself, said Sara. Yes, Marie agreed, without hesitation, she was. And at that same moment Jean was saying: I bet the girls are having a good old gossip. I've heard that before, said Sara.

You're very quiet this evening, said Louise. Eve waited a second before replying. As though still in a dream, and still speaking from inside it, she said: Max and I had a row on the way here. Then: We're always rowing. What about? asked Louise. Everything, said Eve, silly things and more important things, everything. Forgetting to hang a coat up, dinner parties, whether we like each other's friends. Everyone's like that, said Louise. I'm sure they are, said Eve. But I don't know why, these scenes seem to upset me more and more. I must be getting older. I used to forget about them; nowadays I remember exactly what's said, as though we were getting better at hurting each other. We know each other really well, so we've stopped saying things that are hurtful but untrue. Now we come out with carefully chosen truths. All the words get stuck in my head, and spin about in some mad jumble of unhappiness, despair, doubt. I end up wondering if I love Max at all, and the worst is, I don't fancy him any more. I can't make love with a man who thinks what he thinks of me: that's the effect these rows have. Melusine said: You should tell yourself that marital rows are just part of the language of love. Your husband's the only one you have them with, so enjoy the exclusivity. Besides, it's quite funny when you've said 'I'm calling my lawyer' and believed every word, only to find you're still there ten years later. No, said Eve, these scenes are really destroying me – I'm discovering what he really thinks of me. And if I try to talk calmly, not just say what I think, to try and preserve the atmosphere, it actually doesn't preserve anything: because the words that get said have all these other words attached to them, all the words that have been said in the past. Each word is actually this whole string of words. Say one of them, it doesn't matter what, some harmless little thing, and the other person hears the entire string. They get upset about one little word that wouldn't mean anything if there wasn't this background, all these memories, with the words all linked together. Sara said: It's nigh on a miracle when a man and a woman do manage to live together in a single space. Why do you say that? asked Marie. Loneliness must be worse than living together. They're both as bad as each other, said Sara, who knows what it's like to be single, married, and divorced and who doesn't share a flat with Tom because he doesn't want to. In any case it's really hard to have a love life with a man but not live with him, believe me. In fact you stop living, you spend your whole time waiting. You wait for the phone to ring, for him to confirm a meeting, for the time you'll be together. Waiting and dreaming, fearing, crying, being alone. A woman needs a home with a man in it, said Sara. Louise and Melusine laughed. Not just any old man, said Eve.

Eve thought: They've no idea what I'm going through with Max, they think we have the same kind of problems a loving couple has. And she murmured, on the brink of tears at the thought of the miserable state of her marriage: I'm not sure that Max and I are exactly a loving couple. Louise gave herself a shake, like a small bird fluffing up its feathers. A loving couple? she repeated in a comical, rather doubtful tone. Who can ever say that for sure? And what does it mean? Then more seriously: What does it mean, to love someone? Do you think you know? she asked Eve. Do you never have any doubts? You're sure of the difference between loving and not loving? She said: How do people know? Don't they ever have a little doubt somewhere, maybe just because they need the other person? They need that other person so much, said Louise. We've so much vested interest in loving, she said, how can we tell if it's really love? True love should be without strings. It should be all for the other person, their freedom, their life. I've often thought that a happily married woman could offer that kind of love to another man, a man she can't share any of her normal life with. You mean a lover? asked Melusine. Not necessarily, said Louise. A man who might be her lover, she said, but we don't always have the time or the inclination for a lover, or to fall in love once we're married. In which case you have the opportunity to experience true love: I mean a love you have nothing to gain from, which makes no demands on you, simple feeling. I love you, I want the best for you, that's it. Do you think that's possible, something like that? asked Eve. Where do you get these weird ideas from? said Melusine. They just come to me like that, said Louise. You've always been one to ask yourself questions. You've never stopped. And you're right, said Melusine. She murmured: There's no explaining the way some people are happy just to live their lives, while others are always wondering what it's all about.

I've had far too much to drink, said Louise. I shouldn't have, I can't take it the way I used to. She was mortified at having drunk so much wine. Her head was spinning. You were tempted to drink to get into the swing of the party, but why did a party need alcohol? Melusine said: So we can get high. Otherwise there isn't much to laugh about. They all had their woes to forget. All except Marie. Eve was rowing with her husband, Melu didn't know what to do with her life, Louise was childless. I must say, said Louise, there always seems to be something that isn't right. It was turning into one of those conversations between slightly tipsy women. Louise thought: What does it mean to love? To be irresistibly attracted to someone? To be attracted to them long term? To want to touch them and sleep with them? Have children with them? Live with them? Suffer for them? What are you thinking? said Marie. I'm trying to find a definition of 'to love', said Louise. She repeated her chain of thought. Melusine and Eve were listening. They made room for Marie in their little triangle at the far end of the buffet, next to the uneaten ham sandwiches, and the triangle became a circle. To matter to someone? suggested Melusine. To rely on someone? said Eve. To not fight with? said Eve. To be in ecstasy? said Louise. They amused themselves for a few seconds with this idea. To be unable to survive the death of someone? said Louise again. To wait for? said Marie. To do nothing but wait for? said Louise. To want the love of? said Eve. To want the best for? said Marie. To forget oneself? said Melusine. To step outside oneself? said Marie. Yes, murmured Louise, to be free of oneself, that's good. She was gentle in her sadness, whispering, circumspect, like an unseen doe in a forest. So, she said, with a tiny smile, are we women who love? She was asking herself the question. But Marie said: I feel as though I am, very much so. Good, said Louise. I don't. Melusine said: I don't know. Eve said nothing, but thought: Obviously not. Right, said Louise, who'd like a glass of wine? Me, said Melusine. Do you think maybe you've had enough? asked Louise, concerned. It's not very good wine, it'll make you feel ill. I don't care, said Melusine. So what if it makes me ill? I'll go to bed. What else have I got to do with my days? No one's out there waiting for me, not even myself. It's too late. She went on: I drink, I'm an alcoholic, I admit it to myself, I prefer to come out with it, rather than find people talking about me behind my back. I've accepted it now, I'm not going to try and change, not going to set myself straight, I've been far too well-behaved all my life, it never did me any good. Don't you love Guillaume? Marie asked Louise. Not as much as I could, said Louise. How do you know? asked Marie. I just know, said Louise. I try to forget it, I pretend not to know, but a part of me knows full well. Why don't you love him? asked Marie. Do you know what it costs, to love your husband? said Louise. No, said Marie. It costs a great deal, said Louise. She looked at Marie and said: It costs your whole life. Marie said nothing for a moment, stalwart but nevertheless undermined by this remark, because that was what she was doing – giving her life. Then she replied to Louise, saying: We have to give our lives to someone.

IV

At the Height of the Party

I

There was still one person missing from the women's party – Blanche. Her friends were talking about her. Indeed, there was much to be said. Blanche was not so obviously content that it was not worth commenting on. Whatever people like to believe, joy is less readily shared than misfortune. So they talked. One might ask whether they were truly her friends. Of them all, Eve had the greatest appetite for secrets and confessions: her unhappiness made her unkind. Blanche's divorce made it easier for her to bear the loss of love in her own marriage: after all, she was still married and correct; she hadn't burned any bridges. And so she said: I haven't seen Blanche once since the break-up. How is she? She pretended to be concerned, though in fact she couldn't have cared less. She just wanted to bring the conversation round to the split between Gilles and Blanche. Louise was the only one who discerned her hypocrisy. She's working hard, said Melusine. Louise bit her lip: Eve had got what she wanted. People never outgrow this passion for talking about others in their absence. Blanche was getting divorced, and when love dies, people love to talk. Friends get anxious, the bonds between them change, people start to take sides, one or other of the partners gets abandoned, people attribute blame or make excuses. Friendship is opinionated. Friendship is also a kind of mirror. Anyone who sees a friend beset with marital grief will start to ask themselves questions about their own love life. How secure is it? Could it go the same way? You are obliged to weigh up your own relationship. Just as death reminds us that no one is immortal, we see in the end of an affair a reflection of our own loves: fragility, presentiments of failure, expressions of undying devotion, problems. For each of them it was someone else's ordeal. There was a fellowship of separated lovers, just as there is a fellowship of lovers, and one love affair gone wrong was enough to give the lie to all the rest.

So they talked of their absent friend and her divorce and even if their talk wasn't malicious, Blanche would have been hurt had she heard them. Because words reduced everything to pulp: Blanche's long-felt passion, its moment of epiphany so many years before, and then the way the feeling, so evident and strong, had suddenly, unexpectedly burned out. They were the couple I always quoted as an example. No one would have guessed. Yes, it was quite a surprise. And how is she? Not too bad. I think she's very brave. Of course she's bound to handle the divorce well, she wanted it so badly.

Spoken words have a brutality to them, something fatal and cruel. But we must become hardened to it, since the women continued to chatter away: You can want a divorce and still find it very hard. You know it's for the best but it's still really tough. What about her daughter? It's always difficult for children. I think she's taking it quite badly. The child just adored her father. He's the one suffering most in all of this. I always wonder, said Marie, how two people who've loved each other can then live apart. Nothing lasts for ever, said Eve. It makes me wonder if they really loved each other, said Marie. If something finishes, then it wasn't love. People think they love someone, but they don't. That's rather radical isn't it? said Louise, smiling. People change and they don't necessarily change together. Life brings its own surprises, it doesn't hand you everything on a plate. Louise knew what she was talking about: a man had left her because she was sterile. Separation can sometimes be inevitable. Gilles didn't want a separation, he did everything he could to stop it. He still loves Blanche. Still especially loves his daughter. Louise said: Do you know what he told me? No, said the others, what? Louise whispered: I thought it was so beautiful, he said to me, very quietly: I don't think I could ever leave a woman. You know him that well? No, said Louise, not very well, but he noticed I was unhappy and we had a chat, just the two of us, not that long ago, one day here at the bar. Why were you unhappy? said Eve. Guess, said Louise. She couldn't bring herself to say: I'm sterile. It was so ugly. And the phrase: I can't have a child contained the word 'child' and the minute she said the word she'd start to cry. She'd never have believed words could get stuck in your throat like that. She stood there in front of Eve, not speaking. It was the best thing to do. She had already said what she had to say. What else could she have done short of losing her temper and shouting: I can't have children, remember? I don't know. What? said the other woman. Think about it, Melusine told her. Eve frowned. There was a silence. Why's Louise sad? she asked Marie again, in a low voice. You know perfectly well: she can't get pregnant, said Marie. You can understand, she's at her wits' end. But if you've never had any you don't know what you're missing, said Eve. It's not too difficult to imagine, said Marie. Eve said nothing. Don't you think? said Marie. I didn't know it mattered so much to her, said Eve. It did, said Marie, and it still does. She hasn't given up. Compassion certainly wasn't Eve's strong suit. I can understand how he could say that, said Marie, coming back to Gilles' phrase:

'I don't think I could ever leave a woman.' I can't imagine splitting up with Jean. I just couldn't do it, she said. One always thinks that, said Sara, but if everything's in ruins, that's what it comes to. I can't see how people do it without tearing themselves apart, said Marie. They can't, said Sara, but they still leave. I feel as though I could want it, said Marie, but I wouldn't be able to actually take the first step to make it happen. Get the suitcases out. Sort out possessions; divide the books. How can people bear to do all that? They do it, said Sara, because there's nothing else left to do. It's like sorting out the belongings when someone's died, said Eve. It must be ghastly, but it has to be done. Marie grew thoughtful. She was aware how delicate her position was. Her secure, reciprocated love for her husband was always upsetting people with difficult relationships. And yet she said: How do you manage ever to fall in love again? How do you go about it, if all the words have already been used, and the gestures are the same? Dear me, you're so complicated, said Eve. She's a romantic, said Melusine. I understand that, I'm the same. And you love your man, said Louise.

Blanche was climbing the stairs up to the dining room. The women had just helped themselves to dessert. There were lots of different types of fruit tart, and they pulled faces, knowing the pastries were fattening. Blanche heard their laughter as her hand followed the curve of the banister. Unconsciously she stopped for a second, as though drawing breath before confronting the noisy world of these people who were her friends and who naturally talked a great deal when one met up with them, because after all that was what they were there for, to talk, since we are all living the same temporary lives, and it's not always easy, and we expect love, passion, caresses, the devotion of another and conspiratorial laughter, as our due. Who would be there this evening? thought Blanche. She'd forgotten now what Sara had said. She had no desire to see any of those spiteful types who share your pain and secretly take pleasure in it. Blanche was not sure all these women were her friends (or rather, she knew that some of them weren't). She was forcing herself to go to the party, determined not to let herself go, in the same way as she had been determined to ditch her marriage from the time it first occurred to her that she should leave.

From where they were sitting they saw her red hair appear, her head, her chest, then her whole body, silhouetted in the half-light at the top of the stairs. She was a woman of average height, quite broad, but with something striking about her, a fine womanly figure and a delicate, almost angelic face. A Slavic type, said those who knew about her Polish origins, a strong will as well as charm. Her haste had left her breathless (which was why she hadn't turned on the light). She'd had a difficult day – lots of whimpering children, women bringing along their babies even though she'd asked them a hundred times to leave Wednesdays free for children of school age. She'd even lost her temper with one mother whose son had made a mess on the new office carpet. She was puffy beneath the eyes, and she had the grey complexion of a smoker. She didn't in fact smoke, but she was short of sleep. Even so, she'd been determined to come this evening. She disliked the idea that people might talk about her divorce and say that she was hiding because of it (even though that was exactly what she would have liked to do: work all day and then shut herself away in the evenings with her daughter). But before exhaustion had got to her, she'd been looking forward to the party. She'd often felt she'd like to go to the club, and hadn't, for fear of meeting Gilles there. Tonight was a good opportunity. He wouldn't be there: she knew he was out with a woman.

He'd told her about it. He'd told her everything. The vision in red, the smile, falling for her at first sight, the clouds of static, the exchange of glances, his doubt, the problem of the husband, the invitation, the acceptance, the burn of desire, the strange sense that she felt the same for him, the arrangement, and then the endless wait. Everything – right down to her first name. Her name was Pauline. Why had he had to go and tell her the woman's name? Blanche was not a fan of men who talked too much. She liked it when people kept the secrets of their heart to themselves. And usually that was what Gilles did. In fact that was why she'd married him. He must be truly, hopelessly in love, to be giving her all these details. Unfortunately there are phrases you cannot help but hear, and which once lodged, won't go away. Blanche had said: That's a pretty name. But he was already back to fretting and waiting for the day. Do you think she'll turn up? he'd asked the woman who had once been his wife, without regard for the incongruity of the question. She found this new kind of intimacy so strange, so inexplicably painful – to see your own husband in love with another woman. There are two moments of separation, she thought, the first when love dies, the second when it re-ignites elsewhere. Whoever falls in love again first stabs the other in the back when they're already wounded. And yet it's not necessarily a war. The people we love are the same ones who torture us, Blanche André thought. And she often came back to this idea when she saw what happened between mothers and their children. We wear our feelings like crowns of thorns.

Do you think she'll turn up? he asked again, this being the only question that mattered to him. How should I know? she'd replied. It irritated her, the way he caused pain without even realising it. And it was clear to her from Gilles' doubt and insecurity that this was not a flirtation, it was a passion. In short, she realised that Pauline had his love, a fact unknown to Pauline, who was only just beginning to love. You're a woman, you know how women act, Gilles went on. She had objected: All women don't act alike. And then she said: Personally I wouldn't have agreed to meet. She said this, when in fact she didn't know whether she would or not, when in fact it struck her as rather romantic, rather enviable, to be swamped with desire, to fall headlong into an affair heedless of the circumstances. But she had been unable to resist having a dig at this woman she'd never met. How mean was that? At the same time she told herself: I can see it's mean, but I can't help it. It's a feminine thing. Yes, she was in this respect entirely feminine: jealous, competitive. Besides, Gilles loved excessively feminine women, even to the point where the phrase became derogatory. And how old is this Pauline? she asked, eventually. Because that was what she really wanted to know, and that was what he wasn't telling her.

Blanche, exclaimed Eve, rising from her chair, we'd begun to think you weren't coming. I had all these emergencies and it messed up my appointments, said Blanche. And you're tired, said Marie, gently. Why didn't you just go home to bed? I really wanted to come, said Blanche. She was about to add, I never see anyone these days, but she stopped herself, she might have burst out crying. She was so tired that the slightest thing was enough to set her off. Her eyes glanced round the table. Everyone's here except Pauline. I wanted you to meet her, said Melusine. Yes, I know, said Blanche, thinking of Gilles. Do you know where she is? asked Louise. Who? said Blanche. Pauline, said Louise. No, I don't, sorry! I thought you said Gilles wasn't here. I know where he is, said Blanche. And it was perhaps at that moment that for the first time she could *see* her husband and this Pauline woman together. Louise immediately thought: Blanche came because she was sure she wouldn't run into Gilles. And Melusine suddenly said: It's odd, Pauline never misses a party like this. Perhaps then some secret part of Blanche realised that the Pauline whom she'd glimpsed at the club and at school was the enchantress. At any rate, the secret part of her whispered a related question: What about Marc – isn't he here either? Oh yes, said Melusine, he's watching the boxing with the others. Your husband's a big boxing fan isn't he? asked Eve. Yes, replied Blanche. How painful she found these words: your husband. It would be a long time before any other woman would understand how much joy he could get from a boxing match. We'll make up a tray with some food and you can watch the fight with me. I'll clear everything up, you just relax. It was a great comfort for a woman to have a man at her side as she went out to meet the world, too little was made of that: dealing with other people, men, women, in and out and round about town, as part of a couple. She wasn't sure she was cut out to live alone. There'd been a time when she'd known how to get about, organise herself. She'd been the age for it, and had known it wouldn't last for ever.

Blanche's mind spun like a mad carousel – Gilles, Blanche, Sarah, some mysterious woman, loneliness – round and round it went in her head, never letting up for a moment. During consultations the torment stopped for a while, when she was taking care of other people. But here at table, surrounded by her friends, she was very jittery. Come on, said Louise, have a drink, have something to eat. Emotion had turned Blanche's cheeks a gentle pink. Her right hand fiddled with a piece of bread. Though no one had asked her, she said: Gilles had to meet someone. Who's that? asked Melusine, who hadn't been following the conversation. My future ex-husband, said Blanche, attempting a smile. The whole thing had broken her apart, somehow, the whole process of finding oneself deceived, of ceasing to love (or believing one had), of finding life together intolerable, of separating, telling other people about it, divorcing, finding oneself divorced. And yet for a while she hadn't even realised it. You can go for a long time without realising you're wearing yourself out. She had honestly believed she hadn't changed, with her social smile, her sex drive, her curiosity, all these things, she had believed, were untouchable, part of her basic temperament, a gift that couldn't be taken away. Can you lose your own temperament? She had discovered that it can get worn out, dulled by life. How she had changed: sadness had set up home inside her. What am I now? she would think. A stupid question, as if she had only ever been Gilles' wife, nothing more. She had always been more than that, she had had her own private life in addition to their life as a couple, and some of that life was still intact. She had a wonderful job, which she loved. But it still seemed as though she'd lost interest in everything. A man would never react like that, she thought, a man would concentrate on his career, his profession. But there you are. She wasn't a man, clearly. Her basic life force was damaged. For the hundredth time she told herself: No one's died. It was meant to be some consolation, an appeal to her common sense. But it just didn't work any more. A feeling had died. That was why saying this no longer worked: not only did it remind her of Gilles, but it wasn't even true. Her eyes were already brimming with tears. She was so tired. Isn't Gilles with the others? said Melusine, now far too drunk to register anything at all. I thought he was with them. I thought maybe he hadn't come because he was avoiding you, said Eve. No, he didn't go to see the fight. Doesn't he like boxing? Of course, he loves it. So? So whatever it was must have been more important.

The others were talking. The others wouldn't stop talking. Blanche thought: I should never have come, I'm not up to this. The others were brutal. If he had left me it would be different, she told herself. They would know I was unhappy. Whereas now it doesn't occur to them. They think I made a choice and I'm just going to start a new life. And yet Blanche knew perfectly well that her decision was just the surface of a whole broader phenomenon for which she was not responsible: when two people split up it isn't just about the decision to split, there are tremors much deeper than that, out of sight. The person who actually announces the decision is not always the one who has taken it. It is less significant, less irrevocable, to speak out, than to manoeuvre in silence, to cast the other aside, desert them, without saying a single word. She could have screamed: Why isn't it possible to separate out real and imagined hurts? Why should it be like this, when all that was left of love was betrayal, a dying light, the bitter solitude of two hearts no longer joined? At last, the carousel had ceased to turn: Blanche was weeping.

Blanche let herself go. The others passed her paper napkins while trying to find words to calm her. It was a moment for delicacy, for saying nothing. Louise had half taken her in her arms. Don't cry, she murmured, her voice shaking with emotion. You love Gilles, said Marie, who quite clearly could not accept the demise of any couple. Don't say that, whispered Melusine, you don't know. If it's true she'll find out for herself. I'm sure it's true, said Marie, she wouldn't be in this state if she didn't love him. Oh yes she would, said Melusine. Do you not think people suffer when they break up? And that suffering jeopardises their chance of ever loving again. I often think that if we only dared, everything would make us cry, murmured Melusine, happiness as well as grief, being together and being apart, being in love and falling out of love. Tears are our destiny, tears are where it all leads in the end, and yet we never accept it. I've found that all my life, said Melusine. But you cry all the time, said Marie. And she was embarrassed to see that Melusine was drunk.

Louise had put her arm around Blanche's shoulders, Eve and Sara had gone to find coffee and some cups, and Melusine and Marie were clearing some space on the table. The waiter had long since gone home. I feel so ridiculous, said Blanche. You're not ridiculous, said Louise. If you knew why I was crying . . . said Blanche. Why? murmured Louise. I'm crying because he's in love with another woman, said Blanche. As if I didn't know it would happen one day. As if it was not allowed. How do you know he's in love with another woman? said Louise. He told me, said Blanche. Louise thought: Another one with no tact. And yet she had always thought Gilles was a subtle man. He's completely spellbound, said Blanche. Spellbound, spellbound, what's that supposed to mean? groaned Louise, smiling. But she was worried by the idea it might be true. He's in love, said Blanche. So? Let him get on with it! You wanted him to give you some peace. One day you'll fall in love too, said Louise, changing tack somewhat. Blanche looked doubtful at this. She said: He saw her at school, he was smitten, he started taking Sara to school every day. He's just trying to console himself for losing you, said Louise. No, said Blanche, it's not like that, he's got her under his skin. It's physical.

Even if we'd still been together he would have loved her, said Blanche. At this thought she buried her face in her hands and began to cry again. There's no way you can know that, said Louise. What about her? Does she love him? continued Louise, treading on eggshells. Did he say anything to you about that? Blanche shook her head. He looks unhappy, said Blanche. She's married. What a mess, thought Louise. Her name's Pauline, said Blanche. That's odd, Louise thought, but said nothing.

She'd stopped crying. Blanche was drinking her coffee. All she could think of was her husband. He had never been so present in her mind as he was now. It was strange. She found herself increasingly understanding of those couples who divorced then remarried. And in fact this idea was beginning to take root in Blanche André's mind. She felt the need, which she could not dismiss, to gather her thoughts round this possibility, to focus on all the things she'd loved about her husband. Gilles was a true lover; he was funny; he had a look that made her feel beautiful; he never lost his temper; and he laughed a lot. She was thinking like a woman in love. She had wanted to disown their union because she found something intolerable in the idea of being indissolubly bound to a man. And because she was exhausted, justifiably jealous, and furious that he was living the life he wished to lead while she was doing what he refused to do. But all that was so paltry in the context of love. How stupid all her recriminations looked now. I've ruined everything, she thought.

Meanwhile, Sara was saying to Eve: What she needs is a lover. And Marie objected: Just you wait, she'll get back together with Gilles.

Stop poking your nose in where it's not wanted, said Melusine. Then, standing there shaking, with her coffee cup rattling in its saucer and her neck red with the effort of speaking, she exclaimed: There's nothing more unfathomable than a couple when you see them from the outside. No one ever knows who will stay with whom and why, who's happy and who isn't, who makes love, who doesn't. It's better to say nothing. Blanche smiled. She thought: You don't really know what you're going through or when exactly things start to go wrong from the inside either. What was Gilles thinking about just at that moment? she wondered. How could he not hear the echo of her unhappiness, ringing in his ears? How could he smile, and come on to another woman? She felt her heart ache with grief at the thought. But she could hardly start crying again, her friends would get tired of comforting her, she'd have to leave. Blanche pulled herself up straight, picked up her glass of wine and began to talk of the various things that had happened in her day, an exhibition she'd seen, a life full of little details. What stopped her falling apart, what stretched her smile across her face, was hidden deep inside her, no more than an idea, an incredible resolution: she would set out to get Gilles back. She thought about this extraordinary rebirth of her love, born out of his love for another woman. Do we really need life to tell us whom we should love? she wondered. Did a woman need another woman's view on a man before she could choose him for herself? We are so alone, she thought, so alone in our thoughts, our choices, for right or wrong. Perhaps we needed someone else's point of view in order to rediscover our own? I'm so weak, thought Blanche, I'm easily influenced, I can't make up my own mind, I've never really been sure what I wanted, and Sarah will be so happy, and as she thought all this her face settled back into a smile. I'm glad to see you looking happier, said Louise. Yes, murmured Blanche, I just felt really down for a moment. And inside her head the carousel had begun to turn again: I must call Gilles this evening. What's he doing? Where can he have gone? Where did he take that woman? Will he go back to his apartment? She told herself, with some relief, that he would have to go back home, because the woman was married. What time will he get in? She had already disposed of the woman he had smiled at. She was eager to get back home and ring him.

2

He was walking along beside a yellow dress. He was smiling, he was flirting with another woman. Just at that moment this woman was looking upset at not having been able to give him what she thought he wanted. Physical proximity. Suddenly he felt hungry for it. Every now and then he stopped and stood squarely in front of her. He would murmur something to her, as though it was of greater importance than what he had just that second been saying, as though he had to stop walking in order to tell her. Often it was a question. He drew close to her, his voice took on a velvety texture, his eyes focused sharply on her. He stood before her, a powerful man. He danced around her. He came right up close to her, she tried to step back, he still came on. She felt as though she was running away. At the same moment he was gripped by an overwhelming desire to touch her. He could have reached out his hands to grasp her face, her hair, and forced her to kiss him. He stopped himself. But his hands seemed to move towards her anyhow. He stopped them as they reached the level of her eyes: when he became aware of them himself. She was aware of the exaggerated fluttering of his hands. She stood frozen in front of her feverish friend, in a daze he could not have conceived of, delighted to be the cause of such fervour, terrified to find it staring her in the face. Meanwhile he was thinking: She's strange. It's almost as though she's completely passive, just waiting to see what happens. Was she playing a game? Suddenly he wasn't quite sure of the answer. He was not sure of much any more. While they'd been in the restaurant he'd really thought she liked him, even that she was physically attracted to him. Whereas now . . . he no longer knew. And so he set off walking again, puzzled by her shyness. Later he would say: I felt you weren't ready. Why?

No, she certainly wasn't ready to get too close to him. Despite her desire for him, she couldn't accept intimacy or boldness. For all that the intimate voice made her shiver, she could not have kissed him or made love to him. Whereas he could have taken her in his arms there and then and become her lover. Here she stood before him, moved, but unable to summon up a single image of love. Just imagine, she could abandon herself to the timeless dance of love and later, stretched out beside this man she didn't know, clean off the traces of their actions, dress herself, go home in fake and whitewashed innocence, and maybe even lie. But she could not lift a finger. She was caught in a dream. What was it actually all about? Pauline Arnoult asked herself. And thought: flirtation. She despised herself for pouting and preening like this in front of him. She was embarrassed by the spectacle of herself. She was embarrassed by the whole thing. It was all quite ridiculous, right from the start, nothing but posturing and tittering to disguise the basic instinct which held them both in its sway.

But instinct had not won through. The inner voice said: Later. The physical was pushed into the distance, leaving just the heady charm of voice, affinity, laughter, all those things which add to the thrill of seduction, the delight of being the object of attention. She was not a young innocent in this respect, quite the contrary: it was precisely because she was well acquainted with the various forms – both impetuous and precise – of desire, that she took care to protect herself. She felt split both ways: she was possessed by a sweeping passion, but could not take any real action. It was as though her desire was somehow illusory. And yet it was real. But it needed a period of preparation, of formal courtship, of familiarisation with the unknown other. (I felt you weren't ready. Why?) At that moment it seemed inconceivable to her that she would be wide open before this man one day, and yet she surely would: ready and eager.

There was also the question of the child. She could feel it moving. Could one lie with one's belly pressed against a stranger and feel within it another man's child, without incurring guilt, or there being a price to pay? At this thought, Pauline Arnoult's smile disappeared. He saw she was troubled about something, and wondered what it was. But he could never have understood the nature of her struggle between guilt and innocence, nor the opposition, in her mind, between the delight of their attraction and the purity owed to the unborn child. Are you all right? asked the intimate voice. Would you like to go home now? She didn't hear him speak. You're tired, he said, as though it had suddenly occurred to him. And indeed he was thinking now of her pregnancy, which, because it was not visible, he had forgotten. It's unforgivable of me, he said, making you walk when you must be weary. She assured him she wasn't and insisted they should keep on walking. And he found the way she said it, her pretty face all stubbornness and outrage, quite exquisite. Oh yes, she was lovely. He told her: Lovely Pauline. But she still didn't hear. She was lost somewhere between her desire and her rejection of it. Her anxiety was growing: she felt as though she was being dragged into this secret love affair, too late to draw back, they were moving forward now at a frightening pace, already she needed him beside her, and yet they would have to part, and the parting would make her unhappy. He sensed there was something decidedly wrong and he thought of her husband.

We should go to this party, he said, abruptly, stopping in his tracks. I shouldn't be monopolising you. They might be talking about you, about me, wondering what we're both up to. They may even guess we're together. What would your husband say to that? She answered simply: Why should they guess? There's no reason they should. She shuddered at their connivance in deception: such familiarity, all because of a shared secret. You're right, he said, forgetting that he had most unwisely mentioned it to his wife. But even so, I think we should turn up, independently, he said. She murmured, blushing: I'm not sure if that's a good idea, I'm not very good at hiding the truth. He laughed and said: That's what all the best liars say. She knew this was true – although she wouldn't admit it, she was actually someone who lied infrequently but to perfection, and yet she said again: No, honestly, it's not a good idea. Yes it is, he said, it's an excellent idea, you can go first, as though you'd just come straight from a dinner that had finished early. What if I blush when I see you? she said. You won't, because you're the only one who knows about it, and you've no reason to doubt that. Tell yourself that only you and I know about this evening and you won't feel anxious, he said, laying down the law. She said: Mightn't your wife be there? I've no idea, he said, but I don't think she will be; since we divorced she's not been out much. Would you mind running into her? she asked. She had a puzzling desire to talk about his wife. Not since I've known you, said the intimate voice. His voice was so smooth that once more she neglected to tell him that he was overdoing it. But it pleased her that he pushed his apparent devotion so far, and perhaps he knew that this net spun of low murmurs and tenderness would be the thing to catch her with. Come on, he said, as though he needed to convince himself as well, haunted as he was by a vision of a night of passion in a room with a locked door. It's a very good idea. Let's go to the club. She smiled. Do you really think so? she said. She realised she shouldn't have asked this. Where would it lead? She was walking straight into a trap. And indeed, he stood still, took hold of her arm and looking hard into her eyes said: Can you tell me any other way of spinning this evening out? And since she could find no answer to these piercing words, he said: I thought not. So don't let's discuss it any longer. Seeing her look so pitiful, he began to laugh and murmured: I don't want this evening to end. He was still holding on to her arm. The warmth of his grasp gave her a wild voluptuous thrill. Such a tiny gesture. Idylls make idiots of us all.

3

The group of men huddled round the TV set were rocked by successive cries and shudders. The spectators had been whipped to a frenzy by the sheer bravura of the black boxer. The world title holder hid his face behind his fists, and his face was contorted with hate. He was a small, pale, thin man, his appearance not helped by the presence of a moustache which turned down unpleasantly at the tips. And whenever he dropped his guard to throw a punch, the grimace which distorted his features was so cruel that not one single spectator in the whole hall thought of him as a champion threatened with defeat or even as a man simply doing his job: every one of them hated him, and wanted to see him beaten. It's quite wrong, really – it may have been simply because he wasn't a pretty face that he had the whole crowd against him. He's looking for a knockout, said Tom. He's not home and dry yet, he said, meaning the handsome black athlete. He could find himself on the canvas any second. His uncertainty was justified, and heightened the suspense still further. Tom was afraid one of his friends might think the fight was in the bag and be disappointed when the whole thing turned round again. Sport isn't over until the final whistle, he said. He added: There are some people in every sport who are incapable of winning a match – it's called the fear of winning. Does that exist – fear of winning? said Guillaume, laughing – a man who was sublimely successful in his chosen career, and never paused to ask himself any questions. From time to time, Guillaume filled up their glasses. Those who'd had enough covered their glasses with their hands. No one spoke. The black boxer was jogging around on his fine, womanly legs. He might well win, he deserved to, but the possibility of defeat was still there and might even yet cut him down in his hour of glory.

Yes! they shouted in chorus. The gong sounded for the end of the round. The girls in miniskirts got to their feet and set off on their tour of the ring amid the roar of the crowd, who this time showed not the slightest interest in them. Poor things, said Tom, laughing. Pretty thighs soon paled into insignificance next to the spectacle of a good fight. A pity Gilles isn't here to see it. Isn't he interested? Of course he is. He's always been mad keen on boxing, ever since he was a child. So where is he then? Ah! Who knows? With a woman? I'd be surprised. Nothing surprises me in such matters. Ever since Blanche left him he's said he's going to stay single, that if it didn't work out with her it wouldn't work out with anyone. He's really taken a knock over this divorce. He's changed. How do you mean, changed? You talk to him about it, he says he's been a fool, he shouldn't have played around so much. All men think about women at our age, said Tom. We think about nothing else. Don't exaggerate. I'm not exaggerating, I really believe it. I look at women, so do you, you look at their breasts, run your eyes over their buttocks, even if you don't actually do anything about it, you think about it, you wonder why it's not allowed, why it's out of bounds, why having one woman means you can't have others, why you can't look, can't touch. They all laughed. Don't start on that again, said Jean. What a jerk, joked Guillaume, pretending to take a punch at Tom. Let's not get back into that conversation, said Henri. Yes, said Jean, I thought we'd drawn a line under it. At any rate, said Guillaume, divorce doesn't lead straight to a walk up the aisle. It's an expensive business, divorce, he said, merrily. You should know all about that, said Tom. I certainly do, said Guillaume. How much is Gilles giving Blanche? They haven't settled the details yet, but he wants to be generous to her, for the sake of the child. There's no guarantee Sarah'll be the one to benefit. I think he trusts his wife, said Henri. Their discussion was interrupted by Max and Marc shouting Final Round.

They all held their breath. The feeling of being afraid for someone else, and being powerless to help them, was intoxicating. They hated the little white guy. What a bastard! He's after a knockout! Bastard, bastard, bastard! Get back against the ropes, Tom shouted to his favourite. That's right, don't go after him, get back against the ropes! It was the end of the fight. The black man was protecting himself with his fists, the white man was hammering away at him with all his might.

And suddenly the gong sounded, that peculiar noise that signals the end of a fight. The fine-looking black guy was standing against the ropes, removing his mouthguard, raising his arms. He knew the match was his. They all leapt to their feet, arms in the air, laughing. Hold on, said Tom, wait for the judges' decision. Sometimes there's a surprise. They watched the presumed loser put on his robe and leave the ring. His face was white with fury, his jaw locked into a cruel grin. His opponent was carried off in triumph.

With the end of the fight, Marc recovered his senses and his first thought was of his wife. Had she turned up? He worried when she was out alone late at night. It was always a relief to know that she'd got back safely. Pauline mistook his concern for jealousy. But it was genuine concern. So he decided to go and see if she was with her friends, and if she wasn't to phone the house. What time was it? Almost midnight. Dinner must surely be over by now. I'm going to see the women, he said. Oh, let them be for a bit, said Max. I want to know if Pauline's there, said Marc. You're worried she might have bolted, said Guillaume. Naturally, said Marc, with a dry smile. And is that consistent with everything you've been telling us? said Max. I think so, said Marc. Stay and wait for the result, said Tom. They were all standing now, stretching themselves and passing comments on the fight. They were tall, powerful men: it was immediately apparent when they were all in one room together, all these powerful bodies, packed into a small space. Strength like that needs to be exercised. While they waited for the result to be announced, they cleared up the relics of their meal. That was a hell of a fight, Tom said again and, since he was the boxing expert, they all agreed with him. The black boxer was an outright winner. The programme was over and Tom switched off the set. Do you want a drink? asked Tom, to finish up a bottle. They set the room more or less to rights – although there remained a certain kind of male disarray – and went off to join the women. Marc walked on ahead, with his agile stride, delighted at the thought of seeing his wife again. He was never so aware of how much he loved her as when she wasn't there.

4

Is it okay to talk about it, or is it a secret? Louise asked Penelope (meaning her marriage). No, no, said Penelope, it's not a secret. She smiled: Might as well give people time to get used to the idea. Stop making such a big deal of it, said Louise gently. I'm not making a big deal of it, Penelope said. It *is* a big deal. Just you wait and see, she said, you listen to what they say, you won't even dare tell me, they'll be so awful. She stood up. I'm going to get myself a piece of tart, she said, picking up her plate. Life made a victim of this woman. Why was it that some people just seemed destined for unhappiness? thought Louise. Was there some part of their inner mechanism that just wasn't good at life? Part of them chose to be unhappy, thought Louise. It was an insight only, not a judgement. Yes, Louise said to herself, Penelope could have got over her young fiancé after he died, she could have loved again without waiting so long, without choosing a man who would also die. Surely that was why she found she could love him, because soon he'd die, like the young lover. Penelope was the architect of her own self-sacrifice. There was a strange fascination to this unconscious perpetuation of gloom and sadness. What are you thinking? asked Eve. She was sitting in Penelope's chair. I was thinking about what Penelope was saying, said Louise. Eve had a pretty enough little face, a blonde's face, a fine bone structure but a harpy's expression. Louise thought this every time they met: it was written all over Eve, however hard she tried to cover it up with smiles and charm, because that was what she was. Louise put her theory to the test. Penelope's getting married, she said. That's marvellous, said Eve, who couldn't have cared less. She's marrying Paul, said Louise, without giving any clue as to her own feelings. The old guy? said Eve. She pulled a face. He's an extraordinary man, pointed out Louise, faking innocence. I've never met a man like him. Maybe, said Eve, but he's seventy. Seventy-two, in fact, corrected Louise. He's getting on a bit to be a bridegroom, don't you think? said Eve. I don't see why, said Louise. Do you think people run out of love when they get to a certain age? Of course not, said Eve. Him I understand perfectly well (her tone laced with sarcasm), but it's not him I'm thinking of. He's quite right to go for it. But she must be completely off her head! I can understand that you can screw a guy out of spite, that you can say yes to one man because another man's turned you down – you often find men who've bagged a woman because she was lost and unhappy – but even so! I believe she loves him, as simple as that, said Louise. I can't believe that, it's not possible, said Eve. Or if it is, she could just not marry him. Well, said Louise, rising from her chair to put an end to the conversation, you obviously know more about it than I do, all I know is what Penelope's told me. And I'm glad for her, because she looks happy.

The husbands' arrival served to rescue a dinner which was turning sour. Eve was clearing the pudding plates with a disgruntled air. Penelope was still eating. Blanche, Melusine and Marie were still sitting quietly over their coffee. I won't sleep, murmured Marie.

Louise and Sara were taking little sips at glasses of red wine, but not drinking seriously. I hear noises off, said Marie. I can tell Guillaume's laugh from here, said Louise. Sara added: I think they must be a bit drunk. A second later there they were in the room with the women: Jean, Marc, Max, Henri, Guillaume and Tom. So, said Tom to Sara, have you had a good gossip? They all managed to look offended. No more than you have, replied Sara. I bet you have, said Henri, teasingly, putting his arm protectively around Melusine. My darling, he said. It came out sounding to Louise like a bleat. Did he despise his wife? How are you? Did you have a nice evening? he asked, as though talking to a simpleton. But Melusine was actually rather dazed. Mmmm, mmm, she said. Louise was revolted. How could he be kind in such a stupid sort of way? It was no help to anyone, it had certainly been no help to Melusine to be made to feel like a child in the face of this macho, somehow paternalistic kind of love. Yes, macho, she thought. The couples all re-formed. Marie was talking to Jean: Come here you, she said. She looped her arms around his neck and drew him close to her. How come you're so hot? They were laughing. Those two make a real couple, thought Sara. Tom often put his arms round her too, two minutes ago he'd even placed his hands on her breasts. That was his sign to her, she thought, the sign she was *desired*. Did Tom love her? She didn't think he knew himself. If he had, she told herself for the thousandth time, would he have been so unkind as to deny her what she wanted (to live with him)? She watched him now, talking to Blanche. What was he on about this time? You're allowed to be tired, Tom was saying, but not to be depressed. Why not? said Blanche. Because you're a very beautiful woman, said Tom. And what use is that? said Blanche. He had always had a weak spot for her, and now was standing right up close to her. She moved away slightly. It helps in seduction, he said, looking into her eyes. And what use is that? asked Blanche again. It helps us get through life, said Tom seriously. He truly believed this. She didn't. But thanks to him she felt less old, less ugly. If there was one thing she could count on, she thought, it was on becoming old and ugly. And she began to laugh. Typical of a man to come out with daft ideas like that just when she was getting divorced.

Max and Eve were rowing in low voices. Max had remembered they were due to have lunch at his mother's the following day and had just reminded his wife, to check she hadn't forgotten. It was the last thing she wanted to do: she'd seen quite enough of his mother. Too bad, he said, you're coming. I didn't marry your family, said Eve. I certainly married yours, said Max. Stop it you two, said Guillaume. Then he said: What about you, Louise sweetheart? Did you marry my family? He was laughing. Only Marc was silent, surprised and worried to find Pauline wasn't there. He thought she must have gone home, and he went off to call her, without success. He came back to join the others. What he didn't know was that at that very moment a taxi was dropping his wife off at the door of the club, while Gilles was making his way along the street. Blanche was alone as well, sitting a little way back from the rest of the group, which was otherwise all couples, now that Tom had gone back to talk to Sara. What were you talking to Blanche about? Sara asked. Tom didn't dare say that he'd been telling her she was beautiful. He said: I was trying to cheer her up. Marc went up to Blanche. He knew her by sight, from seeing her at the club and at school. He assumed therefore that she must know Pauline. My wife hasn't called? Pauline Arnoult, he explained. She wasn't sure if she'd be able to make it. I was very late myself, said Blanche, but she wasn't at the dinner. She detected his concern. It was touching. Ask Louise, she said with a friendly smile. She was jittery from the coincidence of the two Paulines. The name nagged at her. She watched the husband go over to ask the others. She'd seen him before at school. He sometimes came along with his wife and son. Now she realised exactly who Pauline Arnoult was. She could even picture the child, a little boy, so blond his hair was almost white. And perhaps it was at that moment that she tumbled to the conclusion that the woman he was looking for was the very woman Gilles had found.

5

They agreed that Pauline should arrive first and then Gilles would turn up after her. Wouldn't it be simpler just to say we had dinner together? she said. Do you think so? he said, teasing her. He knew the others would find that very odd. Did you tell your husband this morning you were having dinner with me? he said. He knew perfectly well what the answer was: it was just the first point in the demonstration of his argument. She shook her head. Well then you can't tell him now, he said. He'd never understand why you didn't tell him before. She admitted he had a point. I'm incapable of thinking of things like that, she thought. She hadn't a clue about the real or suspected deceptions husbands and wives committed against each other. On the contrary, she told herself that the simple truth was better than any amount of camouflage. Didn't some things seem unbelievable when in fact they were true? Didn't people just block out those things which threatened to destroy them? But, she said, if I say it like a joke, I was with Gilles André and we went and made love in a hotel, even my husband won't believe me! She had gone a delightful pink as she said this. He noticed this, decided she was sweetness itself, and not seeking to further spare her blushes he asked: Are you sure of that? I think so, she replied. Well then, do it. Tell him what you've just said. I'll stand there next to you and laugh along. The problem is, said Pauline Arnoult, I'm just not capable of lying like that. You mean that if I take you to a hotel now and then on to this dinner you *will* be able to tell them all about it so they'll believe the opposite? She agreed it sounded rather idiotic. It's not that, exactly, I know that's how you're meant to play it (he laughed out loud at this) but whatever had actually happened, I still couldn't lie. Well, if you can't tell a lie . . . he said, in a voice thick like honey. She didn't ask herself what he meant by this. What she heard him say was: If you can't lie it's not going to be very practical. Shame and enchantment mingled. She was quite convinced that she could read his mind.

She understood the things he thought but didn't say. He was thinking: Some loves thrive on secrecy. Not on lies, but on silence, lying by omission. Because they came along too late to be able to be played out in the open. They must flourish in silence. She heard him think: We will love one another in secret. You must be able to keep a secret. A single word fluttered about in her mind: lovers. Words can be our downfall, creating new desires, new projects within us, that have all the sparkle of words, but are all too concrete and dangerous. I will have a lover. These words sent her into a fever of guilt and made her determined to give in and to suffer. He was smiling at her, as though she was a child, and indeed, next to him she did feel like a little girl. Accordingly, she began looking down at her feet as she walked in a rather dim-witted fashion. How odd, she thought, to feel at once so happy and so oppressed. She had never encountered this particular mix of emotions before. With her husband, at the exact equivalent moment of falling in love, she had felt only happiness: the future was theirs.

Pauline Arnoult felt more relaxed out in the street that she had in the restaurant. She was happier talking in the street than sitting brazenly across the table from her companion, in full public view; here the rhythm of their steps seemed to provide an alibi of sorts. Gilles André, on the other hand, gave no sign that he was either embarrassed or moved in any way. He looked – though apparently he did not feel – tired. There was no great plan, no big effort or affectation, he was just being entirely himself, without showing off or putting on an act, but with no false modesty either. And that was so rare in itself that she was impressed. He was the type of person who doesn't pretend to be what they're not, who doesn't compare themselves with others. She felt somewhat diminished herself, in the face of his positive approach to life. Just as she was abandoning herself to the feeling, indeed to the sure knowledge, the pleasure even, of being dominated, that is, to being in the presence of a giant and feeling elevated by his company, he saw a taxi. Here comes a cab, he said, and stepped out into the road.

For the first time she was sitting beside him, her body no longer half-hidden behind a table. He could see her knees and her skin. She had lovely legs, long and shapely, he thought, unaware of the blatancy of his gaze. She felt she was being examined, and was embarrassed. Although she was quite equal to playing the conventional feminine role, she would have preferred not to be pushed into it like this. She was quite irritated to find herself playing it, pouting, being desired, even to feel all of a sudden as though she was being sized up, like prey. She smoothed down her dress over her thighs uneasily. Don't tug at your dress, he said, teasing her. You look very nice as you are. Again she found herself blushing, and sank down into the back of the seat. But she swallowed all his impertinence, she was under his spell, obedient. I'm going to get out before you, and the driver will take you to the entrance of the club, so you'll get there quite a bit before me, he told her. She felt increasingly scared. She was astonished by the little trickles of sweat running down her back: proof of her real intentions this evening. Otherwise why would she be frightened? She said nothing. And he did as he had planned: he stopped the car, gave a note to the driver and slammed the door. Are you all right? asked the intimate voice. Yes, she whispered. She could see the eyes of the driver watching her in the rear-view mirror. He obviously assumed they were lovers who had just spent the evening together in a hotel. She felt indecent, transparent because of her secret. Perhaps her lover guessed as much, for he murmured: No one knows you've had dinner with me, honestly. Again she assented in a wretched whisper. And this time he noticed her distress, her sudden fragility, and an incredible grace that went along with it, and he came back to the car door and stretched his arm through the open window, to stroke her cheek with the back of his hand. He said: This evening, when we're with all the others, would you prefer me to come over and talk to you, or just to let you be? She didn't know. She didn't know how good she would be at covering up. We'll see, he said. He looked at her and said: I can tell you're worried. There's no reason to be. She reflected that she was the only one who knew what reason she might have. Then he said: I'll call you next week. She didn't reply. May I? he asked. She nodded yes, moved by a profound sense of pleasure that he should ask it as a favour. She wanted to be wanted, pleaded with, desired. She wanted to be the one to haunt the sweet, troubled dreams of a devoted lover. And although just at this moment she was none of these things, and although he was neither quite devoted nor troubled but simply as tender and concerned as any man smitten by a woman, the sensuality in his voice led her to believe that he was devoted, that he was in that world beyond petty labels that she had invented for them. She, though sorely deluded, was happy.

V

Full-Blown Lies

I

Pauline Arnoult was a changed woman. Outside and in. On the outside she was more radiant than ever, on the inside she was dreaming. And it was this dream that gave her her outer radiance.

The woman in the summer dress, flat sandals and a yellow scarf still gave off an air of finesse, robust youthfulness and impertinent beauty. But she now carried the weight of an additional man. Even as they parted the evidence lay upon her, a luminous glow, the sign of a secret. Pauline, who had been the object of desire, now shone with reciprocated passion. Later, the man who had inspired it would say: We were lovers in a previous existence. It was a piece of gallantry, but it was also what he liked to believe was true. For the moment he takes note, but says nothing: the sheer force of his attention has made her fall in love with him. Nothing enhances a woman's beauty like mutual attraction. An immediate sense of conspiracy had flashed through her, the kind that makes you believe you can do no wrong. Thus Pauline Arnoult's beauty was enhanced by the ease which comes with a sense of self-confidence. Gilles André might simply have laughed at the idea that there was anything new in this. He was thoroughly familiar with the whole process of liking someone, and the lift it gave you. But a look of innocence, the mystery of a woman in a summer dress, those expressive eyes, the interplay of virility and femininity, the pretence, the trepidation, the masks and secrets, the return of that shyness you thought you'd overcome for good, the way you felt young again, born again, the quickening heart, the speeding up of ordinary life – all this sets the head spinning, so that it is no wonder we fall for it time and time again. And anyway, Blanche had left him, and he needed to believe that this time it was different. After all, this woman had kept him at arm's length and at the same time made it clear she was interested in him. She was shy, without taint of vulgarity, whilst bearing the mark of that indispensable quality in a mistress: a taste for love. This combination had overwhelmed him: he wasn't even sure he could have kissed her now, if the opportunity had arisen.

Pauline had settled back into her seat, her thoughts now in total disarray. The taxi driver watched her covertly, silently admiring. What a beautiful woman, and a woman in love at that. Her new glow was not lost on him. You had only to see the way she melted in front of that man just now. They must be lovers. He was laughing to himself: Does a woman look that way at her husband? He had been married for twelve years and was pretty sure he knew what he was talking about. No woman had ever given herself to him as he'd seen this woman do. With that look of bliss in her eyes. She looked thoughtful since her friend had gone. He could tell she was trembling as the light spread over the entire surface of her body.

She felt numb from all that smirking and smiling and hinting, already gloomy in her solitude. Any route you'd particularly like? the taxi driver found himself asking the lovely, lost-looking woman. She murmured: We're almost there. She spoke distractedly, with her back to him. She was watching through the rear windscreen as his already familiar shape receded. Watching a man who is out in the world, from a distance, may offer the opportunity to gauge the depth of your feeling for him. And she was suddenly quite sure she loved him. She was overwhelmed with the obviousness of it, and with a feeling of dreadful unhappiness. His role in her future became quite clear to her. She knew she must suffer absence and interruption. He would never be a husband to her.

At this thought, she regretted having played up to him. The genuineness of this new feeling was at odds with the mannered atmosphere in which it had come about. I acted the coquette, Pauline Arnoult thought. She was disappointed in herself. It had been uncalled for and yet she'd done it. She hadn't been able to stop herself entering into the time-honoured role of a woman who is being courted. She had to admit it, she had put up no resistance, she had played and pouted, delighted to be found delightful. Seen from the outside, it must be a ridiculous spectacle, she told herself yet again. She thought this every time she saw a couple in full flirtation mode. She met the glance of the driver in the rear mirror. She must truly look like a courtesan to him. She could tell from the way he was looking at her. No sooner had he clapped eyes on her, without a second thought, he had cast her in a role. How awful to become part of some crude generalisation about the most basic urge. When it came to matters of the heart, you could only get past the stereotype if you were familiar with the innermost details, Pauline Arnoult thought. She needed to believe in the necessity which had brought them face to face with one another. Without this force of necessity, the banality of their motives was unconscionably crude. It felt as though only the purity of an almost hopeless love could dignify it. Must their love be hopeless to be beautiful? It must be eternal, too.

The evening marked the beginning of a long, long affair – or so Pauline Arnoult liked to believe. She would have liked to know whether her hero thought likewise, to have that reassurance. He would not have been surprised by the question: women are already thinking about how to make a gift last for ever when men are still thinking about how to get hold of it. This is why a flirt makes the hunter tell more lies than a willing prey: he has to promise a future so as not to lose hold of the present. But her hero was gone. Too late to ask him now. In any case, she wouldn't have dared. She was on fire. Her cheeks were burning, the carousel of images was off at a gallop once more, and her body was in a state of extraordinary exaltation. Just because of a man. When she was a married woman, expecting a child. A fact she had entirely forgotten. She was content to let her mind drift back over the dinner. Certain memories were like sparks: the moment when she had withdrawn her hands and unaccountably taken fright, the awkwardness which had followed, and the words she had said next, incoherent, irretrievable and then the final U-turn, her unconditional surrender to a man she didn't know. I've lost my head, she thought. The evening had to end. The conversation could not go on. I couldn't stand it. But how sad she was to be deprived of his flattering company. As though I have been banished back into the grey shadows of my everyday life. It was inconceivable. The grey shadows of my life. In point of fact, all lives are grey. The speed with which she'd fallen for him, the burning urgency of her need seemed to point to a kind of special election. A lover was entering her life. She had already started wondering when and how she would see him again, even before he had left to go home. She had felt calmer once they had agreed to meet again at the club. He would still be there. She would be able to see him, hear him, feel him watching her, be desired, be unique again.

A charged encounter leaves its imprint: Pauline Arnoult still burned with sensual arousal. She climbed the stairs to the dining room in a blaze of happiness. On the ground floor all the lights were already out. The table tennis room, the children's playroom, the entrance to the cloakroom, were all plunged in darkness. Pauline Arnoult was reconciling two contradictory thoughts: she was about to step back into the spellbinding presence of her hero, but her husband would be there as well. She felt herself already begin to blush. She began to worry she would give herself away. Were her intentions writ as large as the things she hadn't actually done, what she hoped, what she felt? Had she in fact known perfectly well what was afoot when she accepted the invitation to dinner? Her embarrassment alone was answer enough. She had seduced a man, and she was in love with him. She felt strengthened by this realisation, and a little bit bolshy. She would have two men who loved her. She should be glad. The tangled web ceased to be a cause for worry, she was not showing any favouritism, because at this moment it occurred to her with great clarity that she was capable of loving two people, without either love being diminished by the strength of the other. Her bond with her husband was in no way affected. That was a basic and underlying truth. The husband was loved. No doubt on that score. She had not begun to find him less likeable, less attractive, or to feel he was in any way a burden to her. To tell the truth, he was no burden at all. Her husband was not a prison. No – she wanted the lot, and she had the lot. She had won. She was the exception that proved the rule, the rule of all those who clung to the normal conventions of exclusivity in marriage. At that precise moment she was entirely free from remorse, jealousy, moodiness, boredom. She was letting a little sunshine in upon her love life.

This cluster of helpful thoughts paraded through her fevered imagination to the rapid, regular rhythm of her own footsteps as they climbed on up the stairs. Before long she could make out the noise of the other women, Marie's piercing laugh and Louise's lovely voice. What were they talking about? Tempted, for a moment, to eavesdrop, she stood still on the steps. Tom's laugh boomed out. So the men were there too. The fight must be over. Was it as late as that? She glanced at her watch. Twenty past twelve. A dinner that finished that late was something of a giveaway. She could see Marc standing with his back to her, apart from the others. Her heart began to race. She tried to picture what she must look like. Did she look like someone walking in their sleep? Did her beauty flash 'Woman in Love'? Did it leap straight to the eye when a woman loved two different men? She reminded herself of his words: No one knows. There's nothing they can see. She got ready to lie, she had worked out what she would say if anyone asked her, just that she'd been at a dinner for work. Something like a magazine that wanted to buy one of her drawings. She would proffer this without blushing or trembling, would not give herself away, and if no one asked her anything, she would say nothing, neither truth nor lies.

It turned out to be that simple. It was simple because it had to be. Because as long as it remained secret, life would continue to sparkle. The existing, enviable life of Marc and Pauline Arnoult needed this secret. Marc would be saved through secrecy. He didn't demand that she deny herself love, that she should bore herself rigid on one single relationship when in fact she could quite well handle more than one. What right had they to bolt the doors to each other's hearts? Their existing, enviable life did not rule out secrets: it positively required them. She felt a rush of love for her husband, for his wisdom, for his mature intelligence, for their complete agreement on this point. She felt him capable of understanding everything, and to be therefore more forgiving than the outside world, where there are no excuses. Since neither of them was sure they could manage it, they had never sworn to be faithful to one another. Better still, thought Pauline Arnoult, they had disliked the idea that one might be capable of fidelity, it would have meant their hearts were dried up, that there were no possible surprises left. They had sworn to spare one another through silence: live your life, but keep it to yourself. The completeness of their love required them to lie. And what did it mean to lie? For her it was a small thing. Did anyone really believe in transparency? She had only ever believed in otherness, the barrier of the flesh, the inscrutability of another person's face. Could she really claim to know Marc? She had simply hoped that she might long continue to love the image she had made of him, which he had helped to create. Nothing more, nothing less. She thought: We are all destined forever to slip through each others' fingers, and even if we don't set out to lie, we all have our enigmas, our secrets, the wounds we can never admit to, our vast confines of silence. So often we decide to say nothing. Thus her thoughts proceeded as she continued up the stairs. The others had seen her and were calling to her. Pauline, over here! Of course she could hear them but she hesitated a second before reacting. The noise they were making would engulf her secret, swamp her confusion. And in fact she did feel as though her attention was being forcibly dragged from one world into another. Where were you? And:

What were you doing? We missed you. You look so pretty all in yellow and white. And (to the others): Look, isn't she elegant. And: Ahah, she's blushing. So who was all this elegance for? said Eve. Your husband was looking for you, said Louise. Oh look, she said, here he is now. Marc was walking over to his wife.

He kissed her, holding her tenderly in his arms. I was starting to worry, he murmured, as though apologising for the fact. And I got no answer at home. He stroked her long, bare arms. She knew no one as delicate and considerate as Marc. She said nothing. She smiled and returned his kiss with the heat of freshly reawakened desire. He pressed her closer to him. At once he felt her own desire, like an electric current. You smell good, he whispered. You look fantastic, he told her, drawing back a little to look at her. She laughed. Fantastic, he said again, admiring her pretty teeth in their perfect gums. He loved kissing her because she had these rows of pearls hidden behind her lips. You saw me this morning, she said. He replied: But you weren't wearing that dress this morning. She regretted having said it. Once again she said nothing. She had slipped out from her husband's embrace and, returning his tenderness, held on to his fingertips. Voices echoed round the dining room. Tom's laugh was uproarious. As was that of Melusine, who was completely drunk. They've drunk too much, said Pauline. Marc agreed. Louise and Max were chatting quietly. They were still on the conversation about Buddhism. Louise was getting more and more into mediation. Max was trying to account for the sudden popularity of such practices in France. For, after all, the Christian religion offered similar comfort. Louise said: Isn't it because Buddhism is more about the body? Relaxation, concentration – people immediately start to feel better. Max had never thought of that.

Whereas Christianity's more abstract, said Max, less immediately rewarding, harder. Eve barged in on the conversation. That's enough of the Dalai Lama, she said. She always interrupted Max's conversations. She couldn't accept that, as people often said, Max had a better brain than she did. Max was so intelligent, so kind, and so modest into the bargain. People must be blind: he's not that modest, Eve would say. She was jealous of Max's friends' affection for him. Of course, Max was careful about the image he presented to the world. It was just a shame he couldn't pay the same attention to his family. Have you seen the time? said Eve. I'd like to go now. What time is it? asked Max, looking at his watch. Oh my God! And the baby-sitter needs a lift home. Louise, he said, giving her a kiss, I'll see you soon. See you soon, said Eve. They left. Blanche, looking furtive and inscrutable, drank a gulp of wine. Pauline's eyes met Blanche's: the look in them was dark and moody. Her secret filled her with a kind of comradely, feminine shame. A second later, Pauline was imagining herself in Blanche's position, but a Blanche who knew the truth. A young woman had spent a delicious evening with her husband, a young woman who was lying, you could tell by the look in her eyes. Pauline would have given such a woman a deserved slap. She was annoyed to realise that oddly, quite unexpectedly, she was more worried about her lover's wife than she was about her own husband. But then, the mind being quick to extricate itself whenever possible, Pauline thought: She isn't his wife any more.

All the same, she couldn't quite bring herself to say hello to Blanche. She stayed next to Marc, who was telling her about the fight. Pauline could feel the fatal question coming: And how was your dinner? For this reason, she wasn't listening to what her husband was saying. She was thinking about how she would reply. As it turned out, chance was kind to her, almost like a blessing: just as Marc was embarking on the dreaded 'And how was . . .' Gilles appeared at the top of the stairs, and all the men began shouting at him, saying he'd just missed the fight of a lifetime. There was a great cacophony of male voices and female laughter, into which Pauline retreated with her secret, her confusion, her pleasure in looking at this man whose eyes and voice had been all hers, and who was now pretending not to see her. She felt as awkward as a young girl, doubly so as she attempted to hide it. Marc Arnoult imagined his wife must be tired. She wasn't herself at all. He said: It's late for you. Are you okay? he murmured, slipping his arm round her waist. You must be tired. I'll take you home. Then he whispered: You look so beautiful tonight.

2

Gilles had been walking in the soft summer air, as if he'd been walking on the moon. He was floating. He'd been carried away by the moment, he was no longer on earth, everything was soft and hushed, reduced to the expression on a face when he had taken hold of a pair of white hands, and those hands had withdrawn. What a strange character she had, he said to himself, but at that moment he was completely spellbound. Trapped in a fairy's web, he thought.

However, by the time he arrived at the gates of the club, the spell had already worn off. The seducer needed to see. Once he was apart from Pauline, he was released from the enchantment. He came back to his senses. Now with his eyes wide open, the world around him seemed more prosaic than the features of the woman he had recently beheld.

He was going to see her husband, and he might also see Blanche. The thought of meeting Blanche worried him a great deal more than the husband. The husband didn't bother him. He'd have no trouble talking to him. After all, he had not yet done anything which might be in the least bit awkward. But he had actually spoken to Blanche. It was only now he remembered that. Suppose she began to ask him in front of Pauline whether the dinner had lived up to expectations? He pushed open the gate, walked quickly up the drive, the gravel crunching beneath his feet. The scent of roses. He reached out to pick one and stopped short. Who could he give it to? To Blanche. He could have given Blanche a hundred roses. He would have offered them to her with more passion than to Pauline, because the past was still very much with him. He tried to look relaxed as he climbed the stairs, his hand holding the railing that Blanche and Pauline had held, concealing as many secrets as they did, his heart and mind in a similar state of disarray. Then he too stepped into the crowded room.

So much talk: endless strings of words. Anything was better than silence. And afterwards nothing stuck, because it was all so insignificant. Hello Gilles, you missed a fantastic fight. What the hell were you up to, why weren't you here? Playing hooky? Who won? Gilles interrupted. And then, as he had hoped, they at once began to take him through the fight and he kept his silence and his secret. Meanwhile Melusine was saying to Pauline: So, you go out to dinner without your husband and abandon your girlfriends. Absolutely, said Pauline. I don't blame you, said Melusine. I didn't do enough of that when I was young, and now it's too late. Nobody wants to take me out these days, she said. Pauline smiled. Melusine was so innocent. Melusine would never be able to accept that one might have a secret flirt. She had been an untouchable, pure wife. Had it made her happy? Pauline wondered.

Gilles was listening to the men. That way he could keep his distance from the two women: Blanche and Pauline. Blanche was sitting alone, somewhat withdrawn from the room, her gaze fixed upon him. What did she want? He had no idea. Judging by her expression, she was waiting for an opportunity to talk. Pauline was avoiding his eye. At one point he caught hers and within a fraction of a second she blushed violently. He was not bothered by this, in fact he was delighted: it was a declaration of love and of intent. Would she have blushed if she had had a clear conscience? If she hadn't been quite aware of what was going on? He stopped looking at her. Now it was Eve's turn to look at Pauline. She was struck by the look on her face. No one else had looked at Pauline's face, no one had noticed anything. Eve's heart began to pound at great speed. She stole quick glances at Marc. He was saying: Right up to the last moment it could have been a knockout. The security guard was doing his round. Sorry, ladies and gentlemen, he said, I'm going to have to close up. It was one o'clock in the morning.

They all moved towards the exit. Blanche found herself next to Marc. You found your wife, she said, with the same friendly smile she had used to steer him towards Louise. I'm the happiest man alive, said Marc Arnoult. He put his arm round his wife's waist and said: Have you met Pauline? The two women recognised one another and said hello. Thank you for being so kind, said Marc. Gilles was walking behind them. He was looking at Pauline: her hair, her neck, the broad frame of her back, her waist, her buttocks, her calves. She knew he was looking at her. Then he caught up with his wife. You know Marc

Arnoult, said Blanche. The light had just been switched out. The two men acknowledged each other in semi-darkness. We've met in the bar, said Gilles. You must be the one who didn't make the fight, said Marc. Your friends wondered what on earth you could be doing. They couldn't imagine that anyone could choose to be anywhere but in front of the television. How wrong they were, said Gilles.

They all said goodbye in the street. See you soon, the men said to each other. Maybe adding: What a fight! They were all somehow incredibly relaxed in a particularly masculine way. The women exchanged kisses, leaning in towards one another, as though each was trying to make the other into the smaller of the two. Only Melusine wrapped her arms around Louise and pressed her to her large bosom, without need for words. Each couple went off in the direction of their car. An observer might have noticed that they all walked differently together. Jean offered his arm to Marie. Henri held Melusine by the shoulders. Louise and Guillaume held hands. Sara and Tom walked side by side but closer together than Max and his wife. Gilles and Blanche stayed standing on the pavement, talking. Pauline and Marc made their way down towards the car park one behind the other. She didn't turn back to look at Gilles. What about your dinner? said Marc. She tried to concentrate, girding herself up to make the correct response, to look casual, not to look as if she was lying. Was it good? he asked again, when she didn't reply.

3

But do you think they're lovers? Eve was saying to her husband. They were back in the car again. The argument seemed to be forgotten, but it wasn't. It had left Max feeling bitter and Eve anxious. Had she gone too far? She had been asking herself this so often recently that she had to admit she was probably pushing it. And what would happen, what did happen in cases like theirs, where a couple secretly didn't get along? She had no idea. Gilles and Pauline? said Max, laughing. You think I'm imagining it, said Eve. Of course I do, he said. Absolutely. She was both frightened and turned on by the idea. It had perked her up no end. I know what I saw, she said with a decided air. Gilles would never do a thing like that, said Max. He's never gone for the wife of one of his friends. And besides, he said, Pauline's pregnant. How do you know? she said. I didn't notice. Marc told me, he said. And that's why you think she can't be Gilles' mistress? said Eve. Mistress – that's a bit heavy, isn't it? said Max. What do you want me to call it? she said. He didn't answer her question, but said instead: She's very much in love with Marc. So? Is that going to get in her way? You tell me, he said, smiling. I don't know women like you do. I think you can love two people at once, said Eve, rather over-seriously. Max was smiling. Is that a warning? he said. Please! said Eve. She mustn't laugh. Max added: You can rest assured, I don't think Pauline's crazy enough to be unfaithful to Marc when she's pregnant. It's still a sacred moment in a woman's life. Eve was jealous of Pauline for having a lover, something which she herself, for want of opportunity, had never had. She always expressed surprise when another woman had success in this domain. Even so, at that moment feminine solidarity got the better of her and she said: Lots of husbands do it when their wives are pregnant, and that's a lot worse. They go strutting about when their wife's put on fifteen kilos and has got no chance of seducing anyone. I'm almost pleased that Pauline's managed to seduce Gilles. Come on, Max exclaimed. How can you be so sure about it? I promise you, it was as plain as the nose on your face, said Eve. Pauline Arnoult's face certainly isn't plain. He didn't say this to annoy his wife. She really is gorgeous, he said. Whichever way, I win this one, he thought while he waited for her to answer. I don't know why you all say that, said Eve. I don't think she's that pretty. She's got cow eyes and big feet. Max burst out laughing.

Meanwhile, Sara and Tom were driving round the ring road, and since Sara had been unable to stop herself from saying, You should slow down a bit, Tom had gone into a sulk and wouldn't speak. It was a good evening, don't you think? Sara ventured. A great success, said Tom, without softening his ill humour. The night was ruined. Sara thought: I'm not going to make the effort. She had no wish to bring back a smile just so as to secure his sexual favours. You can drop me off at my place, said Sara. Fine, said Tom. And Sara thought of Jean and Marie, their house full of children and the intangible something that existed between them. They had found what everyone looked for: a love that never dies. So how did they manage it?

Louise was asking herself the same question. As she had got into the car she had decided Guillaume was overweight, drunk again, and had a booming laugh. These negative feelings, which seemed to gather despite her best intentions, upset her. Which was why she too wondered how Marie managed to remain passionately in love with Jean. She thought of Pauline. Pauline glowed with loving harmony. Marital understanding was definitely a mystery, thought Louise.

I thought Pauline looked really beautiful, Henri was saying at that moment. Bastard! said Melusine. You'd happily grovel down before her, like all the rest. Her voice was husky and unrecognisable. Her entire personality had dissolved into the alcohol. Her kindness had vanished, along with her tolerance for pain. But Henri kept his cool. He treated his wife as though she were a very sick woman. Darling, you're the only woman I love, he said, laughing. He had come up close to kiss her, and she slapped him. Take that, she said. He laughed. Darling, now why are you getting cross?

4

I was going to call you when I got home, Blanche was saying. Standing there in the dark, facing the man whom she had made her husband, and then her ex-husband, aware that she had chosen both to weave and unravel what they had. She was unsure of what to say but determined to speak. They were standing in front of the gates to the club. But it would have been late, she said, I don't know if I would have dared. She was not lying. And yet she would have called, however late. She couldn't have slept a wink unless she'd talked to him. She was trembling with her need to have him back. I don't want to go through with the divorce. I've made a dreadful mistake. I know I still love you. Could you put off saying such things? Could you put on hold a drama which was in full flow, postpone it to tomorrow? The person you loved needed to know right away that you loved him, that it mustn't end, that it had been a mistake. She wanted to tell him. And she stood there, trembling, breathless for no reason. He was smiling at her. The realisation that he had nothing to say for himself disconcerted her. She murmured: Did you have a good dinner? And she was so upset she didn't even take in his response. Why talk to him about the exact thing she meant to blot out? All she needed to do was say nothing. Why did she always feel she had to say something? She lapsed into a determined silence. He had simply said yes with a nod of his head. But his face bore the signs of happiness, sweet and secret. Blanche was deeply pained to see him looking so content. I've done a lot of thinking this evening, said Blanche. Oh, he said. He wasn't going to help her. He was childlike in his *naïveté*. She had just swallowed her pride. It was no small thing, she thought, as she looked into the night, standing side by side with her husband, who was becoming at once both ex- and future husband.

He looked at her. She seemed truly worn out. You look tired, he said. He'd meant to say, You look on good form, but he hadn't managed it. It would have felt as though he was making fun of her. Some lies are too absurd for one to impose them on people one loves. She must know perfectly well she wasn't on good form. I am tired, she replied, simply. You've no call to be, he murmured. Was he being deliberately boorish, or did he simply not realise? Had she not been caught up with her bid for reconciliation, Blanche would have lost her temper. How could he say such a thing? But then she immediately thought: Let's not start fighting again. I don't know why, she said, but I've stopped sleeping. And since I work so much . . . Once again she found herself on the verge of tears, as she had just now at the dinner table. She began to feel sorry for herself. You're not ill, are you? he asked. He knew her so well. He knew she was saying nothing because she didn't want to cry. And so he suddenly stepped up close to her, put his arm round her and said: Go on, have a cry, let yourself go. She flung herself on her husband's chest and sobbed. I'm so sorry, she mumbled. Sorry, sorry. And then, feeling his hand move up and down her spine, she relaxed. I love you, she said to her husband, with new-found fervour. She had never been so convinced of it as now. She had had to get to the point where she thought she'd lost him. . . . She let rip: I've never loved you as much as I do this evening, she said. The reply came back promptly: I love you too, said Gilles. I never stopped loving you. Relief surged through her. Even when you were completely off your head, he said. She smiled. But she was unaware of what was going on inside him. He was triumphant: his wife was coming back. He was no longer the one who'd been left, who hadn't been able to hold on to his wife. He was no longer family-less, only fit to pay the bills. He was turning into the man who never lost faith in their love, the one who'd been right when she was wrong. The one to whom all future happiness was owed.

Arm in arm they walked. She came out with the kind of random remarks one makes out of complete trust: I threw a mother out of my surgery this afternoon. Sarah's got nits: I had to wash every single pillow. Melusine had a huge amount to drink again; I don't understand why Henri lets it go on. Did you know Penelope was getting married? He expressed surprise. She told him more. They laughed. She seized the moment: I want to get married in church, she said. Gilles nodded. He wasn't keen. She insisted: For me, please. They laughed. He found a way out: Give me time to get used to the idea. She kissed him. He said: I'm on foot. She didn't reply. They set off walking. Just like the old days, he said. And he was happy at the thought of seeing his daughter the next day. You'll see, Sarah's really pretty with her hair cut short. It was an odd thing to say: strategic, combative. A calculating remark disguised as concern. Blanche held a child in her hand. Why not play the ace?

They walked all the way to Blanche's house. Of the two of them, she was the one who gave most thought to the dinner he'd eagerly awaited, to the woman she didn't know. What are you thinking about? he asked her in the end. I'm thinking I'm happy, lied Blanche. I'm happy too, he said.

Pauline Arnoult told her lie and told it very well. The danger suppressed her emotion. She blushed only in front of the man who was its cause. I'm pleased for you, said Marc. The conversation was underway. He remarked: It's a very good magazine. She was about to sell a drawing – no small achievement. She couldn't avoid having the conversation. What price had they suggested? Was that all? She could have asked a bit more. Still, it wasn't important. At this point she was embarrassed to find herself talking into a void. I'm exhausted, she said. You'll sleep well, he said. He was tender with his wife. We're almost there, he said. I'll go to the garage on my own. She would have liked to suggest going with him, as she usually did, but her desire to be alone was stronger than her concern for him. There was a brief silence, which Marc was first to break. Where did you go for dinner? he asked his wife. She settled for the truth. Was it good? he asked. She kept her answers short. What age was this guy? he said. She thought how lying, editing what had actually happened, inventing, re-imagining isn't that hard in the beginning. It is only in the longer term that it becomes more complicated. You couldn't afford to have a lapse of memory, to forget what you had made up. For this reason she said as little as possible. She played safe too on the question of age. I can never tell, she replied. Between thirty-five and forty-five? My age, then? he said. At this she went back to the secret truth, and said: Older than you. She had the strange sense of being in a scene from a film, a moment which existed in parallel to her real life, quite separately. A false moment.

Here we are, said Marc, stopping the car in front of their apartment block. I'll see you in a minute. She said: See you in a minute. He watched her run up to the entrance and go into the building. As soon as she'd vanished into the building, the car pulled away. And of what followed, as of what had happened earlier that evening, he remained forever ignorant: at breakneck speed, she pulled on her nightdress, brushed her teeth, pushed back the covers, climbed into bed and closed her eyes, balling her fists at the sound of the key in the lock, and feigning sleep under the loving gaze of the man who then entered the room. Marc Arnoult slipped noiselessly into bed next to his wife, taking every possible care not to wake her, and was asleep long before she was. How could she have slept? Images were spinning round and round in her head.

VI

On the Phone

I

The next morning Gilles André was at the school with Blanche. They went together with their daughter. Sarah's face glowed with pleasure as she looked up first at her mother, then her father. Each of them held a hand. The happy couple, who had walked so close to the edge, were smiling, victorious, exorcists reunited in the splendour of love reborn. Pauline saw them smiling. It was like a body blow. They looked so close, she thought perhaps he'd told her everything. It wasn't impossible. She couldn't bear the thought that Blanche might know about their dinner the night before, and about the attraction which had led to it. To have a woman privy to a woman's betrayal. So Pauline Arnoult was far from at ease with Blanche André. She turned as red as her coat. Her gestures speeded up in her sudden panic. Theodore looked at his mother in astonishment as she stroked his cheek, looking distraught. Gilles was making for the classroom. But he didn't pass the young woman without saying hello. His behaviour seemed to her, in her confusion, breathtakingly natural. Such self-mastery: she acknowledged him as a master. Hello, he said, in a neutral voice which bore no relation to his intimate voice. He managed, off the cuff, to hit the exact note used by fathers and mothers who meet at school. Blanche immediately went one better, greeting her more warmly than usual, since, as of last night, they were acquainted. Your husband was worried about where you'd got to last night. He seemed most put out not to find you at the club, she said, smiling. I was not lost, said Pauline, and he found me. I hated to see him so upset, said Blanche, but all the same, it was sweet. Very touching. They were talking to each other. Gilles André was horrified. He couldn't remember what details he'd given the one about his meeting with the other, but he was quite sure he'd said too much. How stupid of me, he thought. How had he come to break his golden rule? And when it was so important. He began to try and think, preoccupied by one detail in particular. Had he told her he'd fallen for the woman at school? Yes, he believed he had. How could his wife, who knew the woman was called Pauline, fail to make the connection now? He thought: she must not *want* to make it. He looked at the two women again. Blanche looked very much at ease. Young Pauline, on the other hand, was all of a dither. He recalled how she had smiled across the table at him. Now her teeth were clenched. He was distressed to see the anguish in her face. It augured badly. She took things too much to heart. He hadn't expected that. It always turned out the same, he was an unlucky fool, he said to himself, and yet again he was going to make everyone miserable. But it all happened very quickly outside the children's classroom. The mothers went in together and he slipped away, indicating to Blanche that he was in a hurry by tapping his watch with his index finger. The scarlet blush on Pauline's face as she refused to look at him was his final torment.

That afternoon he phoned her. She was speechless, her voice strangled with passionate grief. She was just discovering the first labour of love, which is to learn to endure and remain silent, even when it seems quite impossible. You're cross with me, aren't you? said the intimate voice. This voice was her ruin and her joy. She never wanted to stop hearing it. And so she gave him his answer. No, why? she said, trying to keep it simple. I'm not going to forbid you to be married. But she would have liked to, actually, and he could tell as much, despite what she said, from the distortion in her voice. He forced a laugh. Goodness me, he said. You can't be jealous, can you? He couldn't believe she could be. He teased her kindly, through a sense of delicacy. She said nothing. Hello? he said. Are you still there? Yes, she said. I couldn't hear you for a moment, he said. I thought we'd been cut off. She became aware of herself: voracious, bewitched. Words deserted her. He realised this, and took charge. Do you love your husband? he asked. It was a false question, to which he already knew the answer, but which would serve as a premise for their conversation. Why do you ask me that? she said. Because you wouldn't divorce him even if I asked you to, he said. Would you? he repeated, simply in order to get her to say no again. No, she admitted in a wretched voice, diminished by her desire to have it all, and her fear that he might disappear. This was how men went about it, she thought. They ensnared you, and then they got on with something else. He said: I'm happy to hear it. That proves to me that you're the woman I thought. Now I'm going to tell you about something that's happened.

And he started to tell her what had happened the night before with Blanche: I don't know how, or why, but my wife decided to call off the divorce proceedings. She wants me to come back to her and our daughter. She told me yesterday evening when we left the club. He broke off, aware that she hadn't reacted yet. Would you rather not talk to me? he said. What can I possibly say? murmured Pauline Arnoult. I don't know, he said. Whatever you like. You can say anything to me. You can always tell me what's on your mind, nothing will shock me, he said with real tenderness. But she fell silent again, so he continued. Life is odd, don't you think? whispered the intimate voice. I've been hoping for this opportunity for months, to the point where only desperation made me think it was still possible. And here it is at last. Of all evenings, the one we spent together, straight after that dinner, when I really felt that I was getting to know you. His way of putting things aroused Pauline's sense of irony. Unaware of this, he carried on talking: But can you imagine I'd want to refuse my wife what she's begging me for, begging me without realising it's what I want too? He stopped for a moment, then continued. I didn't tell you this because there didn't seem any point, but I never thought the divorce was a good idea. The woman I chose to share my life with was strong, loving and sensible and I couldn't understand why she wanted to break up our family. People thought I must be crazy, blinded by unhappiness. They made me feel I must have somehow deserved it. They told me I'd have to get used to it. Do my grieving: that's the big thing, these days. He gave a bitter laugh, and then fell silent again. Pauline Arnoult was running back over his tortuous turn of phrase: that dinner, when I really felt that I was getting to know you. It had almost made her laugh. Why not call a spade a spade? That dinner when he'd seduced her. That was what had happened, though it was true that it was too late to say so now. What bad luck, to get your wife back the very day you manage to seduce another woman, she thought.

They both remained silent, each with the receiver clasped to their ear. His words had brought a lump to Pauline's throat. She was moved by his sincerity. His intimate voice had an irresistible effect on her. As a result, her feeling for this man continued to soar, despite all he'd said to her about his marriage. He said: Don't listen to other people who give you advice. They may sometimes be right. But there are so many things you can only know yourself. The love you feel for someone and, occasionally, the love you've inspired. Oh, I don't know. But I'm happy. There you are, he said. Now you know everything: there's nothing I haven't told you. I can see why you're surprised. I was too. It's a surprise I don't want to spoil for all the world. You can't begrudge me that, surely? No, she said.

At last, she'd spoken. He could tell from her voice that she had remained silent so as not to express a sadness to which she had no right. And so he spoke reassuringly to her. The tenderness he felt towards this young woman and her distress added softer notes to the already smooth timbre of his voice. Do you think it will make a difference to what's happening to us? he said, with admirable rectitude. Pauline Arnoult hadn't dared to ask this question. He, on the other hand, was a model of directness and simplicity. As though nothing could be ugly, shameful or unfitting, provided it could be said. She was grateful for this. I don't know, she said, relieved. I think you think it will, he said. And in an attempt to draw her out of her torment, he lightened his voice and said: You must be crazy. He had hoped to make her smile or laugh, but he had no luck. So he turned serious again. Did you talk to your husband about me? No, she said. You see, said the intimate voice, then don't torment yourself. You're not looking for a husband, are you? he went on, pursuing his argument. No, she said. The one you've got will do nicely, he said softly. He was laughing again. Stop laughing, she said. But she was smiling: they were flirting again.

Alas, it ended. He had finished speaking and she could think of nothing to say to him. See you soon? he said. Yes, she murmured. I'll call you, he said. I promise, said the intimate voice. Thanks, she said, in an even smaller voice. See you soon, he whispered, and hung up the phone. As the humdrum silence of everyday life returned, she burst into tears.

2

As soon as she had a moment free to daydream, she thought only of him. Her entire inner life revolved around him. It was the most amazing sentimental daydream she'd ever indulged. She felt the need to be alone, to gather her thoughts, so that she could go back over her feelings, their meeting, their walk, and all that had been said that evening. She snuggled into her memories like a kitten in a basket and rather let slide those things which weren't connected to her imaginary lover. Sometimes she was aware of the folly of these idle musings. Did other people live in this fantasy land? Couldn't she just stop thinking about him for a moment? She tried to live as she had before. But almost immediately something unexpected would bring Gilles André back to mind. She'd be driving through the part of town where he lived, or where they'd had dinner. She read about the publication of a book on angels. She wore her yellow dress. She met Blanche at school. As is true for everyone, her private world was peopled with faces linked to words. One of these words had only to pop up and bingo! the face came back too, and the whole memory attached to it, carefully woven from the threads of place, names and people. It is impossible to forget your wishes even if you wish to, and there was a long list of words which could summon a lover back into her life.

She gnawed at her secret with questions of her own. Was she a woman like all the rest? Was it degrading to dream in secret about a man who (obviously) was not her husband? Of course she had no answers to these questions. And it was only ever just another way of thinking about him. She could almost hear the murmur of his voice. She could make him repeat over again the sweet words they had spoken to each other. All the words they'd said were still there, suspended in her mind. Each time she thought of them, they flickered into life again, a perpetual humming, trapped in the sensual, velvety texture of his voice. It was quite simple: this man was under her skin. What was happening now, what had already happened, and all that she hoped would yet happen. And she dreamed of this, playing out scenes in her head where she invented his part of the dialogue too. He ate up her life. Better still, his presence was so all-consuming that it became real, and crept down her thighs, a smooth caress rippling the still surface of her being.

Gilles André had gone back to live with his wife. Was he equally captivated? In Pauline Arnoult's dreams he was. But she didn't really believe it. It wasn't possible. Men never put their life on hold for love. Love existed for them alongside whatever else they were doing, in the margins of whatever took up their time and gave them the sense they were important and indispensable to others. It was only right at the start that they insisted and persevered. After that, it was the women who embarked on huge sentimental journeys, sprinkled with tears, hopes and finally the words they found to justify their being deserted. Gilles André was living proof of this: he'd stopped coming to school altogether, he made no attempt to see her. And yet he phoned her every day, at considerable length. Needless to say, she waited for every call. She was hanging on for dear life to the end of a voice, understanding nothing, and he . . . he just let things drift.

His desire had now faltered. He had managed, through a mixture of geographic distance, and good sense, to wriggle free of the spell. He had stepped out of the field of attraction. He could even replace his original vision of her with the image of the woman as she really was: a beanpole, some might have said, a curtain rail. No boobs, no bum. In short, she wasn't that wonderful. And yet he felt connected in some way to this young woman, not just by desire. And then, going back to Blanche, he didn't feel as available as he would have needed to be. He had begun to play with the idea of something other than an affair: a complex and total friendship. He began to try to create it. It wasn't easy: passion deplores anything which is not passion. With a little patience she might follow him, Gilles André thought. And so he phoned her. He stuck to the intimate voice. Pauline was ensnared in the web of whispers and laughter he had spun about her.

I'm lost in a dream. What about you? Do you think of me sometimes? Maybe if she'd dared to question him he could have answered: Yes, I think of you very often. So, they thought of each other. He: very often. She: the whole time. There the difference lay. If he had been being really sincere he could have said: there was a moment when it was a dream, but then life had reclaimed him, and there was just a trace of it left. He managed to live without her perfectly well, but he needed to know she existed. He needed to be sure that she was there, that she was loving and gentle.

A part of his inner life was quite given over to this woman. He made time to talk to her. He listened to her at length on the phone. He sensed she was trembling; he tried to make her laugh. He felt incredibly close to her. He occasionally felt desire for her and wondered if the desire would last. He no longer felt the need to have her as his mistress. But could he bring himself to end it altogether? He didn't have the heart. And was there any real reason to? Because she was unhappy? He wasn't aware of her suffering. He didn't want her to suffer. He phoned her so she wouldn't suffer, so she would have no doubt that they were indissolubly linked. But she wanted more. She had dithered about initially, but now she wanted him, all of him. Whereas he, who had suffered the first rejection, was now free to take things entirely at his leisure.

3

And so they spoke every day. Their closeness survived the physical separation. But they experienced it differently. He was happy that she existed, she was exasperated. Her yearning had been converted into words, waiting, thoughts, tears and desire. And all this at the end of a telephone line. When can I see you? she begged. And each time he replied: Soon. But still they didn't meet. Strange as it may seem, they had not seen each other since the night of the clandestine dinner. I'd so love it if we could have dinner again together, she would say. Soon, he would reply. And with each day that passed she wove a little more of the cloth of her fevered anticipation. He remained deaf to her sad entreaties. He wanted to let her be, and not rush. I've got a lot of work on, he said. I don't have time. You always say the same thing, said the young woman. I'm telling you the truth, he replied. He was the more sensible of the two. He was thinking of the child she was carrying, the husband she slept next to at night, his reunion with his own daughter. He thought too much to abandon himself to passion. She was utterly bewildered. No one's going to find out, she said. I know no one will find out, he said.

He was happy. The bitterness had gone from his life. Not a day went by when he wasn't able to kiss his daughter, and sometimes he even felt as though his wife was truly in love with him. Professionally, the horizon was cloudless: he was praised for his inventiveness, his courtesy, his intelligence. He was a shrewd maker of useful friendships, and earned a lot of money doing something he loved. Towards the end of each afternoon he telephoned Pauline Arnoult, and listened to the melancholic little laughs and the desire of the woman he'd enchanted. Why do you never want to see me? she would say. Are you scared of me? she asked. She thought she must have frightened him off by revealing the turbulence of her desire. Why should I be scared? he replied. This was where she felt she didn't understand. Was there anything to understand? He was a lover who was simply biding his time, prolonging the period of courtship, examining his own desire. But why have you changed so dramatically? she asked eventually. I haven't changed, he said. You know very well you have, she said. But he would never admit anything. We will meet, he would say simply, with calm assurance, as though he hadn't already made this promise a hundred times. You always say that, but I never see you, she said. And from then on she was obsessed by one thing: she had to see him. Her obsession fluttered about her wildly. She could still see his smile on the night of the dinner. It was like a film running through her head.

And what about her husband in all this? Didn't he notice anything? His wife's eyes . . . sometimes his wife's eyes seemed to focus on nothing. He watched her without her knowing. Her eyes began to seem like the sea or the sky, a piece of azure blue jewellery washed by the wind and idle dreams. His wife was a great dreamer. That's what her husband thought. And Pauline was absent. She could almost hear the intimate voice, that peculiarly softened tone in which Gilles spoke to her. She took to her bed, where she could think about him undisturbed. She would wallow in her dream of him. Are you going to bed? the husband would ask. Yes, she said, slipping in between the sheets. Her thoughts alone whipped up her passion. And then it didn't matter, any man would do. Come, she would say to her husband. He would come over to the edge of the bed and bend tenderly over her, caressing her gently. She welcomed her husband with the desire she secretly felt for another, a strange mingling of actual pleasure and fantasy love. The flesh is so difficult to read. I wonder what it'll look like, he would say, meaning the unborn child. He stroked the raised dome of her belly. You're beautiful, he said. A bit fat, she replied. He shook his head at this – she wasn't. And so they proceeded along the path of intimacy, which is paved with habits of proximity, legitimate caresses, secret little words, tender gestures, all those little physical favours whose magic may vanish at any moment, and which disguise the truth of our irreducible otherness, our capacity for secrecy and stealth. You're so gentle, the husband would say to his wife. And she thought then that he too, the other one, would say the same thing, and that perhaps that was what they all said.

4

People who are deeply in love step back from the world to dream, to think of nothing else: Pauline Arnoult neglected her friends. Sara had phoned her a few times, but Pauline hadn't called her back. She knew that Sara wanted to marry Tom, and that he wouldn't ask her. Their common sufferings should have drawn them together, but Pauline preferred to be alone. Besides, she was constantly hoping for a call from Gilles. Sara bemoaned her fate as Tom's lover: I spend the night at his place, we don't sleep until dawn, we go through the whole routine, I promise you. I'm wiped out, I go straight to the office in the morning. I can hear all the women whispering, She hasn't been home, because I'm wearing the same clothes as the day before. The other day one of the editors invited me to lunch. Guess what she does? She comes out with all this stuff about Tom's various affairs. I wet myself, said Sara, I promise you, I was pissing myself. Pauline didn't know what to say to this. But Sara didn't require an answer. Apparently Blanche and Gilles have called off the divorce, she said. I was really glad to hear that. Do you know Blanche André? said Pauline. A bit, but I know her husband better, said Sara. Oh really? I didn't know that, said Pauline. He knows everyone and everything worth knowing in this town, said Sara. Pauline had gone quiet. She didn't want to hear the details. She didn't want to hear anyone's views on him. He was not to be spoken of as others were. And besides, she simply didn't want to know. On the other hand, said Sara, I think things are going really badly with Max and Eve. I've thought that for a while, said Pauline. Their rows had become increasingly frequent and public.

When Sara called she filled Pauline in on everyone's news: Melusine was in detox at a clinic. Henri dined at the club every evening. You go along, you'll see him, him and his carafe of red wine. I bet he won't give it up when Melu gets back. That really gets to me, him doing that, said Sara. Pauline had no opinion on the matter. She hardly knew

Melusine. Sara went on: Louise has had a fifth IVF treatment, and it hasn't worked, again. She's like a shadow of herself, and Guillaume's completely oblivious, said Sara. You don't know that, said Pauline, you don't live with them. Maybe he's really sweet to her. Isn't Marc back yet? asked Sara after they'd been chatting for an hour. What time was it? Pauline looked at her watch. He should be back shortly, she said. And they hung up. It was nine o'clock. Pauline didn't mind chatting at such length, because she knew that Gilles wouldn't phone then. He was with his wife. What would their evenings be like? wondered Pauline. She conjured up images, then banished them again. Marc Arnoult came home, kissed his wife. Is Theodore in bed? He went to check on him. He told her about his day. Pauline told him the gossip from the studio. . . .

Others made scenes. Why do you say you'll be back at eight o'clock if you really mean (she looked at her watch) twenty past nine? Eve was saying at that moment. Because I can't know in advance that people are going to come to see me and that it will take time, said Max. Or that the roads will be busy on the way home. She sighed. I've had it up to here, she said. I do everything round here, you're never there, you've always got meetings, lunches. I don't actually have time to have lunch myself, she said. Think of that. He waited for her to finish the list, which he already knew by heart. She screwed up her eyes in a way he knew well too. Well it seems like good timing then, he said, because I've had enough too. He was firm and resolute in a way he wasn't usually and which, when he managed it, never failed to frighten his wife. He watched as surprise mingled with fear stole across her face. We can swap if you like, he said. You can work out a way to go and earn five hundred thousand francs a year, and I'll stay home and look after the children. You wouldn't be up to it, she said. I'll learn, he said.

I should go out and find a lover, said Eve, that's what I should do. Anything to put a smile back on your face, he said. She didn't react. I wouldn't be the first. You saw Gilles and Pauline at the club the night of the fight, she said. Did you really not notice anything? she said. Nothing at all, he said. Don't drag that one up again! Didn't you notice that Pauline was all upset? she said. She screwed up her eyes again. Do you think they're sleeping together? she said. No, he said, I don't go round imagining that sort of thing. Anything's possible, I'm not saying for definite it isn't true, but it's none of my business. I hate secrets and gossip, and if they are lovers, well good for them, but it's nothing to do with me. Good for them, you say, she said. And good for Marc, while we're about it, she said. I thought Pauline looked pretty as a picture the other night at the club, he said (again taking pleasure from the thought that the compliment would annoy his wife). She said nothing. Yes, he said, there was something luminous about her, there often is, she has that way of smiling with her whole being, that's the essence of her charm. I don't know why you're all so gaga about her, said Eve. She's not that pretty and she's got eyes like a cow. You're all just jealous, said Max. How can you live like that, envying and hating each other, even your friends? We don't hate each other, said Eve. We watch each other. She thought: We learn things by studying each other. And then she remembered the romantic smile on Pauline Arnoult's face on the evening of the party at the club. She played her cards close to her chest, that one, with her icy beauty. And as for her chum, the big blond, he must be happy as a sandboy to have bagged her.

5

Did his happiness come from self-confidence? He had an affected way of asserting things on the phone, as if it amused him. She was never sure if he really believed what he said, or whether he was just trying to get a rise out of her. I don't think you really love your husband, said Gilles one afternoon. She was at home now, on maternity leave. How should you know? she said. She laughed from sheer astonishment. Because you told me, he said. I said no such thing, she said. Why would I say that, since I don't even think it? I picked it up from what you said two minutes ago, he said. He went on: You don't love your husband, you're fond of him, you feel great tenderness for him, you care about him, you're concerned for him, but it's not love. If that's not love, she said, then what is? Ah! he said. It would take too long. Love isn't those things, but it may contain all those things. So you are lacking something, or at least (he corrected himself) I got the feeling you were. And what would that be? she said merrily, insistent but (he thought) not in the least bit annoyed, as though she had accepted – recognised – what he was saying to be the truth. I ought to bear in mind when I say these things who it is I'm saying them to, he said. Go ahead, she said. You have my full attention. He gave her a seductive smile, which she picked up in his voice despite the distance between them. She pulled at the handset and lay down on the bed, so as to enjoy the full naughtiness of their conversation in comfort. The intimate voice made her languorous. He said: I think it's something to do with sacrifice. When she didn't reply he continued: You aren't prepared to make any sacrifices for your husband. You live your own life, you do your designs, you doggedly pursue what you want. You take about as much notice of him as a sock, he said. He was laughing.

She loved hearing his laugh. That's not fair, of course I care for him, she protested. It was virtually a formality. Then suddenly she realised that it was exactly as he said. You're very sure of yourself, she said. I know you very well, he said. You are naked before my eyes. She didn't take him up on this. There was a long silence. She even loved sharing silences with him.

She said: Have you ever been really sure you loved somebody? Is anyone ever certain? I always have a slight doubt, because I can see that when it comes to conjugal love, I'm as concerned about my own pleasure as I am about my husband's happiness. There's so much self-interest and selfishness hidden behind our feelings, that I wonder if it's really a question of love. That's not the real issue, he said. You're so sure of yourself, she said. I do it to annoy you, he said. But I understand what you're saying, you need your husband, and that compromises your notion of disinterested and altruistic love. You're right to be concerned, said the intimate voice – which had re-emerged, along with the seductive smile – because it's true, you don't really love your husband. She was now laughing openly. But it's not your fault, he said. That's what you were brought up to expect, that you'd form a partnership with someone. That's what your relationship is, it's a business with outgoings and receipts which has produced two children thanks to the efforts of two complementary individuals. Because none of that is love, he said again. What about you? she said. Do you love your wife? No, he said. I'm with her pretty much the same way you're with your husband. Have you ever really loved a woman? she asked. No, he replied. No? she repeated, laughing. What about me? she said. Yes, he said, of all the women I've known, you're the most in love. They both burst out laughing, because what he was saying was: You love me. He was telling her as though it was something she didn't know and he did. But she wasn't prepared to let him get away with it that easily. You shouldn't go thinking that, she said. You may get under my skin sometimes, but it's only a physical attraction. That's where you're wrong, he said. I've already told you: it's different with you and me, and it's not sexual. Why was he repeating this? Again she wanted to object: Of course it is. But she said nothing, happy not to keep a score, of progress or regression, of the passing days, of what she had or hadn't got, happy simply with the words he'd said, his confidence in her, their complicity. I don't have what I have with you with anyone else, said the intimate voice. I don't talk to anyone else about the things you and I talk about, she said. I should hope not, he said, nastily. And he said goodbye abruptly, saying, 'Bye, a word he often used, and which struck her as almost brutal, no doubt because if it had been up to her she would have liked never to have to hang up the phone and be cut off from the searing heat of his voice. Phone me, she implored sometimes, in a low voice. A voice can hold things just as a body can. It can enter deeper inside you than a man's sex. What can a voice do? wondered this woman in love. A voice can inhabit you, lodge in the pit of your stomach, in your chest, right by your ear, and nag away at that part of you that so badly needs love, stoke it, whip it up as the wind whips up the sea. Am I in love with a voice? she wondered, suffering.

6

His words reached down deep into the heart of her, like plants submerged in a lake, invisible but there none the less, stirred by the currents in the water, ever denser with time, the fronds growing ever thicker and closer to the water's surface. His words lay within her like tangled branches, creating hidden structures in her mind, a secret, sunken framework: Of all the women I know, you're the most in love. The best thing about you isn't your beauty, it's your temperament. I don't have what I have with you with anyone else. You don't love your husband, you think you do but you don't. You have a partnership. It's not your fault, that's the way you were brought up. His words danced hypnotically inside her head. What was the best thing about her? Yes, their relationship was unlike any other, that was quite true. Did she really not love her husband? True, some evenings he got on her nerves, just by being there. Was that a sign? Had she once loved him, or had she just been deluding herself? A partnership? Well, she'd never leave the partnership, there was no way she'd ever divorce. That's what you were brought up to expect. How could he know all these things, when it was all news to her?

Don't talk about me with anyone, he said. I don't want anyone to know we talk. Why? she said. I told you, I like secrets. That's how I first discovered love, in total secrecy. You believe in secrets? she said. I believe in my secrets, he said. It seems to me all secrets get betrayed sooner or later, said Pauline Arnoult. As if they all one day find the person to whom they must be told. Don't they say a secret's something you only tell one person at a time? she said. Could you tell just one person at a time what you feel for me? he said. He sounded very serious – in a way that struck her as excessive, particularly as the seriousness was basically a question of inflating what she felt for him, taking it for granted, even, since he, and not she, had brought it up. But instead of denigrating him and poking fun, she surrendered yet once more to the caress in his voice, wildly exaggerated though it was.

She said: No, I could never tell anyone. Well then, there you are, he said, spiteful in his happiness. I knew this man, she said, who was always cheating on his wife, and when I told him I thought he was mean never to try and hide it he said: If it's a secret it isn't love. And if it isn't love it's impossible. I suppose what he meant was that if it's love then it's too strong, too involving, too devastating to stay hidden, she said. I expect that's what he meant, he said. I can't really tell since I wasn't there. So? she said. What do you think? Maybe he was right, he said, without giving it much thought. How it pained her to hear him say this. It was as good as if he'd said: I don't love you. With you and me it isn't love. Which is indeed what he thought. He said: With you and me I'm not sure what it is. He'd said this to her the very first evening. He hadn't changed. They were connected, but he couldn't quite say by what. He felt some desire for her, true, and that first evening he had even felt a great desire. But there was something else cutting across his desire. A deep tenderness. The sense that they were secret twins. This woman was a sister, she was out of the same mould. He'd never met anyone so like himself. And so he wouldn't let himself make her his mistress.

And yet that was what she wanted now. Perhaps she also simply wanted to establish his indifference. Since she had no idea what he really thought, since there was also this virile drive in him, pushing him towards her, she found herself bewitched with desire. She longed to be touched and loved. How much did he really want her? To what extent was he holding himself back? He wasn't actually holding back, he was simply dithering, he was savouring a kind of connection which he'd never known before, and he had all the time in the world. Would this attraction towards her last? he wondered. He left it to Blanche to take their daughter to school. He made no effort to see Pauline Arnoult again. She wanted to see him: he detected the fervour of a woman in love in her voice. But her entreaties fell on deaf ears. He kept himself distant, busy stoking the conjugal flames and disposing of a young mistress he was tired of. But he wouldn't let her forget him. He too was weak. He never tired of loving women. I need it, he would tell her later. He phoned her. I'm not disturbing you? What are you doing? Have you had a good day's work? You're sad? I don't believe it. Have you done any drawing today? I'm glad to hear it. You mustn't just sit around doing nothing. That's not your style, never will be. He basked in the pleasure of their phone conversations. He never talked to her about other people, always just about her, about himself when she asked, and above all about the two of them, face to face, two months back, and today, about what they would be tomorrow, about their unique and all-consuming relationship, et cetera. Love wants to hear itself talked about. He was in ecstasy. He laughed with her. In short, he made life joyful. You do such interesting things. What me? Oh, I'm fine. What are you wearing? And while their conversation lasted she remained ever exquisite, ever ardent; the minute she'd hung up she was hopelessly despondent. She was like water over a flame, gradually coming to the boil.

VII

In Bed

I

And so in the end it happened. They met up again. Two or three times, in bistros. These brief lovers' meetings meant so much to the young woman. She loved the bantering conversations which ended in languorous proximity. On these occasions it didn't really matter what she said. Her big blue eyes smiled constantly. And when she laughed, the rows of pearl appeared between her lips. What a picture of gracious youthfulness. And he had made a resounding conquest of this image. She was in full romantic swing. The heart was a dream-making machine. How could he have forgotten that? And so he thought of her. It was odd, this way they had of proceeding in opposite directions. She was walking towards the fire, he had turned his back on it. He had well and truly recovered his senses. She no longer had the same effect on him as before. The second time you look at someone, the purity of their face is less striking, and the slightest fleeting imperfection can disappoint. He found her paler. Of course it was her pregnancy that was tiring her. But this weariness increased her sensuality. She was adamant she wanted to sleep with him. Okay, he said to himself, why refuse her what he stole from so many other women? Yet still he hesitated. She seemed to take everything so seriously. He no longer felt quite the same urge to touch her. Perhaps he hoped that way to keep her longer. For ever, even. Who can say? It was different with her, and he didn't want her to suffer because of him. He had begun to be more fond than desiring. But she seemed to have spring fever. Hadn't he hoped she would develop this ardour for him? He'd courted her: he felt responsible. And so he gave in. It was in September. It was raining the whole time, it was cold. He invited her to his place. Theoretically this was for her sake, not his. He wanted to make her happy, he wanted to put an end to the affront of rejecting a woman who was offering herself. He asked her round to make love to her. As it turned out, things worked out very differently. The moment he put his hand on her, he knew it was a mistake, that he was actually sheltering the flame of her torment, enclosing it, as if in a holy shrine.

She arrived at his house. He opened the door to find her wearing the same red cloth coat which had once so bewitched his imagination. But that was all that was left, the red coat and the memory of his rapture. The image itself was dead, and he would never again recapture that first glimpse of her. Luckily she had no idea that visual impressions could be so fickle. A black woollen hat covered her head and brow, and her blonde hair showed round the edges, gently brushing against her cheeks. Don't stand there, he said. Come on in. Her face was white and tense, the face of a woman who knows she has been outwitted by fate. Her heart was beating very fast. She could do nothing to restrain this mad impulse within her. She was frozen at the very source of feeling, the point from which it all flowed, in the small of her back, the curve of her spine. Her racing heartbeat drenched those parts of her body which always moisten when that string, alert to disaster and delight, begins to vibrate, that element buried deep in the flesh which senses those things greater than the flesh itself. The thing which, through suffering and ecstasy, connects us to our natural gift for self-negation and ultimately to the fellowship of death. Here stood a woman in the grip of the mysterious forces of attraction and fear, thinking she was grasping happiness, when she was perhaps simply the victim of a fleeting illusion. She had longed so much for this moment that now it had almost come too late. It seemed so unfair, absurd even: that just when you had ceased to really want it, the moment of apotheosis should come along and disturb your new-found peace of mind. This was what had happened to Pauline Arnoult. Her desire had been just about to falter. This man was manipulating her. She could now almost think this without it really hurting. She was getting used to not seeing him. It wasn't killing her. Life was beautiful again, now that the shadow of her love had begun to lift from the scene. And so, just as she became resigned, he phoned to set up a lovers' meeting. Had he guessed she was on the point of admitting defeat? Or was he just yielding to her feminine entreaties? She was offering herself on a plate. He couldn't possibly say no: pretty women can count on the fingers of one hand the number of men who resist. But Pauline Arnoult had no idea he was thinking this. At last she had pinned down her lover. That was what she believed.

The lover looked at her. Are you all right? he asked, concerned at her pallor and unable to forget, when faced with her swollen form, that she was pregnant. She said nothing, as though she was completely dazed. Had she really thought she could just come and sleep with a man in his house while his wife was out? Display herself, naked and pregnant, just to satisfy a desire? She was discovering how far one could surprise even oneself. Give me your coat and come and sit down, he said. She wanted to keep her coat. I'll wait till I've warmed up a bit, said the young woman. The heating hadn't come on in the flat yet. He apologised. It's so cold for September, she said. You're not all right, he said unhappily. I'm just intimidated, she murmured with a lovely smile. He wanted to be nice to her, and he squeezed her arm through the coat. He thought she might burst into tears, her smile and her whole face looked so distraught. She had been turned upside down. She could have said to him: I've come from the edge of despair, I've done nothing but wait for you, imagining this moment, and now it's here I'm afraid the reality will spoil it. Tell me truthfully it's as important for you as it is for me. But how could she say that? She'd look ridiculous, like some tragic actress with grand illusions. She realised this. But it was still what she felt. And she couldn't say it. Certain phrases can't be brought into the open, but stay crouched at the bottom of a woman's heart, oppressing and poisoning her. And so, lovesick as she was, she stood there in front of him, admitting neither hopes nor expectations. All she would tell him was that she was strangely afraid. When I'm getting ready to meet you I feel scared, she said. My stomach feels all knotted up, like before some kind of ordeal. What am I scared of? she said. Genuine astonishment led her to ask the question out loud. I don't know, replied the intimate voice. All at once he had become almost insignificant, banal even, because he was confronted with a kind of desire which was itself banal. She refused to recognise this, it was something she couldn't accept, and she continued to pursue her own thoughts. I'm worried you won't like me, she said. I'm scared of your fickleness. I'm scared that what we had has vanished, and yet it did once exist. The greatest happiness is so close to intense fear, she said. She wondered if he was listening, because once she finished he whispered: One of my friends is due to drop by. I told him I might go out for dinner, but I don't want him to see the light on if he does come. None of which had anything to do with what she had just said, but it was far more important to him just then. Come with me, he said, and took her into his office. Not a single lamp was lit. She stood there in silence, her back slightly arched, fresh from despair and anticipation. You look nice, he said. As he said this he stepped up close to her and his lips began to brush against her forehead. She could tell he was moved by her, but only in a way that was habitual for him in these situations – there was an underlying lack of seriousness. If it had been otherwise, the paralysing fever of anticipation would have turned the occasion into a fiasco. The moment demanded that Gilles André be more frivolous than overwhelmed. But she was not a man, and these were things she didn't understand, and she contrived not to think he might be shallow.

Standing before her and her long red coat, he kissed her eyes, her neck, the sides of her nose, tenderly removed her hat and breathed in the smell of her hair. He was slow and gentle. She returned his kisses. The silence of a lovers' embrace. He took her head between his hands and feasted his eyes on her unblemished face. It's been so long, whispered the intimate voice. She melted in his hands, totally surrendered, not to him but to the affinity between them, to the prayers and solemn vows, the delicate movements and forces which refresh and transform us, cause us now to open, now to close. I'm scared, she whispered. What of? he said. Of you, she said. She thought for a moment. I'm scared that afterwards I'll find I love you, she said. You already think you do, he said, laughing. She was too far gone to take offence. Besides, it wasn't at all clear why he was laughing. Perhaps it was joy at being there with her. Or pleasure at the thought that he was loved. Had he ever been this sure of a woman's love? And yet how cruel it was of him to laugh. It wasn't as though he didn't realise what she felt, he took pleasure from the fact that she was so much more in love than he was. That was what lay behind his high spirits. Do you not think you love me? she retorted, which pulled him up short. But preoccupied as he was with this friend who might drop by and disturb them, he wasn't really listening to her, and didn't catch the question. Do I not think what? he asked, after a silence. And she whispered, wretched, pitiful even: That you love me. No, he breathed, with his lips to her ear, kissing her. He didn't want to tell her he loved her. What would be the good in that? And anyway, could he really decide a thing like that, so quickly, in the heat of desire? He began to kiss her again. His mouth was extraordinarily soft and moist. One by one he undid the golden buttons. Once her coat was open, his hands slid inside and found her flesh. The hunger in her was instantly satisfied. It had happened, the thing which had so obsessed her. At last, she thought, he'd caught her, she was his. She let him invade her, as a stretch of land lets in the sea.

His thoughts were vague. He was doing what he'd longed to do from the first time he saw her at school. Things were under way. He could sense that she was full of emotion. He wanted to give her pleasure, he wanted to show her: This is what you're capable of, I knew it from the start, and now, thanks to me, you know too. He knew how to go about it, a movement here, a touch there, a caress, a kiss, and his hands upon her, a woman so gentle it was pure pleasure, even if nothing we do is ever completely harmless, even if there was a danger he'd damage her a little. He kissed her. His hands settled in the crook of her back, and held her. From a deep silent well within her, she felt the approach of the greatest release of pleasure. She collapsed beneath his kisses. This man, who had deliberately seduced her, now refused to say he loved her. But for just this brief moment his desire was as good as his love.

He had his own special way of kissing her. His lips fluttered over her belly. For him, the only uncommon aspect of the situation was that she was pregnant. He'd always made love to other men's wives, but not in the sacred period of motherhood. You're not all that big, he said. He held her breasts in his hands. Even though you're pregnant, you're a little thing, a slip of a girl. He said: They're like cherries. She was laughing. A crucial knot had come undone. She let herself fall into his embrace.

This was what she'd come for. But how could she tell him that? She'd pretended she'd come round for a chat. What a silly idea. A chat. The intimacy of words was hardly going to satisfy the woman he'd awoken. Since the night of the famous dinner, she'd been weaving this dream, a dream of his hands upon her. Her sleeping and her waking were both lit up by the precious sparkle of his desire. It was impossible to imagine that the rest of the world, everything that might be said, done, delighted in, all the other people with whom these things might be said, done or delighted in, had vanished, eclipsed by the radiance of frustrated desire. Why, she had wondered, when their fate was so clear, had nothing happened all this time? Pauline Arnoult had completely lost her bearings. The implacable patience of the world around her had stoked the fire. She wouldn't admit to this overriding obsession with the physical embrace. Even so, it had to happen. And now, head thrown back, her face was radiant, the face of a woman running to meet what she has so long gone without. Is it possible to avoid the consequences of your gestures?

Pregnant to the gills and stark naked, murmured the intimate voice. Are you shocked? she said, drawing away from him. Not at all, he said, and grasped hold of her firmly, sitting her down on top of him. Desire had reasserted itself. He smiled as he looked her over. You are pretty, he said. You seem surprised by that, she said. It surprises me because it's not the thing I love about you, he said. His saying this made her feel attractive and more than just attractive. This man had a way of making actions weigh less heavy, as though he'd known instinctively, with a kind of pagan certainty, what conscience and purity would look like, once stripped of the ornaments draped over them by those in authority. At least, this was what she believed, since it had never occurred to her to see him as a libertine. He was the one who brought her liberty.

There was nothing left for them but action. They had nowhere else to go. They were through with talking, now they would touch. She felt desire like a spontaneous thrust into her damp flesh, a moist invasion which she would not resist. I'm afraid of hurting you, he said. But it was too late to draw back from the hot clutch of this transfigured woman. His normal sensitivity was heightened by the feeling of silk between his hands, drawing him into her body. Instinct took command of his hands. I'm not hurting you? he said again, though already he had lost the power to resist. You're not hurting me at all, she said, in a voice which was scarcely more than a murmur.

They both fell silent. They had never been so close before. She felt the tracing of his fingers on her. At his touch she discovered the outer limit of her body. He was drawing her shape, so that she too could perceive it. You're on fire, he said. She had no words now. She was being shaken by a deep shudder, and silent tears seeped from the corners of her eyes. For her sake, he sought the gentlest possible rhythm, one which throbbed with tenderness, and which may in the end be a frustration, leaving the other begging for the final thrust of violence to achieve pleasure.

He found a way to join their separate bodies in the natural rhythm of a dance. She followed him. So much so that he was amazed by their instant affinity. It was at this moment that it occurred to him that they had been lovers in another life. They knew one another, they had always recognised each other. Everything was simple, immediate, given. He was in tune with her: he could sense what she felt, he was woven into the inner constellation which was coming into being. She gave herself to him. He was disturbed. How could he yet again pretend not to notice that she was in love with him? He wished he were an angel: tender and strong. He moved in and out, happy, but cowardly, murmuring her name, Pauline. She was carried away by the flowing succession of minute gestures and emotions. She drifted away. He heard a silence open up, following upon a sigh. And then the person she had been disappeared. Her spirit narrowed to her obsession and to that soft, slow, continuous pounding. And gradually she sensed, as she entered the fullness of this eclipse, that she was nothing but a cauldron coming to the boil. She had no words for it, no need of any. She was the liquid part of those flames. Her blood was alive. Her skin was soft. Her white cheeks and brow had flushed red. The haughty beauty had turned into a melting goddess.

Her face was a wreck, devastation beneath a mask. She was tousled. You're such a gentle lover, whispered the damp lips between kisses. This time she said nothing. Now it was his turn. She made small lascivious noises, but was inscrutable in the whiteness of her naked, swollen form, which he glimpsed only in part as occasionally he opened his eyes. He tried to look at her but his eyelids kept closing. His body was more conscious than his mind. He slipped in and out of her hot, juicy flesh, moaning, kissing, his hands running free, joined to her by his extremities.

The bodies of Marc Arnoult and Gilles André had nothing in common. Pauline was certainly aware that the two experiences were quite different. This might have led her to feel regret. But love justified everything. She was in that state of wonderment and love which wipes out all sense of wrongdoing or regret. She kissed her impertinent lover. They wallowed in the most basic of sensations, those which teach us wordlessly what it means to be one moment on the inside and the next on the outside, inhabited, then empty again. She was at once mother and lover and molten splendour. He was gliding like a swimmer. The life force in him connected with the throbbing inside her. A woman's heat had invaded his manly body. He kissed her wildly. His kisses were true and ardent – they came from gratitude. And later, smiling, a little sleepy, her arms folded over her breasts, gazing at her rounded belly, even laughing at last, she once more confirmed his sense of what it was to be a woman: to be made for love.

But she was aware that he could have acted just the same with another woman. She said: What you love is women in general, femininity. Not me in particular. He smiled. You're wrong, he said. Every experience is different. But you have had other experiences, she said, with regret. Yes, he said, breathing out heavily. He didn't want to lie to her. That's exactly right: femininity in all its forms attracts me. For a little while, he said. How happy he seemed. There was something brazen in his smiling face. His joviality made her shudder a little. She was already devastated by the thought that she would have to leave him, and here he was, laughing. He could see she was unhappy. He held her tight, saying nothing. She wept, without explaining why, stopped herself, stayed close in his embrace, and he ran his hands up and down her arms, which were plump from her pregnancy. There was nothing he could do for her. Their coupling revealed the difference between them. For a second time he was ensnared by her hot, welcoming body; but this time with sadness, a sadness he could not share with her. Because now he knew, simply from seeing the love in her shining eyes, that she would not leave this bed intact, whereas he would, though he did not know why it should be so.

Were women required to pay a price, to make tribute to the splendour of Eros? Violence, the utmost tenderness, indecency and the low whispers of love – did these all necessarily leave wounds? Was it a curse of the flesh or something sinister, invented by men, which meant that the acts of love carried out with this woman should increase her attachment, her transport, and with them the pain of separation? As though the passage of the body through this place which was, after all, the cradle of life, must sow a seed of love. As though the birth of children, as well as the pumping of a man's sex, opened up in a woman in love whole new pastures of hope. The rewards of attachment. Did it come naturally to them, or did each generation of mothers teach their daughters to hope and wait? All this, in contrast to the flippancy of their lovers. She would not leave the bed intact, she would leave it newly burdened. As she left, he would see that she had changed. She would need him now. He would sense her welcoming this new passion, which, unlike the insubstantial ardour which had overwhelmed her up until now, would be as slow and patient as love. He knew this the second his body merged with hers a second time, like a looter who has just discovered the secret of beauty. He would have to answer to her for what he'd done, and he wouldn't be able to, and would have to watch as a tide of desolation spread across her face. But once she was again moving in his arms, he forgot all this and began to kiss her passionately.

The buzzer at the front door made her jump. He, however, had been listening out for it, and heard the sound of the lift coming up, and stopping at this floor. He put his index finger to his lips, with a smile. Ssshhh, he said tenderly. The young woman was sensitive to every nuance. His gentleness filled her with bitterness. It meant nothing to be tender, it was just the way you acted at a time like this when you were in bed with your mistress. They waited. The buzzer sounded twice more, then they heard the lift door open again. They lay there, naked, side by side, hearts pounding with fright. They were shrouded in silence and gloom. He's gone, he whispered very quietly. She could feel his breath against her cheek. She wanted more of him. She wanted to prolong this moment. She had lost all reason. Were you frightened? he asked. Very, said Pauline Arnoult. I loved it, he said. I didn't, she replied.

He looked at her as though trying to work out how, as a result of this new intimacy, his own view of her might have changed. What image did he have of her – false or true? Had he now transformed her into someone else? He said: The first time I saw you, I couldn't take my eyes off your face. I certainly noticed you were looking at me, she said. And what did you feel? he asked, interested. Nothing at the time, she said. I think I was just flattered. I liked it: it was a nice way to start the day. It was only afterwards, when I thought about it again, and you carried on. . . . What? he pressed her. She smiled, as though she had made up her mind to tell him nothing. He said: I want to know exactly what a woman feels when someone really looks at her. I can't imagine it, he said. But you know it works, she said. And he was relieved to see her laugh. So then tell me, he said. And he repeated the question: What did you feel when I lusted after you at school? I don't know if I can explain it, she said. Try, he said. I've forgotten, she said. I know you're lying, he said. No, I promise you, she said. Well make an effort then, he said. She made another effort, for him. And she said: To begin with it bothered me. Bothered you? How? he said. It troubled me, she said. It made me feel uneasy. And then? he said. And then I was glad. It was nice, and I got used to it. Used to being admired? he said. That's right, she said. Were you sure it was admiration? he said. I thought you must fancy me, she said, turning red. You were right to think that, he said. She reflected for a moment, with the question hovering on her lips: What about now? Do you still fancy me? And since she wanted to ask the question, she must already know the answer: his initial rapture had ebbed away. He said: So what happened when you realised that? She went on: It was as if life began to sparkle again. As if something was going to happen, and I knew it would be really nice. I needed you to look at me. Did you tell your husband? he asked. Of course not. Why did you say life sparkled *again*? he said. She seemed to think this was obvious. Well, because . . . – how should she put it? – because loving the same man for a long time, and falling in love with someone, are two quite different things. Did it feel like falling in love? he said, in mild astonishment. It seemed like a possibility, she said (somewhat vexed). Because you fancied me too? he said. It must have been that, she said. At any rate, I thought you were all right, and as I said, I enjoyed being looked at like that. She said: Meeting someone new is a big deal: you don't do it every day. And you felt you were meeting someone new? he asked. Does that surprise you? she asked, disappointed that he should ask the question. No, he admitted, I felt something important was happening too. She said: Something magnetic. You could put it that way, he said. And then? he said, with a note of happy triumph in his voice. What next? What do you mean, what next? she said. What went through your pretty head after that? He laughed openly. Nothing, she said. I just hoped you'd be there when I went to school. Crafty, he said.

What about you? she said. What was going on inside your little head? He knew that she had turned the tables on him, and he answered the question. At first I tried not to think about you. But I saw you too often for that. So? she said. So I let myself slide, he said. I tried to find some way to get to talk to you, he said. She smiled, as though she remembered it quite well. At first I thought I might ask your son over to play, he said. They laughed. But my daughter didn't seem to want to oblige me by being keen on your Theodore. I had to think again, he said. To find some way of getting close to you, murmured the intimate voice. She was never happier than hearing him talk about them. I didn't think you'd dare, she said. I thought it would be impossible, he said. He laughed, and his laughter was more genuine than hers, because it was becoming clear now that it had been a kind of ambush and that he was a past master in such things. And so you took the plunge, she said, teasingly. Yes, he admitted, I had no choice. I had no choice but to try my luck. I admired you for that, she said. I respected it. Really? he said. Why? Because I've never made the first move with a man, she said. Haven't you? he said. I couldn't possibly, she said. You only think you couldn't, he said. You've never needed to do it. That's true, she said, but I'm a shy person anyway. You're not really, he said. I don't think you're shy. I'm not with you, she said. Do you know why that is? he asked. It was a genuine question. No, I don't know, she said. I just feel at ease with you. Me too, he said. Right from the start. The phrase seemed to please her. But that wasn't why he'd said it. He'd meant it sincerely, and he was glad every time he was able to make her happy without telling a lie.

Have you ever had this kind of conversation with a woman before? she said. Don't keep asking me that, he exclaimed. For a moment he became the mature man, talking to a young woman. Because he had admonished her, she found herself admiring him, and resolved to be quiet and listen. Nothing's ever like anything that's gone before, he said. I've had relationships with loads of women, and each one was different. What about with your wife? she said. What about with my wife? he said. What are you getting at now? He smiled at her, as though at a child. She didn't know how to answer, and there was a silence. Did saying something really help to get it off your chest? This conversation had transformed her view of things. She was forced to accept that she was not the unique, unparalleled object of worship she had liked to think, but simply a woman in the bed of a polytheist. But you were the one who chased after me, she said. She wanted to get him to admit this, but he wouldn't. That's not true, he said. After I'd asked you out for dinner, I left you in peace. But the harm was done by then, she said. You wanted to go too fast, he said. You were the one who begged to come over this evening, he said. She found this attitude ungentlemanly. But all she said was: Didn't you want me to come? She spoke in a small, faraway voice. It upset him to hear her sound so fragile. Of course I did, he said. I thought it was a completely delicious idea, and you're so sensual. . . . The intimate voice, which had suddenly taken over at this point, fell away. He burst out laughing, doubtless as a release for an underlying nervousness. And for her part, she was so hurt that she felt nothing at all.

Are you going to tell your husband? he said. Never. It would just make him unhappy, she said. Yes, he said. I think I'm like you, she said, I'd prefer no one to know about us. I've developed a taste for secrets since I met you. He was happy to hear this: it made things so much easier. She was his sister, his twin. You are my secret lover, she said, pretending to make a joke of it, but it wasn't a joke at all to her. He replied swiftly, seriously: Don't get that idea. I'm not your lover, he said. This remark cut deep with her, since she understood exactly what he was saying. She shouldn't get carried away. She mustn't get over-excited. She must make quite sure she kept her feet on the ground. What they'd just done didn't make them lovers, being lovers meant a lot more than this enfolding of each other's bodies. People became lovers after many such encounters. In their case, there would be no repetition. It was as though someone had switched off the lights at the end of a party. Can you tell me where the bathroom is? she said.

They found themselves out in the street. They walked to the taxi rank in silence. She felt like she'd been crushed in a vice. You're so gentle, he said. She couldn't think of anything to say. She gave him a kiss and got into the taxi. Thank you, he said, and gave her a long, fond look of farewell. Yes, he was finishing it. Without a pang of regret. He was smiling happily. What greater mental torture could there be than to say goodbye to a man who has enticed you into a world of love and pleasure, only to leave you there? What kind of denial was that? She shuddered. He leaned in towards her, slipped his hand behind her neck and kissed her tenderly. See you soon, he whispered. She was quite sure he was lying, though he was not aware of it himself. She had begun to turn it all over in her mind, while he was simply savouring every moment.

2

And she lied, too. She made up her lie as an oyster makes its pearl, in silence, growing around her hidden, painful secret. I'm not asleep, said her husband, as she came in and made her way silently to their room. He was already in bed, but he was lying awake in the darkness. I was waiting for you, he said. Did you have a nice evening? he asked considerately. Yes, she said, very nice. Where were you? he asked, with no trace of either suspicion or authority, simply out of interest. She told her lie quite serenely, no awkwardness, her face as perfectly composed as ever. And then she went off to get ready for bed.

When she came back into the bedroom he was still awake. She'd been hoping he'd already have dropped off. She got into the bed and curled up next to him. Have you been in bed long? she asked. Her thoughts were in turmoil, keeping her mind awake. How odd it was, she seemed to feel happy and sad at once, she had found and then lost the measure of her appetite. A while, said Marc Arnoult. He smiled, half asleep. Did he have any idea what it meant when a woman came home with a face this radiant? She took his face between her hands and greedily kissed the flesh of his mouth, already slack with sleep. It was not the same mouth, and these were not the same kisses. But her desire, by some physiological principle of persistence, was still unquenched.

What's all this? said Marc happily. He shook himself awake. The refrain ran through her head: A man has awoken me. He seized her by the waist. He undid her buttons patiently. He opened, and removed her nightdress. Aren't you tired? he asked, stroking her rounded belly. I love you, he said. I love you too, she said. While thinking: A man has awoken me, and taken nothing away from you. I'm still here. Secrecy is a casket for the preservation of happiness.

Late that night they were still talking, bodies stretched out, touching, half-dressed, as he mechanically ran his fingers over his wife's flesh. You don't mind the fact that you only sleep with me? he said. Not really, she said. I don't find many men attractive, she said. This was true. I find some of them revolting, she continued. She cited some examples among their friends. Take Philippe, for example, she said. I don't fancy him at all. She said this because Philippe was a Don Juan. Or Oliver, or Albert . . . ugh, I just couldn't. They laughed. I quite like Max, she said. But as you see, I'm not exactly throwing myself at them. Besides, she said, I don't think it would be about sex. She was lying on her back in the semi-darkness. Her belly was perfectly round. He ran his hand over the taut skin. The precious tabernacle of her womb filled him with joy. You're so beautiful, he said. And he meant it. To him, his wife was a goddess. I think what I'd like, she said, would be a kind of amorous friendship. Another love in my life, I mean, she murmured. They both laughed at the thought. Yes, he said, I think that would be nice too. The rest doesn't interest me either. Almost all his relationships with women had been long-lasting and deep. He'd never had a purely sexual involvement, and what he was saying to his wife was the strict truth. She knew this. She knew him so well that she also knew the nature of his desires. All the same, she never forgot how timorously, delicately and slowly he had wooed her, and how he had contrived it so that she had been the one to admit her love, and afterwards she thought he simply wasn't capable of taking the initiative and being pushy with a woman. He didn't want to take, but be given to, without having to ask. She kissed him. Dear, complicated Marc. So full of scruples and consideration. She'd never met a man as good as him. He had become the most precious person in her life, a sure foundation from which she could open up like a flower and expose her glorious colours. She had never doubted that he truly loved her, in the way one imagines love should be: he loved her just as she was, for what she was, and as long as she was happy, so was he. Would Marc be capable of taking up secretly with another woman? For the first time, Pauline Arnoult considered it might be possible. Who could resist the urge to fall in love? She knew now what it was all about, and how you should never absolutely count on anything. Her own infidelity made her suspicious.

It was very rare for Marc and Pauline Arnoult to be in complete disagreement. They had a genuine affinity, and when one of them got on the other's nerves, it was often because they were so similar: they were both looking for the same things, and whichever one of them was more successful in the search aroused the other's jealousy. As it happened, Marc had a secret love as well. But, curiously enough, although his potential mistress was safely divorced, and although he had known her, and desired her, for quite some time, he had never been unfaithful. Not because he thought it would be wrong to, but because the situation seemed likely to lead to complications, and he didn't want to make the woman suffer. It was as though he was aware of what Gilles André chose to forget: the legacy of secret acts. And so he stayed faithful to his wife out of love for the woman who could have been his mistress. This woman had chained herself to him. She demanded to see him, confided her troubles to him, and he listened to her. It is possible to be so alone that one other person can come to mean everything in the world. And he was everything in the world to this woman. Perhaps she was waiting for him to cast himself into her arms. But he was an incorruptible soul. Do you think your husband's unfaithful? Gilles André had asked Pauline. No, she said, I'm sure he isn't. Poor chap, he'd said. Let him live his life. I do, Pauline protested. Hmm . . . Gilles André had said.

3

The next morning, the voice was on the phone. At first Pauline found this a bit corny, then she decided it didn't matter. The voice transported her into a world of romance. She gave herself over completely to these voluptuous and insinuating conversations. I haven't woken you? What are you wearing? he said. From his voice she understood that he was interested exclusively in her. I'm in my nightie, she said. What colour is it? he said. White, she laughed. She laughed like a true lover at his silly questions. Ah, you are always so fresh, he rhapsodised. You are incredibly fresh, he told her. These anodyne words reconnected her to the inexhaustible physical passion raging within her. She wanted to see him immediately. I'm alone, she said. Come and see me. You're about to have a baby, he said, teasingly. She didn't find this remotely funny.

He came. She had pleaded and wept. He had given up trying to resist. As she pleaded with him he became aware of the frenzy to which he had brought her. She was tired and alone, and after what had happened the previous day she had begun to indulge in all sorts of fantasies. I might die in labour, she said. She would say anything to keep him by her. He smiled sadly, but did not know what to say. Feeling ridiculous, she continued anyway, declaiming: Thou hast committed fornication – but that was in another country; and besides, the wench is dead. Then, more seriously: What would you do if I died? He said simply: I would be very sad. For a woman it was an inadequate response. He tried to bring her back to reason. You're not really afraid of dying in labour? said the intimate voice. Her heart leapt to hear his tender tone. No, she said. But perhaps I ought to be. You hear so many dreadful stories. Giving birth isn't a casual thing. She laughed with a sort of spiteful bitterness. Suddenly she was in the women's camp, her voice changed, distorted with rage. All the caresses in the world, even the feeble penetration of the body by the male organ, are nothing compared to the disembowelling of childbirth. As she said this, her face was racked with despair. I should have known, he thought. He tried to say so gently but she wasn't listening. Over and over she said: Nothing, nothing, nothing. It was a way of belittling what he'd done, as though, on a woman's path through life, there was always this bitter struggle between love of man and love of children. What could he possibly say in answer to this lesson, which she had every right to give? He said nothing, and was dismayed.

She came and took him by the hand, pulling him towards the bed. It was the bed she shared with her husband, but they didn't remark on this. She guessed that this was something he would never have the audacity, the indecency even, to do. She realised this, perhaps from his glance towards the bed, or an imperceptible step away from it, or because she recalled how he had taken her into his study. What was he thinking? Impossible to say. She looked up at him. He was undressing as though there was no problem; he was relaxed, with a smile that was neither one thing nor the other. And then he stepped towards her. She had the distinct impression he was forcing himself to do what is expected of a man in this situation, but that in fact he didn't really want to. He lifted her white nightshirt. Her belly seemed ready almost to burst, the skin was so taut it was almost transparent. The fine network of blue veins were the only visible sign of the slender thread that keeps us intact. Just above the fleece of her sex, red snakes ran through the distended flesh. I'm really frightened of hurting you, he said.

Do you know, Eve Mortreux asked me if I knew you, he said, just as he was leaving. I forgot to mention it to you. She seemed to be implying something. You didn't say anything to her, did you? he asked. Nothing, said Pauline. I never speak to her except to say hello or goodbye. What did you say to her? she said. Guess, he said. I took Oscar Wilde's advice. I said: Of course I know her. I've always loved other men's wives. I adore you, said Pauline Arnoult. You've got such a nerve. And what did she say when you said that? she asked. The same as you've just said, said Gilles. That you had a nerve? Exactly, he replied.

I really must go now, he said. Are you okay? he asked, since she had gone very quiet. Yes, said her eyes and her smile. It would be a long time before they met again. He suspected as much; she feared it. He knew himself well enough to guess that this would be the course he'd take. She thought that the birth of the child would get in the way of her love affair for a while. But none of us is clairvoyant, and we choose not to believe in the signs we pick up. And so she continued smiling. But she would only hear and speak to him. Their lives would be truly separate. He had no wish to cause the kind of ravages he'd seen in her today. And attraction, once it was satisfied, was not insurmountable. How is it that men, who can sow the seeds of love simply by desiring something, then manage to live perfectly well without it?

4

What did the whole thing mean? Pauline Arnoult didn't manage to get much beyond asking herself the question. She remained in an oblivious state of pleasure. She was happy, she was proud. She had two men in her life. Her life had become extremely sensual. Nothing concerned her much – not the secret she kept from Marc, not the odd lie here and there, not the betrayal of his trust. She was simply full of wonder at what she felt for her lover. The depth of her love was matched by the shallowness of her virtue. It occurred to her that the man who had aroused this feeling in her was not the only one to benefit from it: it increased her fondness for her husband, as well as her enthusiasm for life. With the one man she found day-to-day contentment in a relationship of mutual tenderness, with the other these extraordinary moments of deep emotion, of love. It was thanks to this fulfilment that she was able to keep her secret. People say that women love to gossip, that secrets always burn a hole somewhere. But Pauline Arnoult never breathed a word.

Out of superstition, she changed the sheets.

She made her way round the bed, pulling and tucking, slipping on a pillow case, lost in her thoughts. She wondered what to make of her own behaviour and of his. To have a love affair outside marriage, considering how long life was, was surely inevitable, Marc Arnoult often said. But maybe these were just throwaway words, lightly uttered, the flippant thoughts of a man with a faithful wife. Love outside marriage. It was a nice expression: no ugliness there, just a little breath of fresh air, beyond the prison of the marital vow. The thing they always thought bound to happen, because they had married young, and for life, had indeed now come to pass. Marc worried her though: he was the one who doubted the possibility of fidelity, but he was also the one who succeeded at it. She was quite certain of that. He was a man in love, and the woman he loved was his wife. She had cracked first. She was torn between two ways of looking at it: should she be appalled that she had fallen at the first hurdle? Or should she insist that erotic attraction was the most wonderful thing in the world and be thrilled to be enjoying it once more?

I know you better than anyone in the world, the lover said. This simple fact, on the other hand, did seem wrong to Pauline. By that token, her lover knew something important that her husband didn't. She was an insubordinate, sensual and secretive woman, not ashamed to be so, but ashamed that one man should know it and the other not.

I know you better than anyone in the world. He was so sure of this that he protected her from herself. After his own fashion he did love her. At least he thought he did, which can amount to the same thing in the end. He felt a sudden surge of tenderness at the thought of her sweet youth. It was a peculiar bond, and to him it seemed indissoluble. He had realised, just at the point when her desire was beginning to fully bloom, that he couldn't make her his mistress. Every woman who'd ever been his mistress had been miserable. Not her, he thought. She mustn't suffer because of him. He phoned her every afternoon. But they didn't meet again. Have you had your baby? he would say. I called you and there was no answer, and I thought, She must be at the clinic. Have you had enough of me? she would say, not listening. He could tell she was on the verge of tears. It seemed to be her role in life to wait for him.

At this point, the baby was born. It was a boy. Marc Arnoult was at his wife's side throughout the birth. But her thoughts were with the other man.

Marc was proud. With two sons, a wife who radiated an almost unreal grace, as though she were improving with age, and a thriving relationship between the two of them, he felt like a king. Married people are risk takers. What a victory, to discover you still felt something of that first careless rapture with your spouse. Thus Marc could add his pride in his family to all his other achievements. He was more proud of their harmony, of his fragrant wife and his two little boys, straight as oaks, than he was of the money he'd earned, the jobs he'd held, the decisions he'd taken, the changes he'd made, the women he'd led astray. He'd sacrificed a little money, a little worldly success, a little power and a little pleasure, in exchange for love and offspring. And others who had taken different routes were astonished by the straightforwardness of Marc's. You've got everything, Tom said to him. I've got everything, Marc said to his wife, sitting by her bedside in the clinic on the evening of the baby's birth. Even a wife who lies to you, thought Pauline. He rubbed her hand tenderly, and they both leaned over the newborn baby. I love a man who isn't my husband, Pauline said to herself, but I still love my husband as much as ever. How could she tell whether this was self-deceit? Often one love extinguishes another, but surely there were exceptional cases, exceptional loves?

The moment she got home again, she began to wait for the voice.

5

How are you? he asked. Fine, she murmured. Did it all go well for you and the baby? he said – but it was scarcely a question. She confirmed that it had. The child was adorable. His name was Arthur. She was tired, but happy. I'm happy for you, said Gilles André. I tried to call you before but there was no reply, he said. Why would that have been? She understood that he had no wish to spend his whole life on the phone. I'm so happy to hear from you, she said. But she didn't know how to kick-start the conversation. She had nothing to tell him. She was feeding and changing a baby, she rested while he slept, she went to fetch the older child from school and her husband came home in the evening. How could you go telling all that to a man you looked on as your lover? She wanted to talk to him about things she considered worthy. I don't have time to draw, she said. She hoped to elicit encouragement, arouse his interest, to be revered and cherished as she had once believed herself to be. Instead of which he said simply: You will do, eventually. Then he added: Pauline, I don't have time to talk right now. I just wanted to be sure you were all right. Lots of love to you. She whispered: And to you too. She was in utter despair. It seemed as though the whole thing was over. He was getting away. He no longer cared for her. So how long did the philtre last?

Normal life resumed: mornings and evenings, strung together like pearls. The two children had to be cared for and looked after. She gave herself to the task. She waited constantly for the phone to ring, but the phantom lover didn't call. Pauline Arnoult refused to put her infatuation behind her. The past was her present. It was breaking her heart. Conversations from the past drifted back into her mind. She felt as though they'd been playing a game, like two kittens with a ball of wool. And the wool had completely unwound. Having once imagined that she was a man's single point of focus, the object of his obsession, she was pained to find there was nothing more than ordinary affection. Marc Arnoult thought it was the baby blues. He spent more time at home, and tried to distract his wife. He sensed he was in the way. So he worked longer hours at the office. And in the evening, furtive, tender, silent, considerate, he tried to be more lover than husband. And since that wasn't really possible, he convinced himself that newborn babies took up so much of their mother's attention that their fathers were completely dispossessed.

And so, for the first time, she phoned him. She trembled as she dialled the number. Her fear of the gesture – so simple in itself – revealed the truth about her confused motivation. What would she do if Blanche answered? Would she leave a message if he was out? What would she say to him? In the end, after much hesitation, she dialled the number. It was an answerphone. At the required moment, she mumbled: It's me: Pauline Arnoult. I just wondered how . . . Then there was a click and she heard him say: How are you? She felt a mixture of pleasure and relief. I'm well, she said, and you? I'm very well, he said. Why don't you ever call me? she asked, put out by the idea that he could be well and happy without her. I'm too busy, he told her. No intimate voice there. And there was nothing she could say in reply. And so she showed her entire hand. I miss you, she said. I'm very sorry, he said. Then: You're just bored. But you'll get back to work soon and then you'll be fine. He spoke as though she was capable of living without him in her life. When can we meet? she said, distraught. Soon, said Gilles André.

Why are you so different towards me? she said, suddenly. I'm not, he said. Yes you are, she said. No, honestly, I'm really not, he said. He was quite honest. The only option left was to put things plainly, tell him straight out what was on her mind: the reverence and respect he was failing to show her. You used to phone me every day, she said. He gave a little laugh, as though he could well understand that one might enjoy being adored, and willingly delude oneself that one was. I never called you every day, he said. You're imagining it. How can you say that? said Pauline. Because it's true, he said. He was laughing. She was cut to the quick. You've changed, she said. You know perfectly well you have. Perhaps I'm a bit less attentive. I've got a lot of work on, he said, that's the only reason. Do you mean that when I met you you had more time? she said. I don't remember now, he admitted, but it must be that, if what you say is true. He said: Did I really call you every day? It was extraordinary, the way he kept coming back to the same question. She thought, and then answered in a tiny voice: Almost every day. Ah! he said. You see. How do you expect me to believe you, when you change your story? He was poking fun, she thought, in horror. He wasn't in the least bit bothered by what she was saying. She said this to him. Why should I be? he asked. I often think of you, I don't always have time to call you, that's all. She said nothing more.

Pauline! he pleaded. You must be very tired. You should rest. We'll meet soon, I promise you. She whispered: I'm angry with myself. Why? he asked, in astonishment. Because I flirted with you, she said. I was flattered by your attention, it became the most important thing, and I ended up putting you off. You must have wondered what you'd got yourself into. So you ran away. That's not true, he said. You're getting carried away now. It is true, she said. I've been incredibly vain. I suppose that's quite natural, he said. It's a weakness we all have, though I wouldn't have said it was particularly strong in you. It is, she said. And as they seemed to have exhausted this subject, she changed tack, while continuing to talk about the two of them. When I think about the conversations we had, she said, it feels like we were playing a game. Perhaps, he said. What if we were? She didn't know what to say. Then she recovered her thought. Well, she said, this is all just insincere, absurd, pathetic and cheap. She heard silence. The intimate voice emerged, enfolding her gently. I've never had what I have with you with anyone else.

And so they were back where they'd left off. She could manage to be patient, just as long as she was convinced she was unique. I'll call you soon, he said. Lies are like little excursions into the space beyond love. Sometimes Pauline Arnoult found she hated Gilles André. But never for long.

VIII

Years Later

I

It was ridiculous, but here they were again, sitting facing one another at a tiny bistro table.

She had arrived first. She had deliberately turned up late, and was annoyed to find he was even later. He had been late nearly every time they'd met. It was just a little thing, but it was telling. There was nothing she could do about it: she was bound to be the one left waiting. She felt embarrassed in this place. Her solitude seemed to attract the attention of people who were not alone. Maybe he wouldn't turn up? At the last moment he'd had to stay at home with Blanche or Sarah. Look, there's a woman getting all chewed up about a man who isn't coming. Surely it was written all over her face? She began to fake an interest in a leaflet about forthcoming musical events. Nothing was left to chance or imperfection when it came to this man: Pauline Arnoult must always have her face prepared, her demeanour too. This evening she was looking very beautiful. The colour she wore gave her a particular glow. Her outfit was no more sophisticated than usual, but it had been specially chosen for this meeting. When he turned up, he was wearing casual trousers and a jersey. She admired him for that. That was what it meant to be truly natural: to seek to please only by being oneself, without changing or hiding anything. Even to be prepared to be found wanting, if that was what happened, but just to be oneself, whatever the needs and desires of love might dictate. He looked at her the second he'd sat down, and said, You look marvellous. No, honestly, he added, as though she had demurred in some way. How could she not have known she looked good, since she had taken all the necessary steps to achieve it, to hit him between the eyes with her beauty? I love it when you laugh, he said. I like you best when you laugh, because for once you're not watching yourself. She protested: she never watched herself. Yes you do, he said, sometimes you observe yourself from outside. I should know, he said. I've watched you do it for a long time now. And he said, smiling: I know you better than anyone in the world. That's true, she admitted. I've never understood how it is, but it's true. They laughed again. They had always had an immediate rapport in spite of the agony of the tempestuous early days, and their separate lives, and time, which had run away like a mountain stream. They took genuine pleasure in each other's company. Two or three times a year he accorded her this pleasure, and since it was one they both enjoyed, she couldn't understand why he didn't seek it more often. How do you manage to do without me? she would say. I think of you, he'd say. I know you're happy and that makes me happy: It's enough. She nodded. I think about you for ages, he would often say.

They had a good time, just as they had years previously, the first time they spoke, sitting out on the pavement of a bistro like this in the same student quarter of their capital city. There are moments which come round again, and which are all the more cruel precisely for not being repetitions, for in fact being deceptive: moments of destruction, splitting, the withering of all living things, the cold which gradually possesses all animate and inanimate beings, a sort of incomprehensible, inevitable horror, which we might associate with life itself, were we not so determined to put the thought of death from our minds. If we knew everything that was to come to pass, would we be more or less inclined to laugh? She would never have climbed the slippery pole of shared delight, if she'd known the misery it would cause her to follow the call of a single admiring glance, if she had known how entrapped a woman can become by the charm of a voice and the memory of an idyllic moment. As though she had misjudged that feminine faith which wants the body's memory and the occasional presence of a sound to be enough to guarantee unwavering and perpetual desire in a particular man, enough for what we perhaps choose to call love. All he had ever done was look at her, and speak in that voice which for her was a siren song. Nothing but this velvety texture in his voice, the voice of a man talking with his beloved in the dark, in their bed, before slipping away into sleep. An intimate voice, which had never let up, despite the passage of time, their separation and his refusal to invite her to make love. She had come to him with a woman's light tread: little steps at first, in answer to his call, and later in giant strides. And so she had arrived here at his side. And he had suddenly vanished from sight. Had he fled? No, he told himself, he had just wanted to hang on to what was extraordinary: their complicity, the sense that they were twins, a chaste appreciation of each other, with no need to express itself, or waste itself in flamboyant posturing. But what was the word to describe such behaviour?

He had never cut the cord of her passion. He'd never left it too long before phoning her. But, strange as it might seem, the situation between them never changed. He no longer felt the torments of a craving lover. He simply needed to reassure himself that she was there. And each time, there she was, talking, laughing, at the far end of the line. She was moved to hear him, and so was he, in his own way, for he still considered her the liveliest woman he had ever met. The song of all womankind was constantly upon her lips, a song of beauty which demands to be admired, the lament of all women in love: Stay. Don't go. I need you. What will I do without you? Do anything, but please don't go. These are the words she would have said, if he had been a fickle husband. But since he was only a lover who did not desire her, she asked: When can we meet? I want to see you. You always say 'soon' and then I never see you.

Why can we never meet up? Why can't I simply have dinner with you? she would ask. But for them there was no such thing as simply, dinners couldn't just be dinners. But these things were obvious. How could he point them out? She knew perfectly well what he'd been through. He had no wish to play with fire. This woman had managed to turn his head for a while, and he'd kept her at a distance. All those demands he hadn't met, all those secret tears he knew she'd shed (and it caused him pain), all the things he'd failed to give her and which she still expected – because he'd held himself out like a promise to her, only to vanish like a thief in the night. She had come through all this and she was still there. Year after year, they still met. Let's meet for a drink, he would say, as though they had seen one another only the day before. She accepted this odd relationship with a mixture of mortification and gaiety. She'd turn up, he would be late. She would wait, he would take a good look at her again, and they would laugh.

On this occasion she was sitting quite upright in her chair, open to his gaze, still a beautiful woman, though her face had grown softer with the passing years. All the same, she thought, his voice had changed.

He didn't play around with it as he used to, his words no longer had the same devastating effect as they once had. Or at least, it didn't seem to sound the same to her these days. Oh no, they were quite different people now. Could they ever be those people again? The years rolled remorselessly on. You've always needed me less than I did you, she said. She was relaxed. Her distress had eventually subsided. That's what made me so unhappy. I never wanted to make you unhappy, he said. Far from it, I tried to avoid it. But you didn't do everything you could have done to avoid it. What she meant was: You couldn't stop yourself moving in on me, touching me. But she said nothing, since in fact she didn't regret it. On the contrary, she would have hated it if it had never happened. Only that first glance, the product of mere chance, could be wished undone in a way that nothing subsequent could be. I needed you, he said. I still need you. You wouldn't think so, she said. He clarified his thought: I need to know you exist. She both understood him and didn't. Because she needed to know he existed (even if it had to be without love) but she needed to know he loved her as well. In actual fact, what she had always found difficult was constantly having to play down this need. For she was a woman: women are intemperate in love. You need me to exist, but at a distance, she murmured. She looked at him and smiled. She felt a great inner calm. How strange. What had happened to that magnetic force, pulling him towards her? Had he got it under control? Was it dead? He gave off nothing remotely resembling it. I have no effect on you these days, she said. I wouldn't say that, he said. He didn't want to hurt her, for all the world. It occurred to her that her own desire had lessened too, her very persistence had extinguished it. All that was left was a strong, but abstract feeling. And what about the body? We certainly have no control over our desire, she thought. It makes itself known in spite of us. We are simply its guest, or its indebted hosts, which amounted to much the same thing. Desire invites us to join the party, it warms our blood, but we have no control over the temperature. The force which had drawn him to her was well and truly dead. So was it true, then, that such a force could die? And yet there was no one else who could have sat down opposite her and given her so much pleasure. So there must still be something left. All this occurred to her in the brief moment it takes to think a thought: they had both been dropped by desire, but they had known it, and that could never be taken away. And so she said: Today I'm really sure I love you. I love you in the best possible way: without asking for anything. I love you even though I can't have you. You give me nothing and I still love you. What do you mean, I give you nothing? he cried.

I give you a great deal, he said. He said this quite seriously. She admired the way he revelled in it all. He clearly deluded himself in this way so that he might be at ease with himself, and she was convinced it was self-delusion, whereas in fact he was no more guilty of this than she was. For she got what she wanted out of him: this exalted feeling, even if it was partly due to torment, and this sense of living life at full pitch. Merely by the fact of his presence here now, before her, he gave her something, however distant or cool he might be. Because feelings tend to ebb away unless they are somehow useful to us, and we cling to whatever helps us hold our head high, even if it's only a sense of despair. But she didn't want a big debate, she just wanted to say what she felt. And so she went on: I love you more than my husband, because I expect all sorts of things from him, I have an interest in him. You have an interest in him? he said. He's my life, whereas you're nothing to me, she said, astonished at the idea that he seemed not to have understood. Oh thanks, he said, laughing. She corrected herself, for his sake, although a second later it occurred to her that in fact what she said was pretty much true. What was he to her, really? Not even a presence in her life. I mean that I don't expect anything of you, she said. And yet, she said, I wish you all the best. I'm glad if you're happy. I couldn't bear it if anything happened to you. When you say that, he said, it sounds to me as if you are wishing I were dead. As though you were actually saying: Go ahead and die. I can't bear it, why don't you just die? She said: No, that's not what I'm saying. I can't imagine how dreadful it would be to have to mourn you in secret. Just think: there'd be no one I could talk to about it. But she let this idea drop and went on with what she'd been saying: If all that doesn't add up to love, she said, then I don't know what does.

Hearing her say this word again, he lowered his gaze. What I have with you is completely unique, he said. This was his own way of echoing her words. There was nothing else he could say. What could he possibly produce which could meet the radiant force of a woman's love? He couldn't rise to her level of self-abandon. He didn't believe he thought of her in the same way as she thought of him: often, without expectation, in silence, benevolently. He lived his life according to what he was: a man, greedy and voracious, concerned with success, much taken up with his job, with being an interesting character, with a variety of different mistresses, a man who had recovered his wife and child (who had now grown into a woman). And he kept his secret to himself, this grace, this refuge: a warm and unseen flame, which lightened the burden of life. He drew on it whenever needed. He would call up this woman who was in love with him, every now and again, on top of everything else he had to do, because it was true, he did need to know that she was there, and was devoted to him. Of all the women I know, you're the most in love, he murmured. There was something fervent, something expectant about her. This was what she meant to him. And she was often the one who pointed it out to him. She wasn't so blind as not to realise that the company of someone with this kind of passion could soothe the heart. Sometimes I envy you, she said. How do you mean? he said. Well, I'd like to be in your shoes, to be able to hear you make the kind of declaration I make to you, for instance. You make me declarations? he said. Yes. All the time, she said. True, he admitted. She laughed for a moment, but her laughter came from unconscious despair at having played her final card and discovering it made no difference. He looked at her, but where once there'd been lust and fantasy there was now simply bemused admiration. Yes, there was this fervent, expectant quality, and she knew it, admitted it, in a way that was only possible in one who had given up hope. Someone who says what is on their mind, who lays themselves bare, has given up wishing for things, given up worrying about themselves, about what they're revealing, about what other people will think or say about them. Yes, he said. I'm a lucky man. But you are in a sense what I've made you, he said. Although she found this rather wounding, as though he had been playing at fashioning her, as though her pain was nothing, he wasn't wrong. She didn't reply. I woke you up, he said, I made you into a woman worthy of the name, a woman who could love. You've got your thoughtful look, he said. I don't like it when you disappear.

It was true. Thanks to him she was a woman with real heart. He had brought out every last drop of tenderness in her, the way children do, an undeniable force of love which tolerates weakness and wrongdoing, separation and deceit, which watches over absent friends and the quick and the dead. She looked into his eyes and smiled. He chuckled. You're much more self-confident now, he said. I don't know about that, she said. No really, he said, you're much more sure of yourself. How old are you now? he said brusquely, as though he'd suddenly realised, to his surprise, that he didn't know. I've stopped saying, she said. Even to me? he said. Even to you, she said. I know you better than anyone else in the world, he said. Allow me one secret, she said. She must be almost forty. You're still young, he said. And I'll soon be an old man. You don't act like an old man, she said. Even so, he said, I can't deny the figures. He said: I feel as though I've known you so long. I feel as though you've always been there. But I haven't, she said. I'm hopeless with dates, he said. I'm not, she said. She remembered everything. How was it even possible to remember in such detail? By revealing such depths of memory she also revealed how deep was the well of her love for him. She thought about this in silence. He felt like she was smiling at a child. Indeed, he knew as little of pain as a child did, and this made her feel immensely old and wise. He was nothing to her. He was everything to her. For he represented the high point of love in her life. Desperate love. Abandoned love. The one you never cease to pursue, and which you clutch between slippery fingers. She had not been able to love her husband in this way, quite simply because she'd always had him close to her. Every day, for so many years now, she had been in his arms. Theirs was a love which continued to mature, without losing its object. But a love which could survive absence and deprivation, which could hold onto someone who disappears, runs away, takes a different path, that was love of an entirely different order. The same kind of love you gave children. Was love in its most perfect form always a maternal love?

She said: Sometimes I feel like your mother; I don't think I could still caress you as a lover. He didn't take her seriously. How can that be? he said. I don't know, she said, but it's what I feel right now. I know I love you deeply, she said. But I also know that I'll never touch you again. Tut tut, he said. How can we ever know what we will or won't do? he said. But she was quite sure it was the case, and that it would always be so. You are naked before me, he said. That's why you're happy with me. Yes, she said, I am, but it's my choice. It's thanks to me that we're here together, she said, because I've forgiven you everything, I've never kept a score or given up on you. I've been so unhappy because of you. But I told you, I wanted to avoid that at all costs, he said again. She reflected that he was a rather weak man. What about you, she said, why aren't you naked before me too? Because that's not the way our relationship works, he said. You've never asked that of me. He was so sure of himself, he had an answer to everything. I tell you everything you want to know, he said. He looked around him. What time is it? he said, looking at his watch. Shall we go and find something to eat?

They ate simple, tasty Italian dishes. That was exactly what I wanted, he said. Do you feel okay? he asked kindly. It was almost unbearable that he should be so considerate. She could have wept, had she allowed her mind to think back to the distant past, or forward into the near future, where there was only separation and the tyranny of real life. How peculiar it was, how difficult, to love two people and yet to only have one life. We are loath to believe in anything but serial love. But in fact a new love needn't necessarily kill off the one before. The heart was a labyrinthine network. Do you believe that Vronsky loved Anna Karenin? she said. No, he said, without a moment's hesitation, he didn't love her. She said: That's what my husband thinks too. But I'm not so sure. That's because you don't like to think he didn't, he said. It would be so awful, she said. Do you read as much as you used to? he enquired. I think we're destined to read certain books, she said. You know I think that. I know, he said, smiling at her. And so you should: you're an artist. He was paying her a sincere compliment. She smiled as she listened to him, as though she knew everything he was going to say, and was amazed to find she was so calm with him so physically close. Times had certainly changed. Something was gone for good. She felt a nostalgia for her suffering, the strength of her former feeling. Do you know what? she said to him. I think I've finished being unhappy over you. That's over now. About time, he said. Then I can be sure I have the best friend in all the world. His words cut her to the quick: she had never aspired to being his friend. But she said nothing. And yet from the look on her face at that moment, he could see her disappointment.

You've become very well known, he said, in an attempt to cheer her up. She nodded. I always thought you would, he said. You always had a special style, everything about you. It's very rare, he said, to find someone who has style. It's odd you should say that, she said. It's something I'm very aware of in other people. You have your own style too, she said, maybe that was what made me fall for you. Maybe, he said. They laughed. But she quickly turned serious again. My work was what saved me from you, she said. And I bet I helped you, he said. How do you know? I just know, he said. You are naked before me, he said again. I often used to draw with you looking over my shoulder, she said. I imagined you could see what I was doing. And if ever it wasn't as good as it might be, I'd hear you point it out, or encourage me, and I'd rub it out and start again. All in all, she said, I worked a lot. See – I've been a great help to you, he said. As he said this, he had a wickedly cheeky look. She burst out laughing and said: I adore you. Really? he asked. You know I do, she said pitifully, almost miserably. She did adore him, but she was tired of showing it and getting nothing back.

They went on and on talking until the tables all around them were empty. They savoured the pleasure of sweet reminiscence and complicity, the almost painful thrill of the legacy between two people who once shared a powerful desire for one another. For they had run through all the words, all the gestures, even some unmentionable ones. And as a result all the cherished images that one invariably constructs of oneself had been toppled. Will I be sad to leave you? she said. I hope not, he said. In the past, she said, an evening like this – which you'd never allow me anyway – would have cost me weeks on end of gloom and tears, because I'd know that it would be months and months before I could squeeze another one out of you. He smiled. Why did you never want to see me? she asked again. I never understood that. She added: Once you'd got over your infatuation at the start. He said: I did try to explain sometimes, but you wouldn't listen. There was my wife to consider, she'd just come back to me. And then there was this other woman I didn't seem to be able to break off with. And I didn't want to make you unhappy, as I had them. I knew you were always tangled up with women, she said, smiling. And you wanted to get me even more tangled up, he said. Precisely, she said. I wasn't interested in sharing. What would you have got out of it? he said. Leftovers. I didn't want that to happen. She didn't answer. Then she said: Anyway, it doesn't matter any more, I've given up. This seemed to be true, but he couldn't quite tell. Nor was he quite sure if he minded or not, or whether he had now lost her as a potential mistress. In his heart of hearts he was certain she belonged to him.

I'll come with you to the taxi rank, he said, as they put on their coats. They walked down the street side by side. They walked quite close together, so that sometimes their upper arms touched. At this brief contact she felt the weight of memory and former desire upon her. As they walked in the dusky evening of the capital city in all its modernity, battered by noise, pierced by streetlights and neon signs, they looked for all the world like a pair of lovers. The lovers they had never been, nor ever ceased to be.

They came to the front of the queue of cars. I always forget how tall you are, he said, looking her up and down. Sorry, she said. He let his eyes rest on her, smiling. You're so pretty, he said. And I've always loved the way you dress. She didn't speak. He had looked at her too long, too hard, and now felt himself trembling inside, as once before. For – shame to say, perhaps – his desire was prompted solely by what he saw before his eyes. She held out her cheek for him to kiss goodbye. He took a step back. Let's go to my office, he said brusquely. Don't go home. She knew exactly what he meant by going to his office. I don't want to go to your office, she said. She kissed him. See you soon, he murmured, without thinking for a moment that yet again he was lying, as though the impertinence of a second ago didn't deserve a moment's further thought. And so, seeing the smile on his face, the way nothing ever threw him, she decided she'd been right to say no. She thought this because she had very nearly said yes.

2

No one else ever knew. Eve had never found any confirmation for her suspicions and had forgotten about that evening. They didn't watch the fights any more. They had become old hands, rich with experience, their children now grown into young adults. Time had caught them in its trap. The story of their lives and the bonds between them had developed in ways which made them wonder whether they could have predicted what would happen. They certainly hadn't guessed. And yet everything that happened seemed so utterly inevitable, and was all linked together, for better or worse. Was it that the signs had been missing, or that they had missed the signs, or lacked the courage to read them? Eve and Max had divorced. At first she had tried to kill herself, but had failed. Max had refused to give in – he visited her in hospital, but never at home. Once she recovered, she moved house. The children were independent now. They never said so, but they were convinced that divorce was preferable to conflict. They too, most probably, would marry and divorce. The elder of their daughters had already chosen a man she would never get on with, a man for splitting up with. Eve and Max could see it coming this time, but could do nothing do stop it. Sometimes they met up at one of Melusine and Henri's dinners. Eve and Melusine had never been friends, but Melusine had been touched by Eve's despair. Henri had been one of those who had persuaded Max that he should start a new life. Melusine's drinking had resisted therapy, advice and danger to herself. Strong liquor was still the mainstay of her life. The slightest thing sent her into a rage or reduced her to tears. After she left, Eve thought how love was never enough in itself for anyone. You had to do something with your life. An attractive woman couldn't live like a flower, adored by the gardener, well-watered and pruned, but planted in the earth, unable to move, subject to the wind and the weather.

Eve enjoyed talking to Max about her work. It was a new development. You never really wanted me to work, she would say. That's not true at all, he replied. But I was quite sure you didn't want to. I thought you liked staying at home, he said. I thought I did too, she said. I should have listened to Louise, she said. What did Louise say? said Max. She used to say that everyone is meant to work, said Eve. She wasn't a Marxist by any chance, was she? said Max. I don't know, said Eve, who hadn't the first idea about Marxism. What's she doing these days? said Max. I never see her, said Eve. You know, she said, since I stopped being a member of the club, I never see any of that group, apart from Melu. I wonder if she had a child in the end, said Max. I felt so sorry for her over that. Maybe they adopted one, said Eve.

They drew up outside her apartment. You can pull up over there, she said, pointing to a convenient place which he knew as well as she did. She got out. Goodbye, she said. She smiled sadly. Marriage is no fun, she said. She believed marriage had destroyed what they'd had. Why do you say that now? he said. I'm thinking of us, she said. Don't go upsetting yourself, he said. She hated him saying that. It's not marriage that's no fun, he said. Maybe just marriage between you and me. I think marriage ruins everything it touches, she said. People and feelings. Look at Melusine and Henri. They're destroying each other. She stopped, then went on again, as though refuelled by a moment's thought. It was marriage that turned me into what you resent me for becoming. You loved me before, didn't you? she said. I don't know now, he said. He was ruthlessly truthful. She began to cry. He tried to improve on what he'd said. Don't cry, he said. I can't give you an answer now, but it's not because I never loved you, it's because I don't know what to make of having stopped. Life just seems to be like that these days: split into several lives. She didn't like to hear him talk like this, but she said nothing, just smiled. She hadn't entirely given up hope of his coming back. See you soon, he said. Try and have a talk with Catherine (the elder of their daughters), she said. You know that's not easy, he said. Try anyway, she said. I just seem to rub her up the wrong way. I promise I'll have a go, he said.

Louise had split up with Guillaume. He now lived with a very young woman, a ravishing young woman, so young she really ought to leave him, as Tom said, which was why Guillaume was not happy. Louise had married a man of her own age, who was widowed with no children from his previous marriage. They had adopted two little Chinese girls. There was nothing more they could have wanted of life. Because her happiness was written all over her, Louise felt she couldn't see Guillaume again. She heard about him through Marie. I don't understand why he can't settle down, Louise said. He's too obsessed with beauty, said Marie, as if that was a definitive explanation. Louise smiled. Had she been that pretty too, then, without realising it? I don't think it's that, she said. He's never recovered from making a mess of his first marriage. It set him off on this perpetual wandering. You're too romantic, said Marie. That's rich coming from you, said Louise. They laughed. And what about you? How are you? asked Louise. Wonderful, said Marie. She was the only one of them still living in a world of children, having had seven in total, the last two of whom were not yet grown up. You should give Penelope a call, said Marie. She's so lonely. Ever since Paul died, she's been living in the wilderness. They'd ended up only seeing Paul's friends, and they've all been dying off one by one. It's a process of simple subtraction. Are your daughters well? Marie would ask. She liked saying the words *your daughters*. Sometimes you can know for certain your words give pleasure to another, simply because it's a pleasure you feel yourself.

Sara was waiting for Tom to make up his mind and marry her. What is it you love about me? Will you always love it? Well then, what are you afraid of? she would ask him. But he always answered: Why does a piece of paper change anything? You're so selfish. I've wasted my life waiting for you. You've got your children and your mistresses, and I keep hanging on like an idiot, hoping you'll marry me. I must be the dumbest woman on earth. Yes, I am off again. Don't look like that. I'm off again, and I'm not going stop, as long as you carry on being a great big selfish pig. That's right, off you go, see if I care. I don't care. And when she talked to Pauline she'd say: How's Marc? You make sure you look after him. He's one in a million.

EPILOGUE

It Never Ends

– You look fantastic, really.

– You always say that.

– I mean it.

– It's not as true as it used to be.

– You look the same to me. You look as lovely as you did the first time I saw you, at the school, in that big red coat.

– You remember the red coat.

– As if it was yesterday.

– Since when have you started remembering things?

– Since I turned into an old man.

– Stop that. You sound like someone else when you talk like that.

– Maybe I am someone else.

– But I know it's you.

– In that case I can go ahead and proposition you.

– You never did that.

– I don't know what I was thinking of.

– I know what it cost me.

– You not going to turn sad on me?

– No. I'll try not to moan.

– Well, then, let's not talk about what you've got against me. I wish you'd look at it differently. I gave you so much more than you think.

– What did you ever give me apart from this impossible love for you and all the unhappiness that came from it?

– It's not my fault you were married.

– I was free enough to give my love to you.

– And so you did.

– I suppose so, yes. And you let yourself be loved. . . .

– And it was exquisite. . . .

– Why don't we go to a hotel?

– You always refused to go to a hotel with me, even when I begged you.

– I thought it wasn't your style.

– You should have thought a bit less.

– I want to touch you now.

– What, suddenly, just like that?

– I've never stopped wanting to.

– So why didn't you?

– Because you took it so seriously.

– And you didn't?

– Less seriously than you, I think.

– We needed somewhere we could go. That's what was always missing.

– I don't know what was always missing, but it must have been something.

– That's what's sad about secret affairs.

– I remember the softness of your skin, like honey before you get stuck in it. Let's find a hotel. Would you like to?

– Don't you think we're a bit old for that kind of thing?

– You must be joking. No one knows you the way I do: you're still as strong and willowy as ever.

– We're a couple of old dinosaurs.

– Indeed, my dear. I feel like we've known each other since the dawn of time.

– Though I wasn't always there.

– Stop talking about it and come here. You didn't talk this much when I first met you.

– Silence. . . .

– Silence makes you feel awkward.

– I've always worried that I bored you.

– How wrong you were!

– I've never bored you?

– You're as pretty as a picture.

– Give me a straight answer. Have I ever bored you?

– Never.

– And how have I managed not to?

– I always loved looking at you. In my eyes you were beautiful.

– That's not enough.

– Sometimes it is.

– And now?

– Let's go and make love.

– Are you serious?

– Don't you want to?

– Of course I do, I've never stopped wanting to.

– So what's your problem this time?

– My love for you.

It never ends.

– When I touch you, everything's transformed. You're like a fairy.

– A very patient fairy.

She joined in his laughter. She still had those perfect teeth he'd admired right from the start. Her gums had simply receded a bit. I really love it when you laugh, he said. Then, recalling their little adventure: You're so soft, he said. Soft but a bit out of shape, she said, laughing. Yes, you're right there, he said. She seemed to take this amiss. He said: I'm just following you. You said out of shape, I agreed. He chuckled for a moment, then he seemed to lapse into a reverie, and, looking serious now, he said: Now will you believe that we're linked together for ever? When she didn't reply he went on: We are, Pauline. Though I don't know by what. Never have done. I've always thought of you a great deal, he said. Far more than you think. Nothing could sever the ties that bind the two of us. I've found your love. It's inside me now, for ever. What about me? What have I found? she whispered almost reproachfully. You've found mine, he said. She lowered her eyes. Her heart was racing. He had just told her what she had been longing to hear right from the beginning. Joy leapt within her, the joy of victory: she had not suffered in vain, and their path had been a true one. They were lovers. But her face remained impassive. I so want you to be happy when you think of me, he said. At least I could give you that, he said. But I'm not, she said. Never? he asked. Almost never, she said.

Down the empty street they went. The night was bright with city lights. Think how many miles we must have walked in our time, he said. That's just how it feels to you, she said. All we ever do is sit around in bistros! Don't you like walking? she asked. Not especially, he said. I have to be going somewhere; I need a destination. My husband says that too, she commented. Leave your husband out of it, he said. Is he in this evening? he asked. He spared a fleeting thought for the man for whom he did not exist. I think so, she said. He must be waiting for you, he said. What's the time? It's late, she said. Then you should get home, quick, he said. She nodded. There's a taxi rank down there, he said. They crossed the road without using the pedestrian crossing and he took hold of her arm, as though to lift her off her feet. At the thought that she must leave him, she felt something fracture and burn inside her. How could it be, she wondered, that you could tear your heart out just for one simple gesture? Tenderness was like a poison, a drug you couldn't be without. She remonstrated with herself. It annoyed her that she should be so weak. It had often struck her how attractive a rugged man became when softened by love. Must she be unhappy because she had to say goodbye to this one? Adulterous love and marital love were like two twins to whom life has dealt a different hand.

He took her in his arms and kissed her. See you soon, he murmured. Stop saying that, she said. Why? he asked, astonished. I can't bear to hear you say it, she said. The thought that she must go home alone, feeling dreadful, while he was fine, made her bitter. She said: It brings back the past, and your endless lies. All my lies? he exclaimed. All the promises you never kept, she said. Did I ever make you a single promise? he said, in a serious tone. No, she whispered, and her eyes were awash with tears. She had made the whole thing up in her head. Had she just been a woman in love with a phantom? Had she pursued him simply because she couldn't get hold of him? Wasn't she more attached to her feeling for him than she was to the man himself? Was he really that lovable? There was no answer to such questions. She believed she loved him. It didn't really matter if it had just been a way of not spoiling the happiness of the beginning.

It's well known that you can be held prisoner by your own ideas. It's a question of your basic nature: either you have a taste for coherence and longevity, which are a kind of fidelity, or you don't. Either you accept that things come to an end, or you don't. She had always been resolutely on the side of those who refuse to accept. Anything that must come to an end need never have started in the first place. And whatever has come about must continue. A whole life could spring from a single evening. A woman could decide not to be unfaithful. But what about him? Why had he bothered to keep stoking the flames, to keep them alight? Should she hold that against him? She had never borne him any rancour, despite her sufferings. It had never once occurred to her to break with him. No doubt she thought that this asymmetric idyll was not so much a personal catastrophe as a salutary lesson. Because in the end he hadn't been insincere. He had never led her to believe that she had him pinned down. There had been his looks, the voice he used, but never a single promise, that she had to admit. I only ever made you one promise, he said, seeing her tears, and I kept it. I need to know you exist, and you will always be part of my life, he said. I know, she said. And now get on home to your husband, he said. And smile! he cried, into the darkness. Come on – there's life in us yet!